PENGUIN BOOKS

# ACCORDING TO LUKE

Gerard Stembridge was born in Limerick. He studied English and History at UCD and has lived in Dublin since. His films include *Guiltrip* and *About Adam*. He co-wrote the satirical radio show *Scrap Saturday* with Dermot Morgan, and has written eleven plays. *According to Luke* is his first novel. It was originally serialized in *The Dubliner* between September 2004 and July 2005.

# According to Luke

GERARD STEMBRIDGE

PENGUIN BOOKS

PENGUIN BOOKS

Published by the Penguin Group

Penguin Books Ltd, 80 Strand, London WC2R ORL, England

Penguin Group (USA) Inc., 375 Hudson Street, New York, New York 10014, USA

Penguin Group (Canada), 90 Eglinton Avenue East, Suite 700, Toronto, Ontario, Canada M4P 2Y3
(a division of Pearson Penguin Canada Inc.)

Penguin Ireland, 25 St Stephen's Green, Dublin 2, Ireland
(a division of Penguin Books Ltd)

Penguin Group (Australia), 250 Camberwell Road, Camberwell, Victoria 3124, Australia
(a division of Pearson Australia Group Pty Ltd)

Penguin Books India Pvt Ltd, 11 Community Centre, Panchsheel Park, New Delhi – 110 017, India

Penguin Group (NZ), 67 Apollo Drive, Rosedale, North Shore 0632, New Zealand
(a division of Pearson New Zealand Ltd)

Penguin Books (South Africa) (Pty) Ltd, 24 Sturdee Avenue, Rosebank, Johannesburg 2196, South Africa

Penguin Books Ltd, Registered Offices: 80 Strand, London WC2R ORL, England

www.penguin.com

First published by Penguin Ireland 2006
Published in Penguin Books 2007

1

Copyright © Gerard Stembridge, 2006
All rights reserved

Set in Monotype Dante
Typeset by Rowland Phototypesetting Ltd, Bury St Edmunds, Suffolk
Printed in Great Britain by Clays Ltd, St Ives plc

ISBN: 978–1–844–88114–7

For
Trevor White
who said I should

# Contents

# Journey Home I

The journey from Kerry to Dublin at the end of summer had always been special for Luke. It was a childhood ritual that began in 1980 when his father bought the cottage at Tahilla, and continued for ten summers until Luke was nearly sixteen. As an adult, he had continued to make occasional use of the cottage, but this particular journey home with his parents, sitting in the back of the family Merc, hadn't happened for fifteen years. That last year of course, 1989, he journeyed in official disgrace.

Full circle, Luke thinks now, without pleasure. He waits in the 04 Merc, watching his father appear and disappear as he moves slowly about the old holiday cottage. His mother Norma is silent in the front seat. These lulls, these . . . longueurs have been a feature of their weekend together. They are no one's fault. They just happen, then they pass and conversation continues. It would be easy enough to describe the visit as relaxed, chatty and uneventful, but Luke can't help counting up the tiny giveaway moments of tension, the unspoken alterations in the family rituals. Now, waiting to leave, he wonders if that was the real reason he had made this trip; merely to strengthen his own conviction that something had to be done.

Making arrangements for the visit over the phone, Luke had not told his father that he intended to travel back to

Dublin with his parents. He decided to let him think it was his idea. This manoeuvre was easy enough. Frank Reid always assumed he was running things anyway. Luke knew that as soon as their phone conversation ended, he would be crowing to Norma about how he had persuaded their perversely independent son to take the train and bus to Kenmare, where Frank would collect him. He'd boast to Norma about how delicately he had handled the chat, and how eventually he got Luke to relax and condescend to travel back to Dublin with them. In the present context Frank Reid would see it as a significant diplomatic victory.

Luke had wondered if anything of the old feeling would come back on the day they left Tahilla. Would the joyous muddle of emotions he had experienced on that day every year of his childhood somehow be regenerated? Would it be possible now to feel it without irony or distaste? Even as he had lived it, the feeling on the last day of summer had never been the simple joy of ice cream. It was much more complex. Goodbye and hello. Goodbye to Tahilla, the sea, the luscious countryside, the warm accents, Sullivan's roadside shop, where in teenage years, he and Cousin Barry dreamed pathetically of chance encounters and instant romance; hello to Dublin, the reassuring certainty of the school calendar, Hallowe'en, Christmas, the Leinster Schools Cup, the annual school play and, again in the teenage years, the lonely yearning of tennis club discos.

The morning of departure itself was always chockful of final moments, last acts. Have you had your swim yet? Luke knew it would be out of order to go for his last swim before Dad urged him. That was all part of it. Once Dad had spoken he could stop whatever cleaning-up job he had been given and make the final run to the shore. He never remembered anyone else being there on those last mornings, but there must have been sometimes. When he was eight, and his sister Judy was four, she suddenly decided to come with him. She watched solemnly as he wrapped the towel around himself and struggled with his trousers and underpants. She sat on a rock gazing at him as he stepped in. When the water of the quiet inlet was up to his chest, he turned and waved to her before leaping up and diving deep. But Judy never swam with him. By the time she was eight she had even lost interest in trailing after her big brother. Matthew arrived too late. They never shared Tahilla. He was only a new baby in the final year, and anyway, that morning disgraced Luke wasn't allowed to have a last swim. Little Ruth was the only one who ever got into the water with him. When his baby sister was four and he was a big strong twelve, he carried her in carefully. She wrinkled her face and seemed about to cry, but Luke made her laugh with some seaweed on his head. Serious Ruth clung to his neck fiercely but silently, as they dipped into the sea all the way to their chins. She came with him each year after that. Two years later she was swimming without wings.

Another must-do on the last morning was bringing the cardboard box of leftovers to their cousins, the Phelans. Don't call them leftovers, Luke's mother always said. It would be a sin to throw them out. It was usually tins of tuna and tomatoes, whatever was left of the olive oil, balsamic vinegar, rice, pasta, butter, sugar. He was about ten when something began to nag at him about this little ritual. He didn't know why. Auntie Joan was always delighted. There would be a slice of her apple sponge and a glass of milk. His cousin Barry would drag him away to his bedroom, and they'd talk dangerous talk and have secret laughs for an hour or so. They probably wouldn't see each other until the following summer so it was a bit sad too.

All in all, going to the Phelans was another last-morning highlight for Luke, but whatever had wormed into his head, by the time he was twelve or thirteen he began to find ways of avoiding this little job.

The visit to Sullivan's shop to spend the last of his holiday money on sweets for the journey was the final act before take-off. For nine summers Luke, accompanied by little Judy first, then by older Judy and little Ruth, would mark their departure for Dublin with the purchase of a lethal assortment of sweets, drinks and ice creams. On the final day of the tenth summer sweets were the last thing on Luke's mind. Had Matthew continued the tradition into the nineties as he grew up? It sometimes occurred to Luke to ask his baby brother things like that. He always forgot.

The shop, the swim, the leftovers: little by little the boot of the car would fill up, Dad would do his last checks while Mum shouted reminders from the passenger seat. He would turn off the electricity, lock up, drop the keys off to Mrs Dennehy who kept an eye on the cottage, and then, at last, they could leave.

After a lot of thought, Luke had made the decision to re-enact the journey. If he was never going to step inside the cottage again, he should make one last visit. Luke always believed in context. He thought he should try to remember and, in some way, relive the emotion of those years, in order to place the experience alongside his present feelings. It was only fair, and maybe something would come out of it. It was a big lump of his life after all, from the clinging six-year-old Dad taught to swim in 1980, to the slumped, shamed adolescent on that last tense, silent, ridiculous journey home. The glorious eighties of his charmed childhood.

*

His father finally finishes his checks and emerges to lock the front door. Luke marvels that their little holiday cottage is now worth more than 700,000 euro. He couldn't know that for certain because it wasn't up for sale. He had figured it out by looking in the window of Daly's estate agent's in Kenmare, and noting the asking price of similar properties. The water frontage was the big plus apparently. Several times over the weekend he had nearly mentioned it, but stopped himself just in time. In fact it was extraordinary how the subject of money or property just never came up at all. It used to be a constant topic of conversation with Frank and Norma. Tahilla had cost Frank less than £30,000 in 1980. Of course, back then, that meant something. It sure did, Luke thinks, watching his father fiddle with the door-lock. Either he is perceptibly older and slower now, or Luke is seeing change and significance where there is none.

Frank gets behind the wheel. He starts the car and the conversation. They are off.

'Pity we missed Paudie last night. He'd have enjoyed seeing you again.'

'Yes, would have been nice.'

Luke doesn't say that he had met Paudie earlier the day before. Paudie shook his hand in that ferocious, crushing way of his. He spent most of the conversation telling Luke what an inspiring, great-hearted man Frank Reid was, and how mad about him they all were round here, no matter what, and how he'd never want for friends in Tahilla, or Sneem for that matter.

'Apparently he had just gone when we arrived,' Frank says. '"Not like him to leave a pub before closing time," I said to Jack, winking, you know. "Oh, he do have other fish to fry sometimes," says Jack. "A fish of the female persuasion I'd say," says I, and Jack roared laughing, you know the way he does.'

Frank laughs himself now, pleased as ever at how amusingly he can do a broad fruity Kerry accent. They are well on the way to Kenmare but he doesn't switch on the radio. Instead he talks on as they go, filling Luke in about Paudie and Jack and the doings of all the local gang. He tells him again of Finbarr and Joan's visit a couple of weeks before. They had had this conversation on Friday night when Luke arrived. Frank repeating himself is no surprise; Norma not interrupting and reminding him of the fact, is. Luke suddenly feels himself fill up in a sentimental way; his poor mother and father. He wishes they could be the way they always used to be on those journeys back to Dublin. No sooner were they on the road than Frank would reach for the radio switch. They always aimed to leave by one o'clock, so that he could get the full benefit of *This Week* with Gerald Barry. For the next hour the battle would rage as Frank huffed and sighed, heckled and argued, offered long alternative theories to whatever was being proposed. Occasionally, of course, if the right people were on, only yeses and absolutelys would punctuate the discussion. Sometimes, too, the radio would be entirely drowned out as Frank and Norma mounted their own live debate. For the children at the back, the contents of all this was irrelevant. It was just part of the soundscape of their journey, another signal of the end of summer and return to the serious business of the city.

Luke could not remember much about specific journeys, mostly just fragments of various family combinations. He had a very clear image of when it was just himself and Judy. She was always annoying him, pawing at his book, wanting to know what he was reading. Then they became three, and he recalled once stopping somewhere like Nenagh or Roscrea, because little Ruth had to have her nappy changed. Dad brought Judy and Luke for sweets, while Mum rummaged about in the back of the car.

Luke had been allowed to sit in the front passenger seat twice. The first time he was eight. That would have been 1982. Mum sat in the back with Judy and the new baby, Ruth. It was like he had been promoted; he and Dad, the men, sitting together in front. 'Put on Radio One there,' Dad said as he started the car. Luke reached out and flicked it on, cool as you like. It was the first time he listened closely, intently, to *This Week* with Gerald Barry. After all, Mum was distracted with baby Ruth, so Dad might need to discuss things with Luke. He understood none of it, so he tried to guess its meaning from Dad's responses. There seemed to be definite triggers; certain words and phrases like 'levies' or 'marginal rates of tax' provoked Dad to a kind of ranting displeasure. The name 'Fitzgerald' brought out the humorist in him. His voice took on a sarcastic tone. Luke hated and feared this tone whenever it was directed towards himself, but on this day it seemed really funny. Dad did this stammering high-pitched voice, and made a series of completely meaningless noises. Luke laughed, which encouraged Dad to do it again even more outrageously. Then, returning to his own voice, he became quite serious. 'That's Fitzgerald for you, Luke, a know-it-all, who knows nothing really. You can be too smart, you know. But the man in the street sees through all that.' Luke felt he had been let in on some special knowledge. Something Male and Adult.

The contrast with his second trip in the front passenger seat could not have been greater. For once *This Week* with Gerald Barry broadcast loud and clear to a deadly silence in the car. Luke, lost in wretched adolescent embarrassment and hatred of his parents, heard none of it. Oddly enough, sitting in the front passenger seat had nothing to do with his disgrace – Matthew had been born only a few months before, so his mother had once again preferred to sit in the back with the new baby – but it certainly added to the pain and the tension, with his father's icy presence immediately on his right.

They pass through Kenmare and still the radio isn't turned on. Neither Frank nor Norma is interested in the latest Cabinet reshuffle news. Normally such an issue would be the subject of enthusiastic debate between them. Argument would rage as to whether McCreevy was shafted (Frank), or had landed on his feet in Europe (Norma). Was Cowan the brightest star in the political firmament (Norma), or a big oaf not fit to lick McCreevy's boots (Frank)? Instead, the marvellous meals they had this year in Kenmare offer them another safe conversation topic. They only went to the Park once but it was really tremendous. For regular eating out you couldn't beat the Leath-phingin, if you could get in. They treated Finbarr and Joan to D'Arcy's on the last night of their visit, and it was so good that they went themselves twice more after that. On and on they talk fine meals and fabulous nights out. They agree with each other all the time. The conversation is peppered with 'as Frank says' and 'We both thought it was marvellous' and 'Norma will tell you, tell him, love'. They are well past Killarney when the restaurant chat finally dies away and there is a radio-free silence. Luke can't help feeling he is being a little bit malicious, when he says, 'Put on the radio there.'

Frank's hesitation is tiny.

'Hmm? You want the radio on?'

'Do you not want to hear the news?'

'Ah, I don't want to spoil the chat.'

'Oh. OK.'

'But I mean, if you want it on—'

'Frank – put on Lyric. That'll be nice in the background.'

'Oh, right – Lyric all right, Luke?'

'Yeah, sure. Lyric's fine.'

'We love it. They should have had it years ago.'

Frank switches on Lyric FM. Evelyn Grant is introducing the slow movement from Dvořák's New World Symphony. Frank is delighted.

'What about that, hah? There's a coincidence – "Going Home".'

There is another silence as they listen. Luke wonders if his parents have to bite their tongues as much as he has had to all weekend, or if it is now quite natural to them. Again and again he had found himself about to say something seemingly ordinary, the bread and butter of family conversation over the years, when his brain, acting like a chess master's, had thought many moves ahead and, spotting where the conversation might end up, had stopped him just in time. It was a strain, constantly improvising safe alternative lines of chat. Eventually he found it easier just to take his cue from Frank and Norma. They seemed to know the safe routes by heart. Having now stirred things a little with the radio request, Luke decides to toss another pebble on the water.

'I see you're still taking the Mitchelstown route.'

'You mean the way we're going now?'

'Yeah – through Mitchelstown, isn't it?'

'But we've always gone this way.'

'No, I remember we changed one year.'

'How do you mean?'

'We used to go through Limerick, then one year we changed.'

Luke detects another tiny moment of hesitation from his father. Perhaps he is just trying to recall.

'Ah sure, that was years ago.'

'Oh, I know. I was just noticing you'd never changed back.'

'Never thought of it. We like this route, don't we, Norma?'

'We do.'

It had been such a to-do when it happened. Mum loved stopping in Adare for ice cream and a walkabout. It was another ritual of the journey home. The fact that Adare was a tourist trap, a carefully preserved haven of thatched cottage Irish charm, didn't put her off. At least it was clean and pretty, she'd say, not like most of the filthy lifeless towns on the way back to Dublin. So if there was going to be a pit-stop, better there than anywhere else. Once, on a particularly warm Sunday, they even took the time to drive up to the Manor Hotel and have a drink. So when, in either 1984 or 1985, Luke couldn't pinpoint which year exactly, Dad suddenly proposed a new route home, there was a genuine row between Mum and himself. Dad mentioned it very casually first, as they set off from Tahilla. He had been looking at the map apparently and he thought, just for a change, for the crack, of trying the route across North Cork to Mitchelstown and then taking the straight run up the main Cork–Dublin road. Mum equally casually dismissed the idea. They were grand as they were. Dad persisted though, saying he thought it might be faster. Mum thought there was no rush. They'd be stopping in Adare anyway. Time was not a problem on that beautiful Sunday. Dad said not to be so negative, let's do something different. Mum said she saw no point. They had travelled the Cork road many times, going to and from Cork. There was nothing special about it. At first Luke thought nothing of this disagreement; loud debate on every subject was a natural thing between his mum and dad. But as he listened, he began to sense a different tone, an undercurrent to this particular argument. Dad was definitely quite determined to go the Mitchelstown route. He was getting very tense and frustrated at Mum's opposition to the plan. Mum either didn't notice this, or was actually enjoying the effect she was having. By the time they reached the roundabout at Killarney where the choice had to be made, no resolution had been reached. When Dad just turned on to the Mitchelstown road anyway, and drove on, Mum suddenly lapsed into an angry silence. Everyone in the car now knew there was big trouble, even little Ruth.

Having got his way by force, Dad now tried making up. He started pointing out little landmarks and beauty spots in a tone of cheery surprise. He expressed enthusiastic delight at seeing all the red flags and bunting fluttering from every window and in every street. All the way across North Cork, the county was being urged to success in the forthcoming All-Ireland final. Finally he offered up Abbeyleix as a satisfactory alternative to Adare. They could go for a quick one in Morrissey's. Abbeyleix was a lovely little town, well worth a stop, and Morrissey's was superb. Luke liked the sound of Morrissey's. He was inclined to support his dad in this row anyway. New was good. Different was good. Adare was boring. He watched anxiously for signs of his mum softening. He decided courageously to intervene. His question was innocence itself:

'What's Morrisey's, Mum? Is it nice?'

It worked. By talking to Luke, Mum was able to step back a little without conceding anything. First, Morrisey's was 'just an old pub'. Then it was 'very old, very authentic inside'. Then she began to offer more enthusiastic detail: the old biscuit tin display, the huge pot-bellied stove. Then Luke was told to wait and he'd see for himself, let it be a surprise. The deal was done. They would stop in Abbeyleix and have a lovely time. Luke caught a little grateful glance from Dad, and he was so proud to have helped him out.

When they got to Abbeyleix, there was what seemed at the time to be a typically Irish chance encounter. They had just settled in Morrissey's when his father's name was roared from across the bar.

'Well, will you look who's here, Frank Reid, is it?'

The man turned out to be someone Dad knew in college. Mum seemed to recognize him too. Luke didn't catch his name. He was involved in one of the local banks. Of course Dad sat him down for a drink. Later, when Mum brought the children for ice cream and a walkabout, Dad stayed on chatting with his old pal. By the time they took off from Abbeyleix. Dad was in high good form and Mum had relaxed again. What might have been a day of disaster had mellowed into another happy family outing.

Something from *Don Giovanni* is on Lyric as they drive through Abbeyleix. Today no one proposes a stop. Luke wishes he now had the nerve to say casually to Frank, was that when it all started, that day in Morrissey's, you and that man, whatever his name was? Norma interrupts his thoughts with one of her favourite subjects: Luke's girlfriend, Emma, and how marvellous she is.

'What would she do with herself now while you're away?'

'I don't know. Usual stuff.'

'But she wasn't all on her own for the whole weekend, was she?'

'Emma's well able to amuse herself.'

'Oh I'm sure, but you both work so hard all week, weekends

are precious. It was an awful pity she didn't come down. She'd have loved it.'

Luke hadn't asked Emma to come. He had explained to her exactly why. She completely understood. In fact, she said in the circumstances she'd be a bit freaked out to be there. Luke doesn't say any of this to his mother.

'She would, but she loves doing her own thing as well.'

'Oh I know, she's a great girl.'

Luke listens to Norma praising various aspects of Emma's personality, not least how good she is for Luke. Luke knows that she means it. He knows that Norma completely accepts that they live together. He knows that Emma and he have had romantic weekends alone in Tahilla several times since they first met three years ago, and it was not a problem as far as Frank and Norma were concerned. Still, he cannot bring himself to sleep with her in Tahilla if his parents are there. This particular weekend it would have been even more unthinkable.

Luke knows, though he hates knowing it, that most of this is a problem in his own head, and once again, as so often over the last fifteen years, he remembers Bobbi.

It was mid-August 1989. He and Cousin Barry were cycling lazily along the road close to Parknasilla. They shot the breeze as always but that day there was an unspoken sadness between them; first of all, the summer was winding down, and another holiday had passed without so much as a whiff of any kind of girl action for either of them. Secondly, more importantly, the Phelans were selling up. While Auntie Joan occasionally said bright no-nonsense things like it was time for a change, Luke knew from stuff his parents whispered that in reality the Phelans could no longer afford to keep the holiday home going. Luke wasn't sure if Barry knew this or not. Barry was the kind who'd put on a show anyway. Usually Luke could see through that, but this time if it was a show, it went pretty deep.

A car pulled up beside them. The boys stopped cycling. It was a Peugeot 504, left-hand drive. There were four people inside. It looked like a family: Dad and Mum in front, teenage girl and little boy in the back. The man at the wheel rolled down the window and showed them a brochure. He spoke with a heavy French accent.

'*Pardon*. Where is the hotel? This one.'

Both boys were staring past the brochure to the teenage girl sitting in the back seat, her tiny golden face in repose, pressed against the window.

'Parknasilla? We are in the right way?'

Strangely, it was Barry who had enough composure to refocus back on the man and his brochure, say yes, and point straight on. Less than half a mile, on a bend, he explained. The man nodded, said thank you, boys, with a little knowing smirk, and drove on.

They were silent for a moment, watching the car disappear. Then they looked at each other. Barry said, 'I saw her first.'

This rule had been invented by Barry to decide who would chat up who. Not that in the end it ever made much difference to either's success. Luke tended to let Barry win. Barry was determined to get off with as many girls as possible. He had incredible focus. Luke sometimes worried about himself that he didn't feel driven in this way. Something else made him calmer and more confident, however. He had begun to realize, the way teenage boys do, in an unspoken way, that he, Luke, was more attractive than Barry. He noticed girls looking at him with a certain interest. While Barry was explaining things to the man, Luke had seen the beautiful French girl glance over. He had seen her interest.

'No you didn't.'

As he spoke, Luke realized he had no intention of letting Barry have first go this time.

'Well, you didn't either.'

'I know, we both saw her at the same time.'

'So what does that mean?'

They looked at each other with rising excitement. There was some life left in the holidays after all. Three days later, after much hanging around the woodlands and bathing spots of Parknasilla, 'chance' encounters, longing chit-chat and fun swims, Luke knew that the fabulous French girl, whom they now knew as Bobbi, had fallen for him. He knew it at a particular moment when Bobbi laughed at some remark of his and said, 'I like you, Luke. You are *ironique*.'

That tight thin French 'i' sound. Luke, with his honest green eyes behind designer glasses, and occasional quiet, spontaneous wit, was indeed *ironique*. And very handsome.

Even now, at thirty, Luke cannot imagine an Irish girl ever saying she fancied him for his sense of irony. That was definitely a once-off. His father's waving arm drags him back to the present. Frank is pointing out the wonder of the new Kildare bypass and praising bypasses generally. Luke agrees. He guesses that the joys of the new motorways and bypasses might well ease them conversationally all the way to Dublin. Luke is alert to the inherent dangers in this subject. How will they avoid mentioning dodgy land rezoning, for example? Frank manages this confidently. He focuses entirely on car owners' safety and comfort, and the huge reduction in journey times. He fondly recalls how long it used to take to get to Tahilla twenty-five years ago in the old banger. He laughs now at what seemed like the pioneering quality of their early ventures into the far south-west, to the tigín that was their only shelter. Luke is fascinated how Frank, like the good lawyer he has always been, constructs without faltering this seamless narrative of family life. He is never so crass as to pretend that they had been poor, but casual usages like 'the old banger', referring to the top-of-the-range Merc of the time, and joking references to the lack of basic facilities in what he calls the 'tigín', all serve to imply a simplicity of living, years of joyous endeavour, which if they proved fortunate, was really God's good fortune smiling on them, rewarding their essential decency. Like the roads they are now travelling on, life always seemed to get better, and bypasses were an important part of that success. Luke can hear in Frank's voice just how real the sentimental love for his family is. The narrative which now carries them from the Naas road along the canal towards Ranelagh is nothing but the truth as far as his father is concerned. So close to home, Luke now knows that this journey into autumn has failed to bring to the surface the other unspoken narrative. Did he really think it would?

Luke has already decided that he will not accept the invitation to family dinner that he knows will come. He is taken aback by how genuine and pathetic it is. It is much harder for him to turn down than he expects. The lie that he and Emma have a prior arrangement to visit friends sounds utterly hollow and faltering. He is truly sorry not to be able to see Matthew, who is at home and would love it if his big brother called. A last sad enticement of organic leg of lamb from Kenmare fails. Luke watches them go, then walks to Tribeca for a burger and a bottle of Campo de Viejo alone. He is able to smile at the contrast between his parents' pleading now and his disgraced return in 1989. That evening a crisp, wordless knock on his bedroom door, and a tray of sandwiches and milk placed on the floor outside, had ended the Journey of Shame. For several hours that night he lay on his bed thinking only of Bobbi. He had touched himself, but was too sad to make himself come. Eventually, before sleeping, he had quietly opened his door and picked up the tray of food.

It had all happened the previous night. His parents had gone for a special meal at Sheen Falls. This was a regular end-of-summer thing, a get-together with other Party hacks from Dublin whose holiday homes were dotted about the peninsula. It was always a very late night, sometimes after three o'clock when his mother and father would finally fall in the door.

This year the younger children were all consigned to the Phelans' house for the night. Luke and Barry were going to watch videos and behave themselves at the Reid cottage. After Frank and Norma left, the boys rifled through the drinks cupboard, took careful amounts of gin and whiskey, and started watching *Nightmare on Elm Street 4*. It was all done without conviction, though, because they both knew what was coming. Fifteen minutes or so into *Nightmare*, Luke turned to Barry and said, 'Right. I'd better head . . . listen, thanks.'

'Sure.'

'See you later.'

'Good luck.'

It was a little wistful on both sides. For all the jokes and dirty talk of several years of adolescence together, both were silently aware of the significance of this night. They knew that in all likelihood, Luke was going to lose his virginity. The plan was to meet Bobbi at the entrance to Parknasilla at ten-thirty. Like the good French family they were, the Delons went to bed around ten. Bobbi would sneak out. What would happen after that was not clear, but Luke had the feeling he might be ironic enough to get all the way. The romance of the moonlit seashore was the first option, but beautiful as it undoubtedly was, there was enough of a chill in the wind to prevent the passion from getting too out of hand. Luke had been shocked to hear himself say, 'Do you want to go back to the cottage?'

Bobbi sat on the bar of the bike folded into him and Luke was as happy as he would ever be. Even though Freddy Kruger still had twenty minutes' more rampaging to do, Barry behaved like a true pal. He would cycle up to Sneem, get some chips, hang about, and eventually go home at what seemed like the right time.

Ever since he was a child and noticed how much it looked and sounded like Tahiti, Luke had loved the name Tahilla. It could easily be the capital of some sun-drenched paradise. He always felt sorry for people who holidayed in Kilkee, Curracloe, Ballydehob or any other drearily-named Irish town-land. Tahilla was exotic; it was sun and opal sea, and tropical foliage.

Tonight he knew he had been right all along. He was living the teenage fantasy. None the less, in his bedroom as he and Bobbi unbuttoned each other, and licked and kissed, Luke was still so tense he couldn't believe the evidence of his own erection. As they got closer to the inevitable, an uncertainty about women and virginity was oppressing him. What was about to happen to Bobbi? He began to press cautiously against her, not quite knowing what barriers he would encounter, what messy realities would spill out. Then Bobbi whispered, 'Luke. I hope you do not mind. I am not a virgin.'

Luke did not mind at all. His brain felt lighter and he smiled, kissed her, and let her guide him easily, suddenly inside. He became impossibly hard and started to rock. He wanted to laugh. It was going to be all right. Much better than all right.

The waitress removes the plate and gives Luke the dessert

menu. He is feeling pleasantly ashamed of himself. A significant plan to undergo a journey of rediscovery with his parents, and perhaps confront some present family difficulties, is ending with him alone and tumescent, his bottle of wine nearly empty, tempted by a chocolate ice cream sundae called 'Heart of Darkness'. Why not?

Her head resting on his breast, her arms tight around him, Luke had been whispering the most romantic things he could think of to Bobbi for several minutes before he realized that she had dozed off. He felt himself drifting away too. It was too delicious to struggle against, but Luke did have the presence of mind to reach out and set his alarm for one o'clock before curling himself delicately around Bobbi's soft curves and letting go. They would have plenty of time after waking before his parents returned.

He was wrong. They were jolted awake by a roar of cars arriving, and drunken shouting as middle-aged men and women fell out on to the drive and slammed doors. Luke's momentary disorientation turned to real and particular panic. He looked at the clock. Not even five to one. How could it be? He knew instantly what had happened. His father, high on drink and good times, had decided to invite a crowd back to the house. There was going to be a hooley.

'Oh no. Oh fuck no. Please no!'

'What is it, Luke?'

'They're back. They're all back. There's no way out.'

'But they will go to sleep soon? And then—'

'Are you joking? Oh, I'm sorry, Bobbi. You're French, you don't know these people. They'll be up all night. I don't know – maybe we can get out the window when they're all inside.'

He could hear voices in the house now. He crawled to the low cottage window and sneaked a look out. The last bodies were lurching in the door. There were six cars scattered about. The window wasn't that high. If Bobbi was willing, a sheet might do the trick. As soon as— The thought stopped dead. Luke saw a cigarette being lit in one of the cars, a black Mercedes. The next moment a bulky man hauled himself out of the driver's seat, and leaning over the roof of the car, puffed away. Luke knew instantly it was a State car. They had bumped into some fucking Government minister or other. Of course, that was why his father and mother had decided to have a session. Unless he was invited into the kitchen for a sandwich later, the Garda driver would be out there all night.

A fiddle started up below along with cheers and whoops. At the same moment Luke heard footsteps coming up the stairs. He scurried to the bed, motioning to Bobbi to keep quiet. She didn't need any urging. There was a tap on the door. Luke stopped breathing. His father's voice was liquid and merry when he spoke.

'Luke, Luke, are you awake, Lukey? Guess who's downstairs if you want to meet him? Luke?'

Tap tap.

'The Boss is down below. He's here now.'

The door was tapped a little more forcefully.

'Luke, you sleepy hoor, you'll be ragin' tomorrow if you miss him.'

Since his fifteenth birthday, his mother and father no longer entered his room without being invited. Right now this delicate and unofficial propriety was Luke's only chance. Somehow it seemed a far greater possibility that his father's drunken excitement at the actual presence of the Leader of the Nation in his humble holiday tigín would cause him to barge in the door and rouse his son to share the thrill. Even as Luke thought he saw the door handle turn, relief came suddenly. He heard another voice coming up the stairs and his father's footsteps move away from the bedroom door. There was a God.

'Where's the seomra folcaidh, Frank? I'm in dire need.'

It was a confident, gravelled voice familiar to the entire nation. Luke heard his father telling An Taoiseach where the bathroom was. At exactly that moment the alarm clock rang. It was one o'clock. The shock made Luke jump. It made Bobbi scream; an unquestionably female scream. Luke grabbed the clock. The alarm seemed utterly deafening, yet he heard the deadly click of the bedroom door as it opened. His father stood there, looking at his teenage son, naked on a bed, fumbling with an alarm clock, a naked teenage girl next to him. The Leader of the Nation now put his head around the door. As he took in the scene one quiet, spontaneous, possibly admiring word escaped his lips.

## 2

# *Cousins I*

Barry Phelan hated when there wasn't enough steam. He liked when he couldn't see faces, when it was just male and female shapes moving around in the fog. That was relaxing. That was why he preferred the steam room to the sauna. In the sauna you could see everyone clearly and there was always some fucker looking to start a conversation. That didn't happen in the steam room. Right now he could see the fatso on the other side clear as day, flopped there with his saggy tits and his gut hanging down over his gear. If he would even sit up straight, give himself some sort of shape; what was he doing here if it wasn't to try to make himself look better than he was? Barry shifted into the corner of the steam room so he didn't have to look directly at Fatso. He sat even more erect than normal, his back a hair's breadth away from, but not touching, the tiled wall, feeling the stretch in his long tight muscled neck. He rubbed a hand along his sweating chest, enjoying the hardness of his body. He should complain about the lack of steam. There was always something wrong in this place. It was supposed to be for relaxing in, Jesus Christ, but if it wasn't the steam room not steamy enough, then the jacuzzi was more like a hot bath, or fuckers were jumping into the plunge pool when there was a sign right in front of them asking them politely not to jump into the plunge pool.

Barry closed his eyes and took a long slow breath. He told himself to forget all that. Rolling his head forward, stretching his spine, he could feel no aches. The workout was getting too easy. He'd have to up the regime. He was so fit. You're so fit, Jackie had said to him last night. She did a little dance naked in front of him, supposed to be for a laugh, supposed to be like it was to turn him on, but it was really because she was so horny for him she just had to let it out somehow. She couldn't sit still. He shouldn't have let her stay afterwards. Bad move. She'd expect it now. He had just got too tired to throw her out. He didn't even check his emails like he always did last thing. He just conked out and suddenly it was seven in the morning. He woke and there she was sprawled all over him. That was a real downer having to deal with that, and check his mailbox, so he arrived at the gym late and in a really bad headspace. That's what happened, that's why he wasn't feeling as good as usual. He couldn't even focus on his emails with Jackie hovering around getting dressed and looking for coffee. Jesus, big mistake. Wouldn't happen again. His first thought had been who the fuck was Luke Reid, when he saw the name. Then he realized it was his cousin Luke. What was he doing writing to him out of the blue? Where had he got his address from? Barry opened it and read it quickly.

Tues. Sept. 21st 20.14

Hello Barry

I hope this is the right address. Clever of me to track you down if it is, yeah? Can you believe it's been 15 years? Talk about Nightmare on Elm Street! Mea culpa that I haven't been in touch since you came to live in Dublin. I should have been a better host. I thought I might do something to make up for that with a nice surprise. Something a bit special. I'll give you a hint. Your county's honour demands you get back to me by Saturday at the latest, to take advantage of an amazing free offer!! Seriously, looking forward to hearing from you. I really hope this email gets to you!

Your long-lost cousin
Luke

Jackie came and nuzzled at his shoulder. Anything interesting, babe? That was it. He shut down his mailbox and stood up. First priority was to get her out of his apartment. In the end the quickest way was to leave with her, drop her at a bus stop and drive on to the gym. One small thing stuck in his mind. Nightmare on Elm Street, what was that all about?

Barry left the steam room, slid into the plunge pool for fifteen seconds and then stretched out in the jacuzzi. He checked the clock; nearly quarter to nine. He could stay until five to at the latest. Ten minutes to shower and dress, and he'd still get to Mountain View Road by half nine. He eyed two pale blondish girls sitting on his left jabbering away. The nearest was in a black one-piece, the other seemed to have some kind of pink bikini on. Weird gear these Russians, or whatever they were, always seemed to wear. Was it some fashion left over from Communism or something? The one-piece jobs had their plus side. They were usually cut very high on the crotch and shaped the arse really well. Barry didn't go for the bikinis at all. The bottom part was usually like some kind of hot pants. What Barry couldn't figure was, if they could afford a thousand euro a year to use this place for fuck's sake, why couldn't they buy proper gear, Nike or Speedos? Barry hoped they'd get out of the jacuzzi before he did, so he'd see one-piece swimsuit's arse in motion. She had a good face, with that Eastern European hollow-cheek thing. If the rest was as tasty, he might fuck her. He wondered if she spoke any English. He turned over on to his stomach. Now when the girls looked his way they'd see the tattoo, the angel's wings stretched across his shoulder blades. He knew from experience it was a big turn-on.

Barry had to wash and dress really fast to get the van on the road by five past nine. He didn't even have time to moisturize. He made up some time by slipping on to the bus lanes in Fairview and the North Strand when it was clear, and zipping along for a few hundred yards before dodging back into the main traffic lane again. That made him feel better. Drivers were always pissed off when he tried to get back in the lane, but they still let him. More fool they. He was held up longer than he wanted by roadworks at Westland Row, and the tat-tat-tat-tat of a kanga hammer beat into his brain. That'd be some trick; to cross Dublin and avoid roadworks? Couldn't be done. He should be finished at the Harrisons' by Friday if he kept the pressure up. Five thousand euro in the paw, and free for the weekend. He'd buy one of those shirts he'd been looking at in Brown Thomas. He'd maybe hook up with Lyn or – no, not Jackie, fuck her after last night. Molly maybe. Yeah, better. Or if Molly wasn't around, he could just hang loose and go on the pull Saturday night with his new shirt and a few bob in his pocket. Plenty of time to decide. Barry thought of his cousin Luke Reid again and wondered what he meant about getting back to him by Saturday at the latest. Was that just bullshit to get him to reply or what? It didn't really matter. He had no interest.

Barry got to Mountain View Road bang on nine-thirty. The Xsara wasn't in the drive, so he knew Mrs Harrison wasn't back from the school run yet. Dougal had subcontracted Barry to complete the electrical work for the extension on condition that he was available for the whole week and that he'd guarantee an early start every morning. Dougal was five weeks over schedule as it was, and had already moved his regular team on to the next gig. Knowing the Harrisons were on his case, having forked out the guts of 250,000 euro for the extension, Barry was able to squeeze five K out of Dougal for what was, essentially, little more than a week's work. 'Keep her happy, that's the main thing. I want her off my back for a while' was the instruction. Fair enough. Barry knew that the sight of him perched on the front wall smiling, freshly cleansed, looking fit in a tight French Connection top and stud-fly jeans, would make Mrs Harrison very happy when she returned from her school run.

When she arrived minutes later he even helped her with the shopping bags. She made decent coffee, and they stood with their mugs in the new lounge which was the centre-piece of the extension, discussing the exact configuration of the recessed lighting for best effect. Ailbhe Harrison really couldn't make up her mind between 3 × 3 or 4 × 2 and Barry, smiling, said he couldn't make it up for her, it was she who'd have to live with it. She shouldn't forget though how an interesting arrangement of reading lamps would affect the overall lighting mood. Exactly, she said. Barry loved this bullshit. He knew what it was all about. He was keeping her happy. Was she forty yet? She took care of herself, OK, but he had already decided he wasn't going there, even if he got a vibe. Too much talk for Barry's liking. He had been fitting sockets in the lounge the day before, and had heard her side of a long call.

'She's a complete fool if she thinks that's the way to deal

with it. You know what he's like as well as I do, if she thinks she'll get him to change his mind she's only fooling herself . . . Look, if she asked me, which she won't of course, I'd just tell her, go anyway, book the tickets. Let him paddle his own canoe . . . Of course you can tell her! That's exactly what she needs to hear.'

Barry figured Ailbhe Harrison would be more than happy if he horsed into her, but she wouldn't be able to stop herself telling him which way to lie, where to touch her, for how long, when to come, wait, wait until I'm finished if you don't mind. OK now . . . now, I said!

Just as she decided the configuration for the recessed lights had to be 4 × 2, the phone rang. Reluctantly she left Barry to get on with it. He changed into his overalls, put on a pair of headphones and turned on Prince very loud. Eavesdropping on her gossip had been a bit of a laugh yesterday, but enough was enough.

His cousin's email kept coming back into his mind. Was it really that long since he'd seen him? The truth was, he hadn't thought about Luke Reid for years. Even when they were kids he only ever saw him during the holidays. They got on all right. They hung about together the way cousins do. But once his ma and da had to sell the place in Kerry, they hadn't met again. Straight after his Leaving Cert disaster, Barry went to London, then on to New York. There you go, simple enough, fifteen years flash by just like that. Nightmare on Elm Street, though, what did he mean by that?

Barry began to have a memory of a feeling. He didn't even like admitting to himself that it was there, but it was; an image from a past he thought was long forgotten. He was standing cold in the dark outside his cousin's place in Kerry, watching. The Reids always called it a cottage, but in Barry's memory it was much bigger and fancier than the Phelans' crappy little place. He remembered how he had watched until he saw the lights go off downstairs, and then a little light go on upstairs in what he knew was his cousin's bedroom. Barry had imagined them fucking; his cousin and the gorgeous French girl. The girl Luke had stolen from under Barry's nose. It had made him feel so sick inside.

Barry was surprised at all this stuff coming back to him. It wasn't supposed to any more. It was too far in the past. It was childish. Anyway, his cousin hadn't stolen her. She had chosen him over Barry. Yeah, that was the killer. Barry shook himself out of it. It's all so much bollocks now. So what if he'd love to have been able to say he lost his cherry to a little French dream when he was sixteen? But he never saw Luke Reid again after that night. That was a bit weird all right.

Ailbhe Harrison was smiling up at him through the little hole in the ceiling he'd punched for the recess light. He took off his headphones.

'I got some ciabatta baps. Fancy lunch?'

'Great. Thanks.'

'I'll be about five minutes. Parma ham and cheese, or are you veggie?'

'No, ham and cheese is fine.'

As they ate, Ailbhe looked at him directly and said, 'May I ask you a personal question?'

Oh yeah. Barry smiled back at her. Shrugged.

'Sure.'

'That tan of yours is amazing –'

Here we go. Is it all over by any chance?

' – do you do sunbeds?'

Barry's lips suddenly felt a bit dry.

'Sorry, it's just that Eoin and I are going to St Lucia in October and I was thinking about doing a few sessions before I left, just to get the ball rolling, just so I wouldn't look completely like Mrs White from White City, you know? But everyone says a sunbed tan is really obvious. A kind of shiny red glow off it, you know? So I was wondering, because yours—'

'I went to Greece in June.'

'Oh, right. Well, there you go. Au naturel.'

'But, ah – I did take a few before I left. Like what you said, you know.'

'Right. You did? How many?'

'Ah . . . three, I'd say.'

It was five, and Barry, flustered, knew he wasn't going to mention the weekly top-up since he returned.

'So . . . would you recommend it?'

'I s'pose. It depends. You look great as you are. Your complexion, it's nice, you know. It's you.'

'Thanks. So what are you saying, it's worth it, as long as I don't overdo it, is that right?'

'Yeah, yeah, I suppose.'

They ate on in silence. Turning away from her slightly, Barry caught sight of himself in a mirror at the far end of the room. Maybe his face did look a bit shiny today.

Barry had an idea that the Christ Church route might be a faster way home, but roadworks at Patrick Street fucked that up. It was after seven when he got back. He was wound up tight. He did something he never did at that hour of the evening. He opened his mailbox. There was another message from Luke.

Wed. Sept. 22nd 18.06

Dear Barry
Maybe it's the wrong address. Maybe you don't check your
mailbox regularly and I haven't given you time to reply. Anyway,
just to say I really would like to meet up with you again
generally speaking, but I hope you are free this Sunday in
particular. (Hint, hint!)
If you'd prefer to call, my number is 087-3371978
Hoping to see you Sunday maybe.

Your cousin
Luke

If this had been a girl Barry would already be walking very
fast in the opposite direction. Something was going on. This
guy was a bit too anxious. And what was Sunday? He checked
a calendar – the 26th. Nothing special, apart from being the
last Sunday of the month. He looked again at the first email.
That Nightmare on Elm Street bit still got to him. Had he
heard anything about his cousin over the last few years, any
gossip? Maybe he'd gone a bit weird? The truth was Barry
didn't know because he showed no interest in his family. He
hadn't seen any of them in two years. On the odd occasion he
talked to his mother on the phone he didn't really listen to
anything she said. He had never contacted Luke or any of the
Reid family since he came to live in Dublin, even though his
mother kept hinting that his aunt Norma would love a ring.
Like fuck she would. Anyway, why start now just because his
cousin had decided to bombard him with emails? And if they
did meet, would Luke notice stuff . . . the changes? After
fifteen years Luke had probably changed a lot himself. There

was no point in getting into that. Do nothing for the moment. He'd probably give up.

The following morning, however, he overheard a conversation in the jacuzzi that explained everything. He was already calm, alert and relaxed. Last night had turned out surprisingly well. Molly had phoned after eight, to say that her flatmate wasn't coming home tonight, and there was way too much food if Barry hadn't any plans. He said yes immediately. He always enjoyed fucking Molly. There was something really naive and vulnerable about her even though she was a fox. Once, afterwards, she had snuggled up to him and next thing he realized she was crying quietly. He pulled her into him and kissed her hair softly. It had made him feel horny all over again. As well as stuff like that, the really great thing about Molly was that she seemed to know the deal absolutely. In fact he kind of thought she had a boyfriend that she never told him about, which was fine. She always phoned him out of the blue, and it was always what are you doing right now? He also noticed that if he ever phoned her in the daytime she always answered, but never if he called in the evening. Anyway, whatever, the previous night had been perfect. It was relaxing, it was controlled, they both had fun, and he was home and in bed by midnight, having checked his mailbox. Nothing more from Cousin Luke thankfully.

He woke at seven feeling nice and fresh. He got to the gym with plenty of time to do his workout and relax afterwards. Even the two geezers sitting next to him in the jacuzzi yabbering on didn't disturb him. Two guys in their thirties, really pale and skinny, one of them nearly bald already; why were they coming to a gym? It was obviously getting them nowhere. They might as well stay on in bed, catch an extra hour of sleep before going to their shitty little offices. Whatever they were saying to each other was just so much noise in Barry's head until he heard, 'Of course, all my relations in Castlebar think just 'cause I live in Dublin I have some secret access to tickets.'

'Ah sure, it's a load of hype. Haven't they a better view on the telly anyway?'

Barry's brain went pop. The All-Ireland final! That's what Cousin Luke was hinting at; he had tickets for the final. That was the whole 'your county's honour' and 'hope you're free on Sunday' bit. It all came together in his head. When Barry was a teenager he was way into Gaelic football. He was good enough to be on the school team. And he was from Mayo. Of course, Luke would still be caught up in the past. He'd think that Barry would be thrilled to get tickets. How could Luke know that he hadn't given Gaelic football a second's thought in years? He slid down into the foaming water up to his chin, and nearly laughed out loud. It felt so great to have worked that out. Barry hated not knowing stuff.

Everything seemed right today. Barry had much more grooming time. He washed his hair with Anthony everyday shampoo and his body with Anthony sea salt body scrub. He liked the Anthony range. He liked the straightforward way the products talked at him. 'Objective: Hair so rich it'll pay for dinner. Strategy: Coconut oil moisturizes and cleans, chamomile freshens, wheat protein strengthens.' Thursday was normally the day when Barry topped up the tan, to make it perfect for the weekend. Towelling himself in front of the mirror, he decided he didn't need it this week. So he just moisturized quickly with Anthony glycolic facial cleanser (fragrance-free): 'Objective: Make your face squeak with cleanliness.' He left quickly to give himself enough time to stop off at an Internet café and send Luke an email. There was no messing, he just got to the point:

**Are we talking tickets for Croke Park here, or what?**

**Barry**

He got to Mountain View Road at nine thirty-five. Ailbhe Harrison was already back from her school run.

'Oh, I'm so relieved. I was getting worried . . .'

What was all this about?

'I was afraid something had happened to you, you're usually so punctual. I was just going to ring Dougal to make sure you were OK.'

Oh yeah. Naughty boy. Little slap. No offer of coffee this morning. What a bitch. Barry worked hard and in silence. He finished the bathroom by twelve-forty. He didn't wait for an invite to lunch. He got a sandwich and a Lucozade Sports at O'Brien's in Rathmines, and drove the van up to Palmerston Park. He sat in his van and ate, listening to 98 FM. One more day and he'd be done. He was so glad he hadn't made moves on Harrison. He hadn't given her the satisfaction. As he ate he watched two African women sitting on a bench chatting. He wondered why he didn't find them sexy. They were young and buzzing. The buggies didn't help of course but it wasn't that. Maybe if he was out in the middle of Africa in the heat, they'd turn him on, but not in Palmerston Park on a dreary Thursday. Jesus, they were loud too, even with the van window closed he could hear them. Not much to choose between them and Ailbhe Harrison when it came down to it. There was nothing worse than fucking a woman who talked too much.

When he finally got home via the toll bridge, there was a reply from Luke.

Thurs. Sept. 23rd 18.08

Dear Barry
Bingo! Yes, precious All-Ireland tickets going free. So, is the Mayoman on? B'fheider go bhfuil ticeidi agat?
Your cousin

Luke

This time Barry typed a reply immediately.

I'm on. Where 2 meet Sunday?

Barry

An hour later he found himself tempted to check for a reply. He told himself there was no point. There was no reason Luke would have checked his mailbox so quickly. It might be tomorrow before he answered. Barry took a quick look anyway. There was no reply. He used up some time cleaning the kitchen. He filled the dishwater, he scrubbed the cooker, he scoured the sink unit. Then after eleven, on his way to bed, he tried again. This time there was something.

Thurs. 23rd 22.17

Dear Barry
Excellent! Delighted! The best seats in the house by the way. I felt a bit guilty not being from either county myself, but at least your presence will legitimize me, and anyway we always holidayed in Kerry.

Now where to meet? I hear the Big Tree on Dorset Street is just amazing on All-Ireland final day. What about lunch there and soak up the atmosphere beforehand? It's only about five minutes walk from 'Croker'.

12.30 to be on the safe side?

Up Mayo

Your cousin

Luke

Barry had to smile. The Big Tree. What a hole. Luke really hadn't a clue.

He pressed 'reply' and typed:

Sounds good looking forward to it should be a great day out.

Barry

Then just before sending it, he added 'Hi, Luke' at the start and pressed 'send'.

As he lay in bed something began to nag at him. Luke obviously had this idea in his head that Barry was still a big GAA fan. He probably thought that he was doing Barry a huge favour offering him a ticket for the match. Should he tell him? Would that spoil things? He fell asleep still thinking about it, but woke early with his head absolutely clear. Luke wanted to be at the match with a genuine fan. It was up to Barry to be that fan.

On the way to Mountain View Road he stopped at a garage and bought the *Daily Star*. On his way home that evening he bought the *Evening Herald*. He didn't even mind the Friday traffic hold-ups because at seven, he could listen to Gerard Gilroy on Newstalk 106 previewing the big game. Already he was getting a feel for it: the burning questions of the week, selection issues, injury doubts, the strengths and weaknesses of both teams. The highlight of Mayo's campaign had been the two semi-final encounters against Fermanagh with Mayo lucky to escape with a draw on the first day. Barry wondered if it might be fun to pretend he had been at that match; give Luke a blow-by-blow account.

His mobile rang. He answered without thinking and immediately regretted it. It was Jackie. Fuck! Not now. She hadn't heard from him since the other night, was everything all right? Everything was fine, he told her. He could feel what was coming next so he got in first. He had to go down the country on a job this weekend – leaving tonight as there was an early start tomorrow. He'd call her as soon as he got back. It still took another ten minutes of craptalk before he got rid of her. Now he was tense again and annoyed with himself. He never lied to women normally. He always laid it out straight so they knew what was what. Jackie had caught him at the wrong moment. He knew if he said anything just then, there would be tears and screams and begging to meet her one more time to talk it out. He hated all that and certainly was in no mood to face it tonight. It would have spoiled the whole weekend.

As Barry arrived home he suddenly thought of something really important. He went straight to his mailbox and sent Luke a message:

Luke

will we recognize each other

Barry

It was half nine so he didn't really expect an answer that night. Still, he had a quick check before he went to sleep. Nothing.

There was still no reply from Luke next morning. Barry went into town. He had arranged to meet Dougal in the Long Hall to collect his cash. Dougal was going to Mountain View Road first, to check if the Harrisons were happy. Barry hated this bullshit. He hated contractors like Dougal, keeping you waiting in a pub just to show you who's boss. Still, five thousand in the paw was top euro, so Barry ordered a sparkling water and sat easy until Dougal finally showed up. He had to buy the old bollocks a pint of course, and listen to his crap for half an hour or so while he drank and talked dirty about Mrs Harrison. Finally Barry escaped.

He didn't do much shopping after all, even though his wallet was stuffed. He wandered around French Connection but saw nothing he liked. He went to Blue Eriu to top up on Anthony products. He bought Anthony shave gel (fragrance-free): 'Objective: Enjoy shaving', and Anthony electric pre-shave solution: 'Objective: Maintain your edge.' He was in such good form he had a funny thought. He started describing his own activities in Anthony style. Going to Brown Thomas: 'Objective: Choose between the AJ shirt and the Paul Smith shirt.' Barry had a little laugh to himself, but he still couldn't choose. AJ was 160 euro, Paul Smith was 145 euro, so either way he was pushing the boat out. He had the money in his pocket, he'd been thinking about it for ages. But he left it for another week. Instead he bought the *Irish Independent* with a free sixteen-page All-Ireland final special: 'Objective: Sound like you know what you're talking about tomorrow.' He smiled to himself again. He was feeling right up there today, he was fit, he was buzzing.

He went to Nude on the first floor in BT2 only to find it wasn't Nude any more, it was now BT2 café. He was really fucked off with that. He had wanted a Nude smoothie. He hated the way nothing could stay the same for more than five minutes in this fucking city. He thought about walking down to Nude on Suffolk Street, but he had his *Irish Independent*, and he liked the view of Grafton Street where he was, so he stayed, had a sparkling water and calmed down. The *Independent* went for Kerry but acknowledged a feeling abroad that it just might be Mayo's year. If the Mortimer brothers were on their game they could turn it. Mayo's amazing good fortune in the first game against Fermanagh was mentioned again with more details. Barry felt more and more like he really had been at that game. As he read, he noticed that on Grafton Street below, county colours were already beginning to appear. Little clutches of people up for the weekend were cruising about, getting in the mood. Barry enjoyed looking down on them. He hadn't felt like a Mayoman in a long time.

When he got home Luke's reply was waiting.

Barry

I wouldn't worry. I don't think I've changed much. Still the same old four-eyes. A bit more boring-looking if anything. How about you? Anyway, I'll be the only one who doesn't look remotely like a GAA fan. The proverbial sore thumb. Is the excitement getting to you yet? I'm up to 90 and technically I'm not even involved.

Up Mayo

Your loyal cousin
Luke

As it turned out Barry recognized Luke without any trouble at all. It was Sunday at twelve-thirty and the Big Tree was jammed solid. Fans from both teams were bursting out on to the pavement. County colours were everywhere. Barry pushed his way past painted faces, Viking helmets, jester caps with bells, flags, giant plastic hammers, into the pub itself. He figured it was hopeless. All around him were drunken happy faces yabbering at one another about the match. He had thought very carefully about what he should wear today and even kept the county colours in mind when he tried on various casual tops, but in this awesome crush of red and green and green and gold he could feel himself disappearing.

Suddenly, there he was. It was so weird. Luke hadn't changed a bit. Barry remembered him perfectly, the same quiet, slight worried look behind what seemed like the same spectacles, though Barry knew they couldn't be. His hair was the same length, parted the same way. Was he even any older-looking? Yes, of course he was, and yet in some odd way untouched by time. Barry was struck by how good-looking he was. He had never thought of Luke that way until right now, as he gazed at his cousin sitting quietly, alone in the middle of all this All-Ireland final frenzy. Perhaps a little lost. Barry pushed towards him.

'Are you sure you're in the right place, four-eyes?'

Luke looked up. Barry knew instantly that he didn't recognize him at all.

'Barry?'

'Yeah. Who else?'

'Hey, sorry. God, I wouldn't have known you.'

'That's fifteen years for you.'

'Wow. It's amazing. Like you're – I don't know – listen, how are you?'

'I'm buzzin'. I'm great. Up Mayo, ha?'

'Absolutely. What'll you have? I can't believe how much you've changed. Lucky it wasn't me looking for you.'

'I'll just have a Coke or something.'

'If I can get served. And listen, give you a laugh. I dug out some old holiday photos last night. I brought one along.'

'We can do all that after. So . . . good seats, you said.'

'Take a look.'

Luke took out two tickets and handed one to Barry. They were corporate hospitality tickets for the Hogan Stand. Barry was impressed.

'Jesus, how did you swing these?'

'The fruits of corruption, Barry, what else?'

'Listen, forget the drink here. Let's get the good out of these tickets. Go there now.'

They pressed their way to the door, and as they walked down a crowded, noisy North Circular Road, Barry moved the conversation on to the match, away from the past. He had no interest in looking at some fucking old photo. Luke told him he had done a bit of swotting up so he wouldn't seem like a complete wanker. He'd been reading Sean Moran in the *Irish Times* all week. He was giving Kerry the nod. The momentum was with them, he said.

Barry shrugged. 'Yeah, well, better to be the underdog.'

He offered Luke his own opinions, a rehash of the *Star*, the *Independent*, the *Herald* and Newstalk, but it sounded good coming out of his mouth. Luke listened solemnly. As Barry talked he was pleased with himself at how easily he took on the role of GAA veteran and regular Mayo fan. He did put himself in the crowd at the first thrilling semi-final against Fermanagh. He explained how they had to play with a man down for most of the second half and the incredible tension he had felt watching them hold out. Barry could see that Luke was lapping it up. By the time they went through the barrier at Jones Road Barry had relaxed completely. He had talked himself into genuine excitement about the final. He even started to exchange casual whoops with other Mayo fans as they passed. He began to realize that he and Luke were somehow instinctively picking up some tone from the past, some way of being together. Luke had always been an easy companion. Barry had always acted like the leader. He didn't know how he remembered that. He couldn't have given an example from the past, he couldn't have retold some incident that proved it, because he had never thought about it. But as they strolled into the famous Hogan Stand, he recognized an easy feeling between them. He liked it.

Smiling ladies checked their tickets as they entered, and in answer to a question from Luke one of them said to take the lift to the sixth floor.

When they got out of the lift, Barry nearly laughed out loud. It looked to him like a delegation of Irish farmers had invaded Microsoft Headquarters. It was the same mad heads and red faces, the same dodgy gear and wrong shoes, but they swanned around the carpeted executive area as if they had been there all their lives. They weren't pulling ham sandwiches wrapped in tinfoil from their jacket pockets though; Barry could see over a long balcony a huge queue for a carvery serving lamb, salmon and some kind of casserole, vegetables, desserts – the whole works. He smiled. They were the same old dogs, but he liked the fact that they had learned a few new tricks. This was not the GAA he had grown up with, that he carried in his head. Stripping down to your underpants by the wall in an old field on freezing winter days, with some alco-holic Christian Brother roaring gobbledegook at you, was more the memory he had.

'I think this is our spot,' said Luke, stopping at a closed door and checking the number on his ticket. The room was empty. There was a counter, a fridge, TV and armchairs. Barry fol-lowed Luke out through the glass door. Suddenly they were there, right in the buzz of the big day. Their closed-off section had fifteen seats and looked down almost directly at the centre of the pitch.

Luke smiled at Barry. 'Well . . . is this OK?'

'Not bad, Luke. Not bad. Which is my seat?'

'Take your pick.'

The pre-match parade was just beginning. Barry couldn't help noticing that the other corporate boxes on either side of them were packed as he would have expected on final day. He wondered who else would be joining them and where they were. He was about to ask Luke when the door to the suite opened. A woman and an Asian guy walked in with a large platter of snackie things and a tray of wine and glasses. They put them down and Luke, who seemed to be expect-ing them, nodded his thanks through the glass. They smiled and left.

'Hungry?' he asked. They went back inside. As Barry opened the wine for his first drink of the week, Luke smiled at him again. 'It's only right a proper fan should get some of this treatment.'

Barry was suddenly reminded of how innocent he'd always thought Luke was.

The bite-size snacks were tasty, the wine wasn't half bad, and suddenly the game itself was beginning. Barry downed his drink and took his pick of the seats. It was pretty clear to him now that there would be no one else in this box; just himself and Luke. It was weird but what the fuck, this was the business. He sat back and threw his legs over the empty seat in front of him, like he used to do in the cinema when he was a kid. As the ball was thrown in and a roar went up, he felt a real thrill.

Barry had no words to describe how the day's amazing cocktail worked on him: the game, being around his cousin again, the food and wine, the strange atmosphere of privilege. Even though Mayo were destroyed by a brilliant Kerry performance, Barry was surprised to find that his reaction wasn't dismissive or negative. He just felt sorry for his old county.

Barry had much more practice at getting rid of people than making them stay, so after the game, as they walked down Gardiner Street, he began to realize that if Luke now said good luck, see you, he wouldn't really know how to stop him. Barry didn't want this to end. They reached Beresford Place. There was a silence between them; the first one that day. They had stopped talking about the match. There was no more to say about that, so what now? Seconds ticked by. Barry didn't know what to do – he was out of his depth. Luke broke the silence.

'So do you fancy a drink, or have you—?'

Barry said yes immediately. They went to the Harbour-master Bar.

Luke suggested a bottle of Campo de Viejo 1995. Barry was fine with that. It went down very easily, so they ordered another. As they talked about this and that, Barry realized that he was wondering when Luke would take out the old holiday photo again, because now, for some reason, he wanted him to. Suddenly he heard Luke ask, 'So did you ever see the end of *Nightmare on Elm Street*?'

What was this about *Nightmare on Elm Street*?

'I don't get you.'

'You don't remember?'

Barry shook his head and was delighted to see Luke reach for his inside pocket and take out the old holiday snap.

'It was the same year this was taken. 1989. Do you remember the French girl? Bobbi was her name.'

Barry nodded as Luke passed him the photograph. He braced himself. What was he going to see? He hadn't looked at an image of himself from that time in years.

'We got out a video of *Nightmare on Elm Street* that night. When I brought Bobbi back to the cottage you were still watching it, but you didn't stay to the end. You were a real pal. Imagine, I never saw you since.'

Barry looked at his younger self. He still didn't remember watching *Nightmare on Elm Street*, and Luke's explanation seemed very unimportant now. Barry looked from the image of young Luke to the real man in front of him talking quietly and seriously. It was absolutely the same person. He was still talking, reminding Barry how that same year the Phelans had to sell off their place, and how his father, good old Frank, had done Barry's parents a big favour, paid them much-needed cash and taken it off their hands. Barry remembered all that stuff, especially how his mother used to drive his father mad going on about how lucky they were that her sister had married Frank Reid, and what a decent skin he was to pull them out of a hole like that. He remembered, but he had no interest in any of it. He was thinking of something else. As Luke talked on, Barry wondered whether if he took a mirror and looked from the photo of young Barry Phelan to his own reflection now, he would see anything to link them. What could there be any more? What did Luke see?

Luke was still talking about his father, how he got planning permission for a second house on the Phelans' land, and how he had sold both several years later. His voice seemed very intense. He gripped Barry's arm, asking him if he had any idea how much Frank Reid sold the property for, compared to what he gave Barry's mother and father in their crisis. Barry didn't know and didn't care, but he could tell that Luke was really caught up in it.

'Do you know how much profit my father made from doing this favour for your mum and dad?'

As Luke talked, what Barry noticed was the goodwill in the sincerity of his gaze, and the affection of the grip on his arm. His cousin was on his side. Luke was completely . . . suddenly Barry remembered something else from the old days. Something he always took for granted. He trusted Luke. He could ask him anything.

'Luke . . . does it – does it feel like I'm still your cousin?'

Luke stopped in mid-sentence. He seemed surprised. 'Yes. Completely. Why?'

'Well, you know the way you didn't recognize me when we met. Looking at this photo I can see why. Like . . . how can you be sure I'm him?'

Luke looked at the photo, and looked at Barry.

'You want to know what I really thought? When I saw you?'

Barry nodded.

'I was surprised. I mean, you're right, I couldn't explain it away by just the passing years. I knew that. But you're Barry all right. That's obvious—'

'Really?'

'Oh yeah. Your whole manner, your way of saying things, even the sort of know-it-all attitude. You haven't changed a bit really, Barry. And the other thing . . . how you look . . .

45

well, the only thought I had . . .' Luke paused. 'Am I allowed to say anything . . . anything I thought?'

Barry nodded, his excitement rising. Was someone finally going to say the words? Would Luke be the one to say it out loud?

'I wondered if you'd had, well . . . work done . . . some kind of plastic surgery?'

No one had ever asked Barry before. He had never said it himself. He felt more grateful and relieved than he had felt for a long time.

'Yeah. Two years ago. I had a nose job.'

# 3

# Hallowe'en Nightmare

Emma McCann was at the checkout in M&S when her mobile rang. She was next in line, so she really did not want to answer it, but when she saw 'Mommy Dearest' flash up she thought she had better. The woman ahead was getting her credit card receipt as Emma said hello to Norma Reid.

'Emma, hello, glad I caught you. It's about tomorrow . . .'

The boy at the checkout gestured at Emma's goods. Emma just nodded, concentrating on Norma's voice. She wasn't going to cancel, was she?

'. . . I know I said I'd call round and let you cook lunch for us.'

The boy started to tot up the purchases: two fillets of wild salmon . . .

'That's right, yeah. Is there—'

'And I'm really looking forward to the chat . . .'

Emma was relieved. She wasn't cancelling. The boy clocked up fresh hollandaise sauce and an Italian prepared salad.

'. . . but then I thought, why don't we treat ourselves? No point in you going to the bother of cooking and cleaning.'

. . . Asparagus tips, garlic butter . . .

'No, really, it's no problem—'

'Let's make it an occasion and go to L'Ecrivain.'

An autumn fruits torte and Jersey thick cream completed the tot. Emma loved L'Ecrivain.

'And we're in luck. I managed to get a table for twelve-thirty. So what will we do, will I just see you there?'

Emma gazed at her purchases. The boy looked at her. He was saying twenty-six euro eighty-five cents. Maybe Luke could have the wild salmon tonight?

'Norma, that would be gorgeous. Thanks so much.'

'Great. See you at twelve-thirty. Bye, darling.'

And Norma was gone. Emma looked at the boy who was looking at her, polite but expectant.

'Did you not know you have to pay money?'

It wasn't the boy speaking. The voice came from behind her. Emma turned. The man was large. His eyes bulged aggressively. His fleshy face screamed high blood pressure. Hallowe'en certainly brought some strange creatures into M&S. His basket was filled with Shriek! midnight snacks, Trick or Treacle treats, Spooky teacakes (what could be spooky about a teacake?), and of course an impossibly bright orange pumpkin. No doubt he'd be rushing off to rent Stephen King movies at Xtravision, as soon as he had finished torturing Emma.

'Believe it or not, Marks and Spencer charge money for their stuff these days. It's a whole new idea.'

It was sarcasm of the most unsubtle and unattractive kind. Emma decided to ignore him. She opened her handbag to search for her purse, but of course now, every second it took stretched and yawned. She could feel his eyes, sense his breath. The guy was clearly violent: Stanley Kowalski without Brando's charisma or sex appeal. Emma had noticed that more and more people like this were shopping at M&S, especially at Hallowe'en and Christmas to get their treats, thinking they were big spenders. It was a bit scary. Emma found her credit card and handed it over. But Bulgy Eyes wasn't finished yet.

'Oh no! The servant who packs your stuff must be on holidays.'

Ignore him, ignore him, she thought, then realized she couldn't start packing because she didn't have a bag. As the boy handed her the credit card slip to sign, she said, 'And a bag please.'

Even the boy seemed a little nervous as he said, 'Oh . . . right. That's fifteen cents.'

Emma now had to rummage for fifteen cents, accompanied by a heavy sigh from behind her. She found a twenty-cent piece. 'That's fine, fine.'

But the boy had been trained by M&S. As Emma started to pack away her items, he clocked up fifteen cents and gave her back a receipt and five cents saying: 'Fifteen cents and five cents change.'

Emma snatched the receipt and the coin. She tossed them into the bag and tried to continue packing calmly, as Bulgy Eyes's goods were clocked up and slid menacingly towards her. Then Bulgy Eyes himself closed in on her. He sighed again as he ostentatiously produced his Bag for Life. He placed a fresh fifty-euro note on the counter at the ready. He began to pack his goods swiftly and neatly. Emma realized the Brando in *Streetcar* analogy was total understatement. This was more De Niro in *Taxi Driver*. This guy had real problems. Emma did not want to be part of them.

Bulgy Eyes finished his packing at the same time as Emma, but luckily he had to wait for change from the fifty. She walked away casually, albeit with increasing speed, towards the Liffey Street exit. The Bosnian woman, or whatever she was, selling *Big Issue* at the door, smiled at her like a long-lost friend, but Emma, normally the kindest of souls, was in no mood. She fired past her. Once outside she quickened her pace even more. She didn't seriously think that Bulgy Eyes might be in pursuit, nor was she going to give the scenario any more credibility by looking round, but still she yearned to reach the calm and security of the back of a cab. This trip into town was becoming a nightmare. It was also now pretty well completely pointless, since Norma had phoned with her brainwave about L'Ecrivain. It would have suited Emma perfectly not to have left the apartment in the first place. She was no longer the girl who felt she had to be first to see the latest new film/play/gig/exhibition. She was not the Emma who had swept into Dublin ten years before to do her post-grad in twentieth-century American drama; the Emma who considered it a night wasted if she wasn't out soaking up the city. Being with Luke had relaxed her about those things. Thanks to him, Emma now felt that her life rhythms were more mature. The Theatre Festival remained her big blowout of the year and a complete must, but once it ended, this calmer, more casual Emma McCann enjoyed the simple luxury of *not* having to battle her way into the city centre. Her pleasure was a quiet walk in Herbert Park, or a lingering coffee at the Breakfast Club. At night she savoured the delights of sitting in, lounging, drinking wine and watching rubbish on the box. The languid, self-consciously low-brow aftermath of Theatre Festival time was almost as pleasurable, though obviously not as exciting, as the Festival itself. Even the seasons turned a corner at this time. Before the Theatre Festival, summer still lingered in the long golden late September evenings; after the Festival, there seemed to be just that hint of chill in the air, and the longer nights demanded real fires and comfort food. This year, as far as Emma was concerned, the Luke problem seemed to chime with the deepening gloom. In fact the Theatre Festival itself had brought things to some kind of crisis point.

She flapped her arms wildly on the corner of Liffey Street and the Ha'penny Bridge. Thankfully the passing taxi was able to pull up. She flopped in, gave her address and immediately took out her diary, examining it closely. Emma found this the absolutely best way to prevent taxi drivers from talking to her. She remembered how on her first trip to New York she had seen a printed list of her entitlements as a customer in a Yellow Cab. She had instinctively sneered at the tweeness of it, but then was totally impressed when she read, 'You have the right to a silent journey.' Yes, yes and yes again! she had squealed in her head. It should be law in Ireland. It should be in the Constitution. She started thinking now how it was typical of the Irish to swallow whole the American version of Hallowe'en, but not take up a really good American idea, like people's inalienable right to a silent cab journey.

Emma was amused at her own thoughts, and wondered if she could work the idea up into a smart five hundred words for the weekend *Herald*. Tie it in with the presidential election, which would provide ample opportunity for Bush jokes. Editors were always stuck for decent witty material, and let's face it, they couldn't afford to turn their noses up at writing of Emma's finesse. But no, she shouldn't allow herself to be distracted from her present purpose: lunch with Norma and a serious talk about Luke. Even if that meant burrowing into some dark family corners. Actually Emma was also getting quite excited at the prospect of a second outing to L'Ecrivain. Her only slight hesitation was that for her it was the perfect setting for celebration, congratulations, making merry; not really the appropriate ambience for a downbeat heart-to-heart about family dysfunction. Still, it was good of Norma to stump up, she had to admit. Maybe that in itself should signal to Emma that perhaps she was being too sensitive with her fears about Luke and the latest Reid family crisis. On the other hand, Emma was keenly aware that she of all people wasn't the kind of person to over-dramatize things, so she was quite certain in her own mind that there was no way she could be entirely wrong about this. After all, who knew Luke better than she did? Call it a premonition, call it a sixth sense, whatever, Emma *knew* there was a very real problem. She was even willing to have lunch with Mommy Dearest in an effort to get to the bottom of it.

The phone message from Luke only increased her already heightened sense of a drama unfolding. She arrived back at the apartment, relaxed after her silent taxi journey, planning the evening ahead. She had no intention of telling Luke about her rendezvous. It would be a long evening during which she had to make sure not to let anything slip. How to do this was on her mind as she pressed the button to listen to the only phone message:

'Hi, Em, are you there? . . . you're not . . . OK. Listen, don't wait up tonight. I'm meeting Barry so I'll be late home. Bye.'

Emma was so enraged at this that it was another minute or so before she realized that Luke hadn't phoned her mobile to tell her. He did it the coward's way. He wanted to avoid talking to her. She smelled a big fat rat. What was this with him and his cousin Barry anyway? Emma couldn't for the life of her recall his name even being mentioned in the three years she had been with Luke, and then suddenly out of the blue there was this All-Ireland final business. Next thing she's been shown holiday snaps of the two of them when they were teenagers, which was a total joke, because when she did actually meet the great Barry that one time three weeks ago, those old photos might as well have been of some Romanian orphan for all the resemblance there was to the repulsive reptile creepo she had had to entertain impromptu right here in the apartment for several hours.

Sometimes Emma wanted to scream. Did nobody else notice? Did nobody in the Reid family see that *something* was wrong? Something was the matter with Luke. She wasn't being hysterical about this. She knew she wasn't. Ideally the person she would have liked to talk to about the whole situation was Ruth. Mommy Dearest was certainly not her first choice. Emma respected Ruth. Ruth was intelligent and sensitive and definitely the one closest to Luke, despite the eight-year gap. He loved her. Emma felt frustrated and even slightly guilty that her effort to talk to Ruth about Luke had ended so abruptly because of what Emma meant to be a jokey remark about Barry. She thought Ruth would laugh, not laugh out loud of course, because Ruth didn't tend to do that anyway, but at least find it vaguely amusing. Even if she had thought Emma's characterization of Barry was a bit unfair and had said so, then fine, Emma would have dealt with that smoothly enough, but to more or less slam down the phone and then not answer when Emma rang again to explain herself? That was a bit too like putting Emma in her place. In fact, though Emma was really sorry for the remark if it upset Ruth so much, none the less, frankly, deep down, Emma didn't actually think it was over the top at all. If the truth hurts, so be it, was how she really felt. Naturally if Ruth was to get back to her even now, she wouldn't go into all that. She would just offer a simple apology, so they could move on to the actual important issue of Luke's strange behaviour. Honestly, the Reids were like something out of Eugene O'Neill sometimes, which didn't bode well for her lunch tomorrow with Norma, but there was no choice now. Emma really was so concerned about Luke; she was actually frightened for him.

She tried his mobile but of course it was switched off. So Luke was avoiding her. What was he doing with Barry? Where were they? He wouldn't bring him back to the apartment again, would he? No, that would be too much. The image returned of her first sight of Barry Phelan, the twenty-first-century edition, sprawled on the sofa when she came home that night three weeks before. She was more sure than ever that her characterization of him had been far from over the top. He did look like something out of the *Rocky Horror Picture Show*. Emma vividly recalled that for those few moments, those seconds before Luke introduced his cousin, she had no premonition of who, or indeed what, was sitting there in her apartment. Nor did she like him, it. Had she been a dog, Emma would at that moment have emitted a long, low growl.

'Hey, we listened to your review, great stuff as usual. This is Cousin Barry. Barry, this is Emma.'

This was Barry? His cousin? Was Luke sure? The smiley country kid in the holiday snap had turned into this? Ravages of time and so on, but Emma didn't think so. What if it was someone else? Was it someone just pretending to be Barry? If so, what did he want from Luke?

Barry smiled and shook hands. Or rather, he felt her up. That's what it seemed like to Emma. When he took her hand and shook it and looked at her, she sensed he was feeling her up. She found herself recoiling from his aura, the cheap glare, the highlights in his hair, the tight clothes, but most of all, the ridiculous tan. And what was it about that face? Emma didn't know how she managed to disguise her inner revulsion. What was Luke doing with this alien? OK, they were cousins, if he really was Barry Phelan, but to miss *Steppenwolf* because he felt he had to meet with the mutant side of his family for . . . for what?

'Sounded like a decent production.'

'Yeah, yeah, well, you heard my review, so I won't say it all again.'

'Barry was saying you sounded really relaxed on the air. He hadn't ever heard you before.'

'I'm not really a theatre type, you know.'

Well, hold the front page! Emma thought as she went into the kitchen, ostensibly to make some coffee, but really because she couldn't stay another second in the same room with Cousin Barry. He called after her, 'Hey, and the sister from *Roseanne* is really in it, yeah?'

Emma sighed. Typical.

'Yes.'

'And come here, does she really get the kit off?'

Oh, Christ.

'Both actors do.'

'I always thought she was steeped to get that part in *Roseanne*. It must be great to be in a show where the star is so ugly she makes you look really fit.'

Emma was literally in shock. Had he actually said that, or did she imagine it? What was going on here? She tried to take it step by step in her head to make sure she wasn't being unfair to Luke in all this. First, Luke announces one Sunday morning that he's going to meet his cousin that afternoon to go to the All-Ireland football final. A GAA match! That alone was about 8 on the strange behaviour scale. He's gone all day. He comes home drunk. No big deal in itself, but again for Luke, at least 6 or 7 on the s/b scale. Then, over the next week, Cousin Barry becomes like some spirit inhabiting their space. Luke keeps mentioning him, even starts meeting up with him. Finally, one evening, out of nowhere, Luke produces photos from Kerry in the eighties to show Emma the young Barry.

His voice sounds a little strange when he says, 'Of course he's changed a bit since then.'

Oddly enough, what Emma was really noticing when she first looked at the photo was the young Luke. How serious and innocent and pretty he was. It reminded her yet again of her little secret; how all those years ago, when she first came to Dublin, she had noticed Luke in college. She really fancied him but somehow they never met. So when they did fall in love years later, she felt this strong sense of destiny unfolding. She had never revealed this to Luke. They had met in a theatre foyer three Festivals ago. It was one of those accidental encounters, casual introductions typical of a night out at the theatre. She chatted happily enough to this new stranger for about five minutes during the interval. She was already finding him pleasantly intelligent and interested and even passionate about theatre, when she suddenly felt this irresistible surge. It was nothing less than a charge, a current. She knew this person. Yes! It was . . . no, it couldn't be. Luke? Yes, Luke. Luke was his name. Luke what? It was the boy from college. Unbelievable.

Looking at the old holiday photo, Emma realized that this pale, beautiful fifteen-year-old was much closer to the boy she first fancied from afar in UCD all those years ago. Was he really the same person as the handsome, well-read and rather diffident twenty-seven-year-old who had become her lover during the 2001 Theatre Festival? Was her confident sense of destiny about this relationship just a chimera, a trick of space and time?

Such sudden doubts about the meaning of her secret history made the present situation more frightening. As well as being the busiest time of the year, when she was on the air reviewing every night for two weeks, Emma always thought of Theatre Festival time as their anniversary; time for them to celebrate together. Luke's special love was American drama and Emma thought, let's face it, how often do you get a chance to see one of the best American theatre companies perform in Dublin? *Frankie and Johnny in the Clair de Lune* might not be up there with *A Long Day's Journey into Night* – the eponymous rock and roll hit is probably more culturally significant than the play, she had rather wittily suggested on the radio earlier. But . . . but it was sweet and romantic, the performances were sublime, and it would have been so lovely to have been there with Luke. He was always passionate about what he saw and it would be perfectly normal for them to debate and share for hours after a play. He often drove her to the radio station and waited outside, so as she broadcast, she could summon up this beautiful image of Luke sitting in the glow of the car radio, his thoughtful eyes gazing into the middle distance as he drank in her words. She liked that. It made her performance even better, she felt. But that night not only did she not know where he was – had he even bothered to listen to her review? Then she arrived home to find Freak Man sitting on her sofa drinking her wine and making crude remarks.

Satisfied that the situation was indeed as eerily unpleasant as she feared, Emma had thrown back an espresso before making herself a cappuccino. Her main hope was that Barry would go soon. The kitchen door was ajar and through the tiny gap she could see his face peeping up in profile over the back of the sofa. He had the oddest gestures. He touched his eyebrow every now and then with his middle finger. It was like he was checking his make-up. Was he wearing make-up? When he cracked a laugh Emma didn't believe it. The sound was all wrong, his face looked all wrong. Right now she just wanted him out of their apartment. The more she looked at him from this disconcerting angle, the odder the whole setup became, the more hurtful and more worrying was Luke's cancellation of their evening out at the *Steppenwolf* show in favour of . . . yes, what?

No sooner had it suddenly crossed her mind that Barry was gay, that there was something going on with Luke, kissing cousins or whatever, than Emma told herself, whoa! hold it now. She really was letting her emotions get out of hand. This was borderline hysteria. She would have to calm herself before leaving the kitchen. None the less, paranoia apart, there was something not right about this guy. He definitely didn't like women. Emma had seen it in his eyes, she felt it from his whole presence. Just as she did not want him around, she was sure he did not want her around. So he mightn't be gay, but he was something scary; fucked up in some way, and Emma frankly wasn't interested in finding out. OK then, she decided the sensible thing was just to get this encounter over with, get past it. There was nothing to be gained by any kind of scene. No one was afraid of Virginia Woolf here. So she had picked up her cappuccino, sailed back into the living room and played a blinder: Luke's happy partner.

Was that really only three weeks before? It seemed so long ago. So much else . . . Afterwards Emma had kept her feelings about Barry to herself. Even when Luke passed up yet another Festival opening night because of some arrangement he had made to meet his cousin she said nothing. Fretful though she was, it wasn't until Emma found out the real story behind the tickets for Croke Park that she decided she had to do something, talk to someone.

On the night the crisis deepened, the situation couldn't, on the surface, have been more normal. They were both home for the night. Luke was working in the spare bedroom they had turned into a joint study. Emma had lit a fire and was waiting for *The Sopranos* to start. There had been many such nights since she and Luke became a couple. The ad break began, *The Sopranos* was next. They would watch it together as always. Emma went into the study to tell Luke. As she kissed the top of his head, she saw he was working on a long list of figures on two pages. Money figures with old £ signs and dates all from the eighties and early nineties. Emma couldn't resist asking, 'What's all that about?'

'I'm trying to work out what my childhood cost compared to Barry's.'

He said it as simply as if telling her he was doing this year's tax return. Emma stared down at the mass of figures and annotations. She didn't feel well. What was happening with Luke?

Emma had never been so conscious of how often 'family' was talked about in *The Sopranos*. Tonight she could not focus on the story, she could not admire the elegance of the episode's structure or the crisp intelligence of the dialogue. She did not even cringe at the sudden moments of outrageous violence, and bury her head in Luke's chest as she usually did. Instead she kept seeing Frank Reid, Norma Reid, all the Reids. She saw Barry Phelan lurking dangerously in the shadows, madness in his eyes. She saw a dinner table with all of them silent, as they passed from one to the other, newspapers with headlines naming and shaming Frank Reid. Emma knew with clarity and certainty that this was at the root of it all. Luke was obsessed with his father's disgrace. Did he feel personally betrayed, let down? Was he worried that people now thought badly of him? Surely not. How much did he hate his father now? Why would he not confide in her? She had never felt the tension of his silent presence next to her as keenly as she did now. One thought emerged and grew stronger, as Tony Soprano's cousin, also Tony, ruthlessly gunned down a couple in a car and limped away: Barry Phelan had entered the equation, and was going to wreak havoc with Luke's delicate mind. He would drag him down.

Emma couldn't stay silent any longer. 'Luke, why did your cousin get in touch with you all of a sudden?'

'He didn't. I contacted him.'

'Oh . . . and he is definitely your cousin?'

'Yes. Of course. I wanted to invite him to the football final. You know he's from Mayo? He used to be a really good footballer.'

'Oh, right. So . . . it was you bought the tickets?'

Luke shook his head. He smiled a ghostly smile. 'My father's firm has a corporate box. He'd promised it to some Kerry clients of his. You know the way it goes. But I thought Barry should be there, so I phoned them and cancelled.'

Emma suddenly felt a chill up her back. Luke was looking at her expectantly, but she didn't want to ask any more questions. There was a silence. Then Luke spoke as if in reply: 'I didn't ask my father for the tickets. I just took them. I don't even know if he's found out. He hasn't said. He might be afraid to confront me.'

Luke suddenly moved very close to Emma and looked steadily into her eyes, holding her frozen in fear.

'You know, as far as I can work it out, I mean, I can't be absolutely certain, a lot of it is just memory stuff, but according to these figures, my childhood cost between five and ten thousand pounds a year more than Barry's. Add it all up and it's probably around a hundred thousand pounds more. It's a lot, isn't it, when you think about it? But I want to be as accurate as I can with the figures.'

He got up and went back into the study. That was the moment Emma decided to contact Ruth. This was too scary. She knew now she couldn't cope on her own, and frankly why should she? This was messy family stuff. She was little more than a member of the audience here, but she would do what she could.

Emma worked out a plan: give Ruth a casual call and invite her out. There was an American play at the Project called *Top Dog/Underdog*, which sounded like it might be right up Ruth's alley. It was billed as a portrait of family dysfunction, so that might lead nicely into a heart-to-heart about Luke over a drink after the show. But then Emma's unfortunate Barry comment meant that encounter never happened. It took her another week of agonizing before she faced up to the fact that she had to talk to someone in the family, even if it had to be Mommy Dearest.

Ask her a thousand times and Emma still could not put her finger on why she disliked Norma Reid so much. That was probably why she had never even told Luke this. In fact she had never said it to anyone. What would be the point? OK, so imagine if she did, then whoever she confided in would ask why. Of course they would. What else do you say when someone announces out of the blue that they hate someone? Plus, frankly, Emma had no reason, no intelligent or logical or sensible reason, why Norma should have this effect on her. The nearest she could come to a description of how she felt would be some kind of comparison with the movies, some psycho horror, the kind when you sense as soon as a particular character appears on-screen that he or she is going to turn out to be loony, even though the movie itself is doing everything to disguise that fact. Of course you know already what kind of movie you are at, and that someone has to be a psycho, which isn't the case in real life, but it was the nearest analogy Emma could come up with in describing the intuitive nature of her response to Norma. If it was a movie, the great advantage would be that as it progressed, she would eventually start to see genuine clues, small but significant indicators, plot points which would serve to confirm the initial unsupported suspicion. Usually it would be something like an unexpected and unnecessary moment of ill-temper, or surprising cruelty, typically involving a domestic pet or a waiter. Frequently the psycho would find some sad event inappropriately funny. Sometimes a tiny unimportant lie would be exposed. This was how alert punters could gauge that a horrific event in the movie was imminent.

In day-to-day reality, however, over the three years Emma and Luke had been together, Norma offered no such clues, nor exhibited any of these telltale traits. In fact she was unfailingly kind and friendly to Emma. She seemed to like the fact that she was a country girl. She clearly approved of her as a potential daughter-in-law while managing not to be pushy about that either. Norma was intelligent, well read, could be amusing. She was an excellent hostess. She did good work for charities without ever being a sentimentalist. Yet Emma knew that she hated and (yes, oh yes!) *feared* Norma, though it seemed that her feelings were doomed to remain at the intuitive stage. She had thought about it and turned it over in her head enough to know that if she ever dared open this conversation to another soul, and explored aloud what was in her head, what she would end up saying, entirely without evidence, was this: She was convinced there was a selfishness, buried deep in the sealed tomb that was Norma Reid's heart, which, if it ever emerged, would be terrifying to behold.

No wonder Emma went to bed uneasy, frightened, thinking of her secret lunch date with Mommy Dearest the following day. The firework explosions outside kept her awake and nervous for another hour. By the time she fell asleep, Luke still had not returned home. When she woke in the morning he seemed to have left for work already. Only a bump in the pillow and the ruffled sheets told her he had been there.

The smile with which Norma greeted Emma was warm and generous. Emma had seen Norma put on an act, and while it was very good, she thought she could recognize the real thing. This was the real thing. Maybe the L'Ecrivain atmosphere helped. They were brought to a gallery table. Emma was delighted as she settled in under the slanted ceiling. From here she could glance over the rail and look down at all the diners. She would get a fantastic high-angle view of what everyone else was eating. This was where she had sat on her other fabulous visit to L'Ecrivain almost a year ago. It was a full Reid family outing, a three-line whip, and they were all there: Luke, Matthew, Ruth. Even Judy had come back from Washington. And she, Emma, was included. It was only a thirty-third wedding anniversary, but Frank was behaving like it was some sort of jubilee. He was on top form, bantering with his children, showing the sort of wit and spirit that made Emma realize he might just deserve the reputation he had as a raconteur, instead of being the smug old bore she had always secretly, guiltily thought he was. Of course he had to make a speech – Frank couldn't not – though in deference to neighbouring diners it wasn't a stand-up job. He sat leaning forward, holding his glass to indicate this was really just a quiet toast to family life. He spoke of the day he and Norma were wed.

'Apparently a number of significant events happened in 1970, and I've noticed that in recently published histories of modern Ireland our wedding that year doesn't even rate a mention, which came as a bit of a shock to me personally.'

Pause for family chuckle. Slight change of tone.

'But that doesn't alter my conviction that it was, and always will be, the most important date in our history. Wasn't it Paddy Kavanagh who said – Luke will correct me here if I get it wrong – "Gods make their own importance"? Well now, I've never claimed to be God, though some might say I occasionally act as if I am . . .'

Pause again for family chuckle.

'And let's not forget our little event in 1970 was important enough for a certain old friend of ours to organize himself time off during the arms trial, to come and see us hitched.'

The knowing tone of the chuckle told Emma that this was a familiar family legend. She felt a sudden tingle. It was fascinating to feel her body react like this, but the excitement was real. She'd never felt more like the country girl thrust into the buzzing throb of the capital. More than that, she was through the looking glass, now inside looking out. As Frank called the toast 'to Norma, wife and mother', and all the family clinked quietly in a murmuring intimacy, Emma couldn't help glancing down at the other diners below, pitying those not in the magic circle.

The present lunch by comparison was hard going. This had nothing to do with Norma, who chatted to Emma with an easy intimacy, and certainly nothing to do with the food. The problem was, how could she properly savour the piquancy of her aromatic spiced duck breast with apricot salsa, or relax and enjoy idle chit-chat with Norma, if, frankly, she was just sitting there waiting for her opportunity to move the conversation on? A very sensible voice in her head told her it would probably ruin everything to start talking about Luke. If she spoke her mind now, what appalling vista would open before her? The prospect was beginning to terrify her. Could the sentence burning in her brain really be spoken in these circumstances?

'Norma, I think Luke may be suffering from depression—'

Ouch! No. Better throw the ball her way.

'Norma, have you noticed anything . . . unusual about Luke lately?'

Hmmm. Maybe she should come from left field completely.

'Your nephew Barry has become great pals with Luke again recently. They're always out together.'

See what Norma would do with that. This last strategy seemed like the only serious proposition right now. Even this was difficult for Emma to negotiate, however. Norma's tone was so upbeat, her topics so frivolous, her enjoyment of the meal so full. Emma kept listening for some shift in tone, a remark or even word association that would allow her to nudge the conversation in the right direction. When the opening came, it was so sudden, so obvious, it totally threw her.

'So what is it you want to tell me?'

Norma smiled encouragingly. It was a straightforward direct invitation out of the blue, as they waited for dessert. Emma was dumbfounded.

'What – sorry?'

Norma smiled again, almost roguishly – not a word Emma ever expected to use about her. Then she spoke again. Now the appropriate word to describe her tone was much more in keeping with the Norma Emma knew: brisk.

'Oh, come on, Emma, you invited me to lunch. Just you

and me. You were even going to cook for me. You have something important you want to tell me.'

Fair dues to her, Emma thought.

'Well, yes . . .'

As Emma hesitated again, Norma actually leaned forward and touched her hand. Then Mommy Dearest showed her teeth.

'It's all right. Can't you tell from me? I've been hinting to you all through the meal. You have nothing to worry about. If you're pregnant I'll be thrilled. So will Frank.'

Dessert arrived. During the necessary pause Emma felt her face grow hot and red, while she saw Norma's smile of encouragement glow even brighter. As soon as the waitress left, Norma continued, 'In fact you probably know that right now it couldn't be better news. We've had such a terrible time of it recently, and Frank's taking it all so hard. I don't mind telling you I've felt like slapping him a couple of times and telling him to snap out of it. These things pass. Look, I said to him, people went out and elected Bertie again, for God's sake! Nobody cares these days. There are so many in the same situation anyway. But you know, Frank is a big softie. He lets it get to him. I'm going to tell you something now you must not ever whisper to anyone, and I mean anyone, Emma. He actually thinks he's not respectable any more. He really does. He's gone completely in on himself about it. Emma darling, this news is just the tonic we need. The first Reid grandchild.'

It was the movie moment in real life. Emma was the heroine in the thriller, and she was staring at the psycho, revealed. But who would believe her? She had no witness.

Back at the apartment Emma stood gazing out of the window, trying to assess the damage. The best she had been able to manage, while not denying a pregnancy, was at least to inject a note of caution. 'Nothing's, you know ... well, certain yet, you understand?' had been the pathetic effort. She now repeated this over and over in her head, to convince herself it would offer some kind of lifeline in the future, even though she knew that Norma wouldn't even recall her saying it. Norma was too busy weaving her own reality. Frankly, the more Emma thought about it, the more she was convinced that Norma knew absolutely that Emma was not pregnant. She just hoped somehow to make it happen; to impregnate her by sheer force of will. It did seem to Emma right now that the easiest and best solution *was* to become pregnant.

The night was drawing in. Already some children were appearing on the street outside, fully costumed for trick or treating. Emma knew she would not be responsible for her actions if any child came banging on her door just now. Some innocent would pay for her own sense of abject failure. She had looked into the eye of the monster and had retreated. There was no avoiding the conclusion that she was a moral cripple, but what could she have done? Across that elegant dining table, with the scent of mango and basil sorbet moist about her mouth, how might the crisis have been averted? Should she, Emma McCann, have reached out and shoved her hand down Norma Reid's throat and pulled out the lungs and liver and heart of her family life; laid them on the table before her?

Fireworks were exploding every few seconds now. A mauve circle of sparkling light revealed a slight figure approaching through the gloom below. It was Luke. Why was he walking? Where was his car? At that moment he saw her. He stopped and waved a little wave. A sad wave. He walked on to the entrance. Among the few true words Emma had spoken that afternoon, she had impressed on Norma that she hadn't told Luke 'anything' yet. So Mommy Dearest swore herself to secrecy until Emma had 'sorted things out' at that end. Of course she did, the witch, Emma thought, her conviction growing that she was the helpless pawn in a bigger game. Her panic increased as she realized she hadn't worked out what to say to Luke yet. Maybe nothing. Maybe just lure him into bed and get him to fuck her brains out. Pregnancy changes things – she had the whole history of Irish literature on her side there. Babies are a source of joy in the world. Yes. Maybe, just maybe . . .

The key in the door turned. Luke came in. He stopped and looked directly at Emma. He seemed to be trying to make up his mind about something. Tell me you love me, Luke. Emma tried to work some magic. Tell me you love me and it will be all right.

'You're probably wondering why I wasn't driving.'

Emma had forgotten about the car. Yes, where was the car?

'I sold it last evening. Barry helped me organize it. He put an ad in *Buy and Sell*.'

Emma just nodded. Events were moving beyond her. She had stopped trying to control them or even cope. For some reason she sensed an end coming, but she had no idea if it was an end of scene or act or – surely not – the drama itself. When Luke spoke again it was in the tone of someone saying 'I cannot tell a lie'.

'I think I have to leave you. It's not fair what I'm doing to you and it's only going to get worse. You tried to help, Em, I know. Believe me, I did notice. Don't blame yourself.'

He hugged her. Emma just let all her weight fall against him, no fight left.

'I'll collect my things some other time.'

And he left. Out of the blue Emma recalled an occasion very early in their relationship when Luke was reading her MA thesis, 'A Question of Morality: Modern American Drama', and had lavishly praised a particular passage:

Whether it is the centuries-old instinct of an essentially puritanical society, or the more glamorous influence of early Hollywood Westerns, in the great American plays of the twentieth century a moral imperative almost always takes precedence over a personal need. In the end the heroes of American drama 'do the right thing' in a way that almost never happens in Irish drama of the same period.

Emma remembered how warm the glow of his praise had felt, as now she watched Luke's dark figure drift across the front lawn into the fog. There was a barrage of firework explosions as he stopped, surrounded by three tiny masked Super-villains. He reached into his pocket. Emma was sure she saw him empty the contents of his wallet into the maw of the children's bag of treats.

# 4

# Bleak Midwinter I

Ruth Reid came home from Benjamin's winter solstice party to find a most embarrassing and uncomfortable message on her answering machine. It changed Christmas for her.

There had been some warning. Earlier, as she arrived at Benjamin's for the party, she had received a text from Emma: 'Happy Xmas. Please ring'. Odd. She would be seeing Emma on Christmas Day, wouldn't she? Luke hadn't said otherwise. Benjamin opened his door and smiled welcome. Ruth forgot the text instantly. Later that night there was another one: 'Please ring!'. Typical Emma McCann to expect instant response. She probably wanted to clear the air before they met on Christmas Day. Again, typical Emma. Ruth was not going to be bullied into calling, that was certain. By the time she stood arm in arm with Benjamin and all his friends, out in the little Rialto backyard, and gazed up at the Northern sky, Emma was no longer on her mind. Benjamin of course had done his homework. Checking his watch, he said it was 12.18 a.m., the exact midpoint between sunset and sunrise on the longest night of the year. It was Ruth's favourite kind of winter night, cold and clean, crisp enough to bite an icy chunk out of it.

Benjamin said to her, 'This feels so strange for me.'

Ruth understood immediately. She was pleased that for once she had been so forward as to make sure that she was next to Benjamin when they gathered for the group embrace, and had her arm around his waist. Now she wished she had the courage to press her fingers that little bit tighter against Benjamin's hip, just enough pressure to let him know how she felt; that she wanted him to turn and kiss her, to feel his beautiful lips press against hers like that day in the National Gallery, but this time to go further and let his tongue tease gently into her mouth. It would be even better if the signals flowed from him; if the hand that now rested on her shoulder in a friendly way should suddenly quietly caress the nape of her neck, telling her, 'I want you, Ruth.'

The group embrace broke. As Benjamin formally hugged all his guests in turn, Ruth watched jealously, but was eventually satisfied that there had been no special intimacy with anyone that might crush her hopes. So yes, she was reasonably content with how the party had gone. She felt that she and Benjamin were inching closer every day. She had decided definitely to take up his offer and move into his house early in the New Year. When she said goodnight to Benjamin, insisting that she wanted to walk home on such a beautiful night, he said, 'About the free room, can I call you tomorrow to talk about it?'

Ruth nodded, thinking they could talk about it later in bed, if only Benjamin would read her signals. Instead she walked home enjoying the canal and her thoughts. She tried to turn the twinge of regret that she was not now with Benjamin into a kind of delicious romantic melancholy. In truth, the glacial tranquillity of the canal bank walk was snapped again and again by lonely muttering drunks staggering home empty-handed or passing drunken boys roaring at one another. One boy had his penis out and was pissing openly on the pavement: he hadn't even bothered to seek the darkness of the nearby trees.

Ruth sidestepped the trickling steaming urine as she went by. Christmas in Dublin.

The walk home had made her feel slightly deflated. Emma's message was rather more of an assault on her emotions. Not too far below its calm, reasoned surface, Ruth could sense the raging undercurrents: hysteria, resentment, frustration, petulance, that ego-driven passive-aggressive determination, badger-like in its inability to let go. Emma McCann was in dire straits. It was also clear from the message that Emma thought Ruth knew all about the breakup between herself and Luke. In fact Ruth knew nothing.

She sat down and played the message again.

'It's been seven weeks since I've seen Luke . . .'

Seven weeks? Ruth tried to remember how often she had met with or spoken to Luke since that time. She immediately remembered Saturday, 6 November. That was easy. It was only a few days after Bush's re-election. It drizzled all day, the kind of miserable spray you could hardly see, but which soaked in relentlessly. Ruth had felt so black. If she hadn't arranged to go and see Benjamin's house, she probably wouldn't have got out of bed at all. There just seemed no point.

She encountered Luke on the LUAS. She was sitting staring out at the end-of-day tatters of the fruit market. It was only half two but it was so grey it seemed almost like night again. She turned away from the window to find Luke standing over her. To her shock her first instinct, the very first impulse, was to wish he wasn't there. She could scarcely believe she was feeling like this, even if for a part of a second. Not with Luke. Then he grinned his beautiful big brother grin. Under its glow, Ruth's heart lifted. She stood up and they embraced.

'That fucker Bush,' Ruth whispered in his ear.

Luke nodded.

'I couldn't believe it, could you?' Ruth continued. 'I mean, I was afraid that's how it would turn out, but I thought . . . I mean, I didn't really think . . .'

Luke sighed. 'No, I knew he was going to win.'

His tone suggested some desperate inevitability in these political events. Ruth fell silent. What a dreary day. She suddenly wondered why Luke was travelling on the LUAS. As had always been the case since childhood, he seemed to read her thoughts.

'I sold the car. I'm glad. I like this.'

Ruth was surprised but genuinely pleased to hear that. The fewer cars in the world the better as far as she was concerned. Then Luke asked, 'Where are you off to?'

Ruth lied because if she had told the truth, that she was going to visit Benjamin at his house, Luke would have detected in her tone the urgency and uncertainty of her emotions. Her desire for Benjamin would have been obvious to him. He might even have gained entrance to that part of her mad brain that imagined a scenario of urgent spontaneous afternoon sex that very day. Ruth believed her beloved brother could see into her very soul.

A lie seemed simpler. Glancing quickly at the list of stops above the doors, she said she was going to St James' Hospital. Immediately she realized her error. How could she have been so brain-dead as to use a hospital excuse with Luke? Luke, who cared about every little thing on earth. Luke, who used to pick up a spider when it scared five-year-old Ruth, and carry it gently out of the cottage in Tahilla, which was full of spiders, especially at Christmas or New Year. He would hold Ruth's hand and carry the creepy-crawly in his other hand, as they went out into the freezing dark. Then he would find a big rock, and explain softly to her how spiders loved hanging around rocks, and he would meet his friends there. Luke would gently place the spider on the rock and get Ruth to wave it bye-bye, even as it scampered away.

Now, for such a little lie, Ruth had to suffer a seemingly endless series of concerned questions, spawning further deceit upon deceit. Visiting a college friend – no, he wouldn't know her – what? Oh . . . a sports injury – not sure. Leg . . . or shoulder maybe – basketball – in her history tutorial, just a casual acquaintance really, but you know, you feel you should – hey! Here already. Out! Out! Out! She hopped off so fast they didn't even kiss goodbye. As the tram moved on, Luke made an 'I'll ring you' gesture.

Because Ruth rarely thought of Emma at all, it was only now, listening to her sad message for the third time, that she realized Luke had said nothing about Emma that day. He had not mentioned her which, to be fair, did not count as a lie. The only one who had lied that day was Ruth.

'. . . I just wondered if you could get him to call me. Just to like, you know, say Happy Christmas. I have a stupid present for him. Nothing special, you know. Just to say happy Christmas, that's all . . .'

The LUAS encounter had been short and a little agitated. The breakup might not even have happened by then. Seven weeks? Maybe. But the phone conversation days later lasted over an hour. Emma's name came up. It was Thursday afternoon, 11 November, the day Arafat died, and the day after she and Benjamin had kissed in the National Gallery. Ruth was still in bed staring out of the window. From where she lay, she could see the tops of some trees. The leaves were golden in the winter sun but the wind was whisking them away one by one. Ruth had counted twenty-three blown off in a long, long game of 'He loves me, he loves me not', when the phone rang. Thinking for some reason – no, hoping – it might be Benjamin, she picked up.

Luke was calling from work. Ruth was glad of that. She liked to sense in the background the calm silence of the museum, the mildly comforting timbre the high-ceilinged rooms seemed to give Luke's voice. It turned out to be a really nice chat, one of their best in a long time. Luke had said that all his life since he could remember anything about anything, Yasser Arafat had been a presence in the world. When Luke was a very little boy he thought he was Mother Theresa's son because of the headgear. Luke could always make Ruth laugh, but even he couldn't disguise the black bitterness in his reply when she remarked on the fact that Bush and Blair were meeting to clap each other on the back, instead of going to his funeral.

'They are vulgar people. Yasser Arafat might have ended up vain, corrupt even, but he was changing the face of Middle Eastern politics when Bush was still falling over at frat parties. They haven't enough dignity or sense of history between them to know they should at least mark the end of an era.'

'It feels hopeless to me, Luke. Why did they elect him again?'

Luke's voice stayed lighthearted. Ruth knew it was for her sake. He said he never wanted to hear the word Ohio again. Did she notice that all its anagrams sounded like cries for help? I ooh! O hoi! On election night if he left the room to make a coffee, the last word he heard was Ohio. When he returned the first word he heard was Ohio. A CNN expert put him to sleep analysing voting patterns in key Ohio precincts. As he woke again, some anchorman was saying he still could not 'call' Ohio. Ruth, laughing, said all that night she kept remembering Daddy's party piece when they were young.

'He had a party piece?'

'Yeah, sometimes, yeah. Don't you remember? "The banks of the O-hi-o".'

She sort of sang it down the phone. She wouldn't have tried this with anyone but Luke.

> And only say that you'll be mine
> In no other's arms entwine
> Down beside where the waters flow
> Down by the banks of the Ohio . . .

Luke said he had completely forgotten about that. He must have blotted it out, like some terrible nightmare. 'Speeches, yes. He'd deliver homilies at the drop of a hat on any occasion. Never remember him singing.'

'He did. Definitely.'

'Mind you, I know that song from somewhere. Didn't he kill the only woman he loved?'

'"Because she would not be my bride,"' Ruth quoted in mocking country music patois.

They laughed so much throughout this conversation, yet after the laughter had subsided, they both found themselves admitting sadly that they didn't know why they had bothered staying up all night watching, as if in shocking slow motion, this huge political motorway pile-up. Luke said it was because people see one thing but still, somehow, want to believe it is something else.

'You saw those queues of people waiting in the rain to vote? For a tiny while we thought we were looking at a new generation stepping out to vote for change, but instead it was an evangelical army holding the line.'

Just as they were saying goodbye, Luke suddenly asked if

she wanted to meet, as he put it, with what Ruth thought was rather Dickensian formality, her long-lost cousin Barry. Ruth said sure, and would Emma be there?

Luke had simply replied, 'No, just us.' He didn't even say her name. Did that count as a lie?

The night out with Luke and Barry turned out to be the best fun in ages. They met on 27 November. It had rained all day, leaving Ruth feeling so dull and heavy that she decided to ring and make an excuse not to go. Then the dreary beating on the windowpane beside her suddenly stopped, just as she was hovering by the phone. It was an immense relief and in truth, Ruth's curiosity to meet long-lost Cousin Barry became the strong desire.

Being a Saturday, Ron Black's was teeming. Ruth assumed that Barry had chosen the pub. She couldn't imagine Luke even knowing about this opulent split-level New Dublin temple. From the moment quite early on when Luke introduced the subject of Barry's plastic surgery, and Barry told the whole story in gruesome thrilling detail, she knew it was going to be a special night. Ruth was only eight years old when she had last seen Barry. She had no visual memory of him at all. The first thing that struck her when she saw the two of them sitting together was how unlikely a companion for Luke he was. Barry smiled, showing off his brilliant teeth, and gave her a hug that lifted her off the ground. She felt the hardness of his body, and even the kiss on the cheek had a wolfish quality about it, but his words were pure familial affection. Where was the skinny little twerp? What gorgeous creature had she grown into? Lucky she was a cousin or he wouldn't be able to control himself. To her shock, Ruth found herself saying that in Jane Austen novels, cousins fell in love all the time.

Barry laughed. 'Don't tempt me.' And he literally planted her down beside Luke and asked what she was having.

Ruth loved this immediate physicality. She found Barry instantly fascinating and exciting; an exotic, strange-faced, over-tanned animal. Luke's presence was that of a reassuring zoo keeper. He made it OK to approach and even touch; she was perfectly safe.

The plastic surgery story was the icing on the cake. Barry was very funny about it, in the way Irish people always enjoy being funny about the odder aspects of American life. Ruth also detected a delicate halting undercurrent of loneliness. She would have loved to explore what this urgent need in Barry to change himself was, what dissatisfaction with his inner core caused him to alter the surface. She gauged that tonight, in the casual buzz of a Ron Black's Saturday, was not the time for such a conversation. She was sure that Luke would know the answer, as always, and she looked forward to discussing it with him. Right now she was gumming for a fag. Luke, of course, goody-two-shoes, had never smoked a cigarette in his life. It was the one significant point of difference between Ruth and her beloved brother. They had both always loved humorously emphasizing it, as if it was proof of their independent existence. When she mentioned going outside, Luke said work away, with that withering sigh he employed whenever the subject of smoking came up. To Ruth's delight Barry said that even though he hadn't smoked in two years, he couldn't let his gorgeous little cousin stand out in the freezing cold on her own. He would go with her. So Luke had to follow.

Outside there was the usual polite nudging to get as close as possible to the heater. Ruth noticed, not for the first time, that a curious consequence of the smoking ban was that people now talked about smoking all the time. This surface text had become chat-up line, political discourse and psychology game all in one. There was even, inevitably, a compound word for it: smirting. It was the lingua franca of single life in modern Dublin. Ruth began to expound at length about how the hardships of the ban had in fact made her more determined to smoke; from being a casual, largely uninterested, indeed disinterested smoker, she had become a committed participant. It was for her a symbol of her citizen's rights. Standing outside freezing with her fellow-smokers, puffing proudly, had become for Ruth a bit like the anti-war marches she had been so enthusiastic about the year before, or her attendance at the recent court hearing in support of the lesbian couple who were asking the Inland Revenue to acknowledge their marriage. In truth she was a protest junkie and she loved it.

As her monologue continued, Ruth became aware that she was showing off. She knew she was amusing Luke. She hoped she was amusing Barry. She was thrilled beyond measure when, as she flourished her pack of Marlboro to light up a second, Barry asked her for one.

'That's it. You've convinced me. I'm going to smoke again.'

He took the cigarette and held it for Ruth to light him up, then enjoyed a long theatrical drag and sighed contentedly. Luke was horrified or mock-horrified: for once Ruth couldn't tell which.

'What have you done? This man was on the straight and narrow. The one true path. You have dragged him down.'

'And it feels good, doesn't it, Barry?'

'Sure does, cousin.'

All in all, it was becoming the happiest night out Ruth had had in a long time. She suddenly felt Christmas in the air. She looked up, thinking it might even snow. Why had she not had a night like this with Benjamin? That would do it, she was sure. If they could once move beyond their brains, flirt not discuss, the rest would be easy. She didn't know how to make this happen. In fact she knew, though the knowledge frustrated her, that such things could not be made to happen. One just had to be in the right mood at the right time in the right place with the right man. The very moment she had that thought, her eyes met Luke's and he gave her the secret wink, the wink that since she was a little girl had always made her feel that no matter what, if she cut her knee, or if Mummy had one of her headaches again and couldn't be spoken to, or if Daddy was shouting curses at someone down the phone – anything – it would all be made right. Her big brother Luke would make it so. That he should wink at her at that moment made her feel that, once again, he had looked into her very soul. He was telling her not to worry. He, Luke, could make anything happen.

The night ended full of Christmas joy, walking together, arms linked, down Grafton Street under the big red lanterns: The Lion, the Tin Man and Dorothy. They stopped outside Brown Thomas's new secular Christmas display, and loudly bemoaned the absence of Nativity scenes and fairy tales. Luke and Barry put a giggling Ruth into a taxi at the Trinity College rank, and she blew kisses at them through the back window.

They had talked and laughed together for five hours that night, and Luke had never mentioned Emma once. That omission surely constituted a lie? Should Ruth now be angry with him? What did it mean that he was no longer including her in his private world? Emma's message finally ended in a sort of whining fall:

'. . . so anyway, Ruth, I would really appreciate it if you could at least pass on the message to Luke. Don't even worry about getting back to me – although I'd love to hear from you of course. It's just, you know, don't feel you have to. I mean, if you're busy or whatever. It's pretty hectic at this time of year – and ah . . . yeah . . . like, obviously Happy Christmas . . . OK . . . ah . . . yeah . . . well . . .'

What should Ruth do? This pathetic message had brought the longest night to a dreary conclusion, but even someone of Ruth's disposition could hardly guess that it would signal the beginning of a downward spiral that would leave her three days later, on the afternoon of Christmas Eve, unable to face getting out of bed. A golden winter sun pushed through cracks in the curtains, but she couldn't face the light. It was on her mind that she still had one more present to buy, but could do nothing about it. What might she buy her little brother Matthew that he didn't have already anyway? She knew he loved Franz Ferdinand, but he owned every Franz Ferdinand artefact in existence so there was no point. She hated just giving him money, but what else was she to do now? It was all a disaster. In just three days everything had gone awry.

The morning after the winter solstice party, Ruth could scarcely wait to tell Benjamin she had decided definitely to take up his offer and move into his house. Before dialling she hovered over the phone for a little while, searching for the right tone of relaxed enthusiasm. She need not have bothered. Benjamin interrupted the carefully crafted opening sentence announcing her acceptance of the offer. He was really sorry, this was what he had wanted to talk to her about. His house-mate had decided not to go home in the New Year after all, so the room was not free yet. She was still intending to leave the country sometime soon, but he didn't want to leave Ruth dangling. He was really sorry. Ruth said she was really sorry too. Benjamin was very upset because he had been really looking forward to Ruth living in the house. He knew they would get on really well. Even in her wretchedness, Ruth noticed herself focusing on Benjamin's underlying tone, listening closely for some hint of intimacy or romantic desire. Something to hold on to.

That same night she had to confront the reality of Daddy's drinking. It was not long after ten but she was already miserably in bed when the phone rang. It was her mother, who sounded as though she was choosing her words carefully.

'Can you come over? Daddy's had a fall. He's collapsed.'

'Where is he? What happened?'

'He's here in his study. Can you come over?'

'Of course, but—'

'Soon as you can.'

Her mother put down the phone. Ruth wasted no time getting out on the black sleety street in search of a cab. By the time she arrived at her parents' house, her mind had turned over every possible horror. All she really wanted to know was if Daddy was in mortal danger or not. Anything less than that and she could cope.

Her mother opened the door quietly and ushered Ruth into the study.

'Have you phoned for an ambulance?'

Norma just shook her head and nodded towards Frank. He lay curled up on the floor, snoring gently. Ruth was slightly puzzled. He seemed to be just asleep.

'I can't get him upstairs on my own.' Her mother sounded just a little too matter-of-fact. Yet the more Ruth looked at her father, the more obvious it became that there didn't seem to be anything much wrong with him. His breathing was noisy but fairly normal. Moving closer, Ruth caught a strong whiff of single malt. The smell of his breath even cut through the heavy presence of recently smoked cigars.

Ruth tried to stay calm. 'You said he collapsed.'

Her mother spoke almost in a whisper. 'Well, he did. He was sitting in his favourite chair reading, and next thing I came in and he was on the floor.'

'So you just need to get him to bed?'

'I couldn't leave your daddy there, could I?'

'No. Where's Matthew?'

'He's in his room. I'm sure he's asleep. Anyway, I couldn't let Matthew see his father like this.'

Ruth decided now was not the time to confront that one. Her anger was receding; her sadness, increasing. It was a terrible situation. She felt so sorry for her father. She knew this was all because he felt so guilty. She wondered whether if people could only understand the depths of his despair they would continue to be so vengeful. She knew poor Daddy must have sat there alone all night in his favourite chair, drinking and smoking, his brain turning round and round the twists and turns of life, of the road he had taken, of the wrong deeds committed for the right reasons. Ruth loved her father as desperately as she knew he loved her. He loved all of them. His family was everything to him. She knew that prison or fines, or anything like that, could never make him suffer the way he was now making himself do. He must have drunk . . . she looked at the little table by his chair, but there was no bottle of whiskey there. Or glass. The ashtray held several cigar butts – Ruth recognized the distinctive red bands of his favourite Cubans, Partagas series D. All evidence of alcohol had been removed.

The two women somehow succeeded in hauling Frank off the floor and between them, dragged him to the bottom of the stairs. Ruth felt keenly the close presence of her mother. Occasionally, over the next few minutes of the step-by-step struggle, their fingers brushed as they adjusted their hold on her father. Sometimes they would both be pulled forward, so that briefly they came face to face, their noses almost touching. Mostly it was a grim, silent haul up the stairs. Norma was particularly anxious as they pulled Frank past Matthew's closed door. Ruth imagined him on the other side, lost in porn on the Internet. She wanted to kick the door and shout, 'Come out and help, you spoiled brat.' But of course she didn't. It wasn't his fault. How could he help? How could he even have opinions, if he wasn't told things?

Once they rolled Frank on to the bed, they stood in silence. Norma said that was fine, she'd get him into bed now, meaning Ruth was to leave, preferably for home

Ruth didn't even suggest waiting downstairs. 'See you Christmas Day,' she said.

The words sounded quite hopeless on her lips. She closed the great black front door silently so that Matthew would not hear. She walked softly down the gravel path, then stood on the road looking back. What was this house? Was it the happiest of childhood homes, or was its red-brick respectability an elegant lie? Was it a restored gem, a tribute to the care and sensitivity of its owner, or was it a smart investment guaranteeing the future wealth of all the family? In truth, the latter was the more frightening prospect for Ruth. Her father had already bought them a golden childhood and he certainly intended to secure their future. She could not reject him now, but her heart felt sick and old.

Ruth cried most of the following day. In between she managed to wrap a few presents but she took little pleasure in this although she was always the best wrapper in the family. Everyone – Daddy, her mother, Luke, Judy, even little Matthew – would ask her to wrap presents for them, because she did it so neatly and tastefully. The Christmas she was ten, she actually took complete charge. She gathered everyone's presents together in the front room where the tree was and spent the happiest afternoon of her whole life in there, squatting on the floor, lost in tags and sticky tape and coloured paper, wrapping for the whole family. Today she scarcely knew or cared what she was wrapping, or for whom. Still, she had not yet reached her lowest point. That came just before she went to bed, when she checked her emails.

Judy had sent a short, cool message home, CCed to her and Luke saying sorry, but she and Alan couldn't get away from Washington after all. She'd make sure to phone on Christmas Day. Happy holiday. Ruth was devastated. She simply couldn't believe it. Judy must know that Daddy really needed the whole family to be there this year; the cowardly bitch, and her Bush-loving merchant banker husband.

Ruth slept badly and woke before eight on a pitch-black Christmas Eve. She just lay there as the light came in and inched round the room. Mid-afternoon she awoke from a lonely doze with a sudden determination to contact Luke. She had to ignore the fact that he had told her nothing about his breakup: and simply pass on Emma's message, even plead for her. Maybe if she did this one selfless thing, something of Christmas might be salvaged.

She tried his mobile. It was out of service. Now three o'clock, it would be dark soon. The museum was closed, so Luke wasn't at work. She didn't know where he lived now, and she couldn't contact him by phone. An immaculate winter sun was turning her bedroom deep orange. Ruth still lay there, unable to get up, unable to fall asleep and forget it all; in truth, scarcely able to go on living.

Then she remembered where Cousin Barry lived. He had mentioned it: Venetian Hall, an old seventies apartment block in Killester. Barry would know where Luke was. She had left them both together at the taxi rank that night. Maybe he was even staying with Barry. It was a lifeline: Ruth was energized by this sudden late inspiration.

It took over an hour to get through the Christmas Eve madness to Killester. It seemed as though it was all worthwhile when Ruth stepped out of the taxi at the entrance to Venetian Hall, to be rewarded immediately by the sight of Barry in the parking area, loading something into the back of his van. He closed the double doors and turned as Ruth approached. He could not disguise his shock. He glanced at his watch.

'Barry, sorry for turning up out of the blue like this. I'm trying to find Luke, but his phone isn't working, and it seems he's not living with Emma any more . . .'

'Right, yeah . . .'

Ruth could tell he knew all this already.

'I wondered if you have any idea where I might find him. Do you know where he's living, or if he has a new number? I don't understand it.'

'Sure, sure, listen, sorry, I can't invite you up . . .'

Is Luke here now, Ruth thought immediately. Is he in Barry's apartment?

'I have to go out . . . ah, he's given up his mobile, I know that—'

'What?'

'Yeah, but I can give you his new address.'

'Oh, that's fantastic.'

'Sure. Have you a pen?'

'Yes.'

'OK – oh and ah . . . Merry Christmas by the way.'

'Thanks.'

'I have a little present for you, is it OK tomorrow?'

'Barry, you shouldn't have. Are you calling over?'

'Yeah, Luke said to come for dinner. I'm looking forward to it.'

Ruth wondered if her mother knew. She couldn't be bothered thinking about that now. The address? Barry pulled out a pen and scribbled on a scrap of paper. Ruth looked. Oh God. Kilmainham.

'All the way across town? He definitely has no phone?'

'No. Listen, sorry I can't give you a lift but I'm—'

'It's fine. I'd better shift. Thanks a million, Barry. I'll see you tomorrow, OK?'

'See you, gorgeous.'

Barry now seemed relaxed again. He flashed a smile at Ruth, showing his beautiful teeth. As she hurried back out on to the road, she noticed that he stayed by the van watching her go. He checked his watch again.

It was now quite dark. Ruth went to the nearest bus stop, but prayed for a taxi. Then she saw the heavenly glow of an approaching roof sign. Maybe it was all going to work out fine.

The taxi stopped. As Ruth got in and gave the address, a bus approached from town, slowing to a stop across the road. A dark figure hopped off. He was hidden behind the bus as it pulled away, but then reappeared just as Ruth took off in the taxi. A second either way and she would not have realized that the dark figure was Luke. He had some kind of rucksack on his back. Ruth shrieked at the taxi driver to stop and he braked hard, cursing, as she turned to stare out of the back window. Luke turned into Venetian Hall. She just jumped out of the cab, forgetting to apologize, and ran back.

She was just in time to see Luke go through the entrance door and disappear into the lift. Now what to do? She was suddenly aware of how cold it had become, too cold to think with clarity. Should she buzz Barry's apartment? Demand an explanation from both of them? Forget everything and go home? Stand there all night silent and still, letting the cold seep into her until she just seized up? Ruth felt so alone, so stupid. All her life, whenever she felt bad about anything, she had always turned to Luke. This time it was Luke making her feel this way, whether he knew it or not. Was Barry telling him now about how she had turned up suddenly, how he had tricked her into going away? Were they laughing at her?

Luke and Barry suddenly stepped out of the lift. Ruth ran for cover, pressing herself between a bush and a wall. She watched her brother and cousin emerge. They were well wrapped up; Luke still had his rucksack, Barry carried a bag. As they reached the van Ruth realized she had to confront them now or not at all. Barry started the engine and she was tempted to run in front of the headlights, arms flailing. But she could not move. She just stayed shivering in the shadows as the van drove away.

# 5

# Christmas with Franz Ferdinand

Matthew felt so free. Christmas Eve had never been like this before. Being sixteen is pretty fine: he held that thought as he lurched towards the lift on the top floor of the Millennium Tower. It wasn't a profound thought, he told himself solemnly, but he figured he was entitled to the occasional not-so-profound thought, and anyway, it was a true thought. He clicked on Franz Ferdinand. Since the Old Guy had bought him the iPod, Matthew had downloaded over 4,000 tracks but 80 per cent – no, more like 90 per cent – of his time right now was spent listening to just eleven tracks from the greatest, smartest, most fuck-off band in years. Actually twelve tracks including their Internet exclusive. Smart boys.

He stabbed at the ground-floor button and fell against the back wall. He went down fast. Christmas Eve rocked. That was the best party venue ever. Ronan's dad was going to be seriously fucked off if he ever got to see the state of his new penthouse. Ronan wanted them all to come help with the clean-up on the 27th. His dad had new tenants coming on New Year's Day. It only seemed to occur to Ronan towards the end of the night that there might be a problem, when Jake forgot to get to the bathroom before puking up. 'Ah, guys, guys.' Ronan with his chubby crying face.

It's so much better on holidays. The serious upside of the Old Guy being so depressed, and the atmosphere at home more miserable than a Dido album, was that there was no more Frank and Norma holding court on Christmas Eve, with sherry, cigars, carols, and boring Fianna Fáil Law Library pricks asking him how the old school was, when really they just wanted to tell him what it was like when they were there back in nineteen-sixty-zed. Definitely there would be no six-hour trek to Kerry this year for a damp post-Christmas in the old cottage. The old folk hardly even raised the energy to ask Matthew where he was going tonight. 'Ronan's place, a few of the guys,' was mutter enough. 'I'm so drunk, I'm drunk, I'm so drunk,' Matthew droned happily as the lift hit rock bottom and he aimed himself at the street.

What chance a taxi? About 3.9 per cent. Taxi drivers? Do they know it's Christmas-time at all? Matthew loved that gag. He started it a couple of weeks ago in history class, when Raggy Boy got annoyed because of Dara (prize moron) not knowing if De Valera was for or against the Treaty. Raggy Boy really boiled over, making like a crazy person. Matthew leaned over to Eanna and whisper-sang in a sad voice, 'Does he know it's Christmas-time at all?' Eanna creased.

Matthew decided that on such a beautiful night he would walk. He looked up for a star in the east, but no luck. He bobbed happily towards Shelbourne Road, thinking about Sarah. She'd definitely seen him looking at her, Matthew knew for sure. She was sitting on the sofa with Eanna, and OK, it looked like he was well in there. Everyone thought that was a done deal, but Matthew couldn't help looking. The way she stretched her body when she reached for her drink, so that even more of her tight little tanned midriff was begging Matthew to reach out and run his finger along it. Except he was on the other side of the room, listening to Seona talking about integral calculus, and was his maths teacher as brilliant as hers? Matthew wondered how he was supposed to know, as he had never sat in a maths class in Muckross. Shane had put on Dizzy Rascal for the zenth time, and at that stage just about everything was getting on Matthew's nerves, when Sarah noticed him looking at her. The thing was, Matthew was 95 per cent certain she was glad. Maybe, just maybe . . . no, she was definitely with Eanna. Tonight anyway. And tonight was the night. Tonight was Christmas Eve. He should have found a way to tell her. He should have told her tonight. Eanna and Matthew were good mates, but if in fact, she preferred Matthew, what was the point in Eanna hanging on in there?

Now here he was, three o'clock Christmas morning, alone. On the mean streets of Ballsbridge. But Matthew was feeling too good to feel bad. This was the best Christmas Eve ever. This is what they would all be like, now and for ever, even to the end of time. Freedom Christmas with your mates. Better again, getting laid. Thinking it through, Matthew figured in the greater scheme of things, in the life plan, it was OK that he didn't get laid this Christmas. As long as Eanna didn't either. Sixteen was like a probation year. Next year when he was seventeen he'd expect real action. He wondered would it be Sarah? Or would he have moved on? Maybe he had moved on already. For the last hour or so before he finally fell out the door, Matthew knew in his secret, deep down honest place, he wouldn't be leaving with her. That was OK. It was actually pretty cool to say silently across the room, 'I know I won't be leaving here with you.' He still continued to stare at Sarah on and off, having this 'I say, you say' conversation in his head, which always ended with him leading her out the door with his hand on her ass. He put away about half a bottle of Southern Comfort in that last hour, so it was fine.

Franz Ferdinand's energy kept him moving, even though some kind of giant fist was now pressing hard on his head, and it was really cold. Matthew cheered himself along by thinking about his presents. Would he get the Vespa? He was 75 per cent confident. The Old Guy would totally want to make him happy this year. He'd give anything for a big hug from Matthew and see him be majorly chuffed and thrilled. Matthew was sure that he had left both of the Aged Ones in no doubt that there were no viable second choices this year. A Vespa 125 was his little heart's desire and hey, 5 A-ones and four A-twos in the summer exams, *and* the lead in *A Man for All Seasons* next term? They couldn't argue with that. Since October he had charmed and maybe ever so slightly blackmailed. It was fair enough: Luke hadn't called to the house for months, Judy was keeping well out of harm's way in New York, and whenever Ruth dropped in, the tension between her and the Old Darling sent the Old Guy running to the study for the Laphroaig 30 y.o. Matthew was a lifeline. He was their precious little baby. He just hoped it was the right colour Vespa. He knew all those things could be changed, but it was so cool when everything was perfect on Christmas morning, and for him, racing green with tan seats was perfect.

Matthew had a bit of a laugh thinking about what sad gay present Ruth would get him. He had bought her *Adrian Mole and the Weapons of Mass Destruction*, because he thought, instead of moaning about Iraq and Bush and Blair all the time, could she not have a laugh? He knew she'd have got him some CD of African bongo music, or a poncho made by a peasants' collective on the banks of the Amazon. Ruth just didn't get it. She was only twenty-two, not exactly in the Luke category of ancient bores, but she totally missed the point, asking Matthew why he was obsessed with labels, telling him he was a slave to Global Capitalism. Matthew had long ago stopped trying to explain that it wasn't a question of logo or no logo. He had thought through all that. He was beyond logo. He was post-logo. He was the master. His world his way. He would buy or not buy. He would wear or not wear. Freedom to play.

He got a text. Yes! Sarah. He knew it. Christmas Eve rocks! It just said, 'Cool Yule. Phone me.' He had been absolutely 100 per cent right. He wanted her with him now, walking along Herbert Park, his arm around her. Why couldn't he touch her now? Why couldn't he have her? He should have done something about it. He stopped and looked back the way he came. Maybe if he went back? No, it was too late now. Fuck! Fuck! Fuck! Fuck! Fuck! Fucking Eanna.

Matthew didn't know how he came to be sitting on the ground screaming, but he was. He wasn't sure how sick he felt. He wasn't going to throw up, he was sure of that, but something was wrong. He staggered up and tried running. 'Cheating on You' was playing, so that really helped to drive him on, move him on, away, away from Ronan's party. He'd get home, get to bed, hope the Old Darling wouldn't wake him up too early in the morning. He'd have to let himself be dragged to Christmas Mass, he knew that, especially if he got the Vespa, then all day he'd have to be St Matthew, patron saint of tax-dodgers.

The running was good. It worked. He took in huge gulps of icy air as he went. He could see the house up ahead now. It was a black silhouette, like some old haunted monstrosity in a spoof horror movie. Go for it, he grunted. He increased his speed and hit the gate, gulping and gasping and heaving but feeling a lot better. He took out the mobi again and looked at Sarah's text, 'Cool Yule. Phone me.' The part of him that was already a serious poetry lover, confirmed cineaste (*A Bout de Souffle* was his present favourite film) and practised sceptic, felt just a little contemptuous at 'Cool Yule'. But the part of him that burned for Sarah's golden midriff, and dreamed of her tongue trailing down his bare tummy all the way, decided that now was not the time for Schadenfreude (his present overused favourite word). Anyway, Sarah had got loads of As in her juniors, so in fact, she was no blonde.

He didn't want to go into the house now. It seemed so old and dreary, with sad old fucks lying asleep inside. Burn this city, burn this city! The family was more or less grown-up now; why didn't the Aged Ones retire to Kerry full-time, sell this tomb, and give everyone a million each out of the proceeds? The place was worth 6 million easy. Matthew could buy a pad with a view in Grand Canal Dock. Perfect set-up for college. He knew one thing: if he had his own place he wouldn't be having puke parties with Ronan and Jake and Eanna and the rest.

He pressed the key in the door. Easy, easy, shhh. They had left a little hall light on to guide him in. The Christmas trees and decorations made an evil forest. Matthew crawled around the floor to find plugs and sockets. He turned on the tree lights and lay on his back in the magic kingdom, jerking with the music. The Old Darling had laid out 20,000 euro to get gay Eric to decorate. The concept, apparently, was traditional Teutonic midwinter fest: 'Stille Nacht, Heilige Nacht'. Eric had explained his vision at length to Matthew one day. He kept calling him 'young Mr Reid' in a roguish, mildly camp way. Matthew figured it was the combination of school uniform and his unkempt blond hair that turned Eric on. It was the first time he had ever been chatted up by a gay guy. He liked the attention. He liked the power of being desired and not caring. Here was this guy, older than Luke, but actually really fit for his age, babbling like he was coked up about Tannenbaum and handcarved Nativity angels, and St Nicholas, but his eyes were saying, 'Come dance with me, Matthew, come on, dance with me.' The fact that it was happening here in the Aged Ones' house, surrounded by ten-foot trees and berries and baubles, added to the thrill. Why couldn't it be like this with girls?

In the moment's silence between tracks nine and ten, the phone rang loud. Matthew looked at his watch. After half three. What was going on? Four more deafening rings, then it stopped. Either whoever it was had given up, or one of the Aged Ones had picked up. Matthew decided he had better get to bed fast. They might hear him. He didn't want one of those 'What kind of state are you in?' encounters. He slithered up the stairs pretty quietly. He had reached his bedroom door, when the door to the Aged Ones' room opened suddenly. Snared. Unbelievably, at the very moment the Old Guy should have seen him, the Old Darling spoke from the bed. He turned back to reply. It gave Matthew just enough time to open his door and slip in.

'You're not seriously going to drive down there now, are you?'

'I have to. I have to see for myself.'

Matthew heard the Old Guy stumble downstairs. Then the Old Darling followed him, saying, 'Well, at least let me make you something for the journey.'

Then it was just muttering downstairs. Matthew thought it all sounded kind of nervy and pathetic. He stepped out of his room again and held himself up by the wall as he slid towards the turn of the stairs.

'Well, be careful on those roads. I really don't see any point in you dashing off in the middle of—'

'Will you shut up, for Jaysus' sake! I'm going. Look, I'm out the door and that's that!'

The door slammed. Matthew tiptoed quickly back to his room and peeped out the window to see the Merc take off. Only now did he realize that Franz Ferdinand was still blasting in his ears. He took off his earphones. The silence felt like the loneliest thing in the world. Matthew lay back on the bed trying to get it together enough to work out what was going on. Before he had finished framing himself a coherent question, he was unconscious.

Matthew couldn't believe it was after eleven-thirty when he woke, still in his clothes on top of the duvet. He had never slept so late on Christmas morning. As a kid he was always up at six to see what Santa brought, and more recently, Jussi Bjorling blasting out 'O Holy Night' over and over would drag him awake. Today there was no sound. Peace on earth. He powered on the mobi; Sarah's text was there. He looked out the window; the Merc was not there. So far his memory was 100 per cent accurate. It was time to check out the joint.

He undressed and sprayed himself. He found clean clothes. He combed his hair. He didn't feel so bad, considering, except for being mildly freaked out.

He went downstairs. Now he could hear a bit of a low murmur from the kitchen. He opened the door. The Old Darling was sitting at the table with Ruth. Both were drinking coffee with something in it, judging by the bottle of Remy Martin on the table. Ruth of course had a face as long as the Great Wall of China, and her eyes were puffed up. Does she know it's Christmas-time at all? Matthew decided to be the slap-happy teenager.

'Happy holiday, everyone. Merry Crimbo. Cool Yule.'

The Old Darling's head dropped. Ruth came to Matthew, curled her furry paws around him, and gave him the big eyes. Now Matthew felt a cold chill.

'Hey, what's up?'

'Daddy got a call in the middle of the night. Tahilla. The cottage was on fire. Daddy drove down to see the damage. He just phoned. It's completely destroyed. Burned to the ground.'

And Ruth did the big hug thing again. Was that it? The old guy drove six hours in the dark on Christmas morning to find out what anyone could have told him over the phone? Isn't the place insured, for fuck's sake?

Just then the front door opened, and Luke's voice called, 'Hellooo. Happy Christmas, everyone.'

Matthew, mainly to untangle himself from Ruth, went to open the kitchen door.

'We're here.'

Luke wasn't with Emma. Instead, standing next to him, was a person Matthew had never seen. He looked like he might have just pipped Victoria Beckham for the World's Most Embarrassing Tan award. Luke smiled brightly at Matthew.

'Matthew, your cousin Barry Phelan. Mum, I brought Barry along. Emma won't be coming so I figured there would be room at the inn.'

Luke was oozing Christmas cheer. Of course he hadn't heard the news yet. He gave Matthew and Ruth a kiss on the cheek, and an envelope each. The Old Darling shook hands with Barry like she was handing him a dead fish.

'Ruth, of course you know Barry already. Where's Dad?'

Ruth didn't put her arms around Luke or give him the big eyes. She didn't tell him about the cottage. She just stared at him sulkily. As Matthew opened the envelope he assumed contained a book token, he wondered what was eating her now.

'Where have you been, Luke?' Ruth asked.

Luke just smiled at her sharpish tone and said, 'I'm not late, am I? I said I'd be here around twelve.'

For a fraction of a second, Matthew thought Ruth was going to slap her beloved Luke. But of course she didn't. That would have been just too amazing. Matthew took a card out of the envelope. It told him that as his Christmas gift, Luke had contributed 100 euro on his behalf to Focus Ireland. The charity for the homeless offered Matthew Reid their grateful thanks.

Dickhead, thought Matthew.

# 6

# Bleak Midwinter II

Luke watches his father's hand shake as he strikes the match. It might be just the cold. It might be age. It might be the tension of his elder son's presence. Luke watches him turn the Partagas slowly full circle, as he puffs and carefully lights it all around. Luke knows that if he closes his eyes now, he will once again see the cottage in Tahilla blazing. He will hear Barry shouting at him from the van to hurry up, they had to go now, even as he breathed in the complex incense of his burning childhood. If he closes his eyes he might even feel all over again the deep spiritual peace of that moment.

Luke does not close his eyes. He keeps them fixed on his father, who is smiling and saluting a passing parent. The wind is bitterly cold in the open space of the school car park. It will be hard ever to find that peace again. In fact, it was only in the last couple of hours, while watching *A Man for All Seasons*, that Luke had decided to continue with his plan at all. Now suddenly here he is, alone with his father for the first time in months. Perhaps now is the time. His mother is still in the hall chatting to the young teacher who directed the play, waiting for Matthew to emerge triumphant. Yes, maybe now is the time. His father blows Cuban smoke into the freezing air and, because he can never bear silence, speaks.

'I have to say, I was surprised, were you? I mean, I don't mean to say I thought he'd make a fool of himself or anywhere

near it. No, I was confident he'd be up to the job – technically.
He's a smart lad, he has it up here, you know. But where I got
the surprise was . . . I mean, looking at Matt on that stage
tonight he really had that something extra, didn't he? . . . What
was it, there was real . . . command, authority. None of your
teenager moping around, you know. I remember the young
McCann, back in the sixties, the way he could dominate a
stage, the way all eyes would be drawn to him. I know, I know
I sound like the proud father and all that, and I'd never say
anything like this to Matt in a million years, but . . .'

Not that Matthew would know or care who Donal McCann
was, Luke thinks drily. He was the finest actor of his generation, Matthew. Oh, right, yeah. Cool.

'. . . but he reminded me of the young McCann. Really
now. As good as that.'

Luke silently agrees. Matthew had been a revelation. Watching him perform had lifted Luke from the dark place he had
sunk into since Christmas. He had first seen the film of *A
Man for All Seasons* when he was only eight. It had remained
special. For Luke at that age, Paul Scofield *was* his father. The
connection was absolute and literal on every level: Scofield's
penetrating but gently understanding gaze; the calm and logic
of Scofield's arguments; the steel of his moral certainty. It
was the first time Luke had encountered anyone as good as
his dad. Matthew's performance had reminded him of that
innocent time.

His father is beginning to relax as he talks and smokes.
Despite the icy wind, he shows no inclination to take refuge
in the car. He happily returns salutes and compliments from
other parents as they pass. Luke suddenly realizes what is
happening, or at least what his father feels is happening. Frank
Reid is tonight enjoying a little public respectability again.

Thanks to his younger son's performance, his father feels free to stand tall, to plant himself near the entrance to the school car park in full view of all the departing audience, to puff on a Cuban and wave regally. It must seem so very nearly like the old days. Frank always loved occasions at the old school. Luke remembers his infectious joie de vivre at any event in Luke's school career. He would bob about, winking proudly at his boy, pressing the flesh with priests and other old classmates, cheerfully handing out cigars. He could smoke them anywhere in those days. The Jesuits were only too happy to join in, their eyes dancing at the hilarious daring of it all, puffing erratically as his father lit them up over tea and biscuits in the refectory. 'O, Jesu, the mad days we have seen!' someone always seemed to misquote to general amusement.

'Now he's not exactly Paul Scofield of course, but for sixteen it was bloody impressive. Even you'll have to admit that, Luke.'

'Even I?'

'You know what I mean; you're such a critic. You can't compare a lad of sixteen with one of the great actors of the British stage . . .'

Luke hadn't done so.

'. . . but you'll have to admit when Matt turned to that lad playing Richard Rich tonight – who was desperate by the way, wasn't he? Jesus, his poor parents – when he did that bit with the chain of office, and looked the poor young fella in the eye, and said, ". . . but for Wales?" I mean, you have to say fair play, it was as good as Scofield did it in the film, wasn't it? That little raise of the eyebrow, the teeniest ironic inflection in the voice. Well, I thought to myself, for the first time ever mind you, "He'll have a jury in the palm of his hand some day."'

He smiles proudly at the thought. He takes another long slow drag. Luke feels ever so slightly mean for thinking that at this moment, the phrase curling round his father's brain is, 'Not off the ground he picked it.'

His father twinkles at him. 'Wonder where he got it from, ha?'

Luke steels himself. Yes, definitely now is the time. Matthew would surely be out soon with his mother. There would be a polite but edgy exchange as his father would inevitably try to capitalize on the success of the moment to suggest some impromptu celebratory outing. Luke would say no, clearly and firmly, without even bothering to offer an excuse. Matthew, no doubt intent on partying with his mates, would tell some lie. His mother would make no effort to dissuade either of them, and Frank's little fantasy of a great family occasion would dissolve pathetically. Even the very real pleasure of Matthew's genuinely fine, upright performance of Sir Thomas More would be diminished, tainted and spoiled. Yes, it must be now.

Luke is unsure how to begin. He understands that he will have to be the one to introduce the subject of the fire in Tahilla. His father certainly will not do so. Norma would have given him strict instructions not to open his mouth on that subject. Under no circumstances, she would have told him. Not tonight. Luke is certain of that. He cannot help but admire his mother's proud silence since Christmas Day. It was so sealed off and self-contained that Luke could not judge whether it was because she somehow divined the truth and blamed Luke and Barry directly for the fire, or simply found Barry's presence at the Reid Christmas dinner table so galling in the dismal circumstances of the day, that she was punishing Luke for his lapse in family protocol in bringing him to her home unannounced. His mother had always been unforgiving when it came to social lapses, as many in her circle of friends had discovered in the past. When she had a circle of friends, Luke thinks, and is instantly disappointed at his own malice.

With every new thought these days he is discovering things about himself. Not all of it pleases him. On Christmas Day he had been surprised and a little guilty at how events had thrilled and excited him. He had always intended that whatever plan of action he would carry out would be done scrupulously, with disinterest and purpose. The only measure of success would be the end result. Yet throughout Christmas Day he and Barry had exchanged excited secret looks, like when they were teenagers, enjoying the current of conspiracy between them. Luke felt real pleasure at his mother's cold anger, his father's pained bewilderment on his return, exhausted from his fourteen-hour trek to and from Kerry, his brother's barely contained petulance at this spoiling of his spoiled life. Luke found it harder to cope with Ruth's bitter, reproachful looks and ambiguous questions. He could tell she seemed to know exactly what had transpired, but for the life of him he could not work out how she knew.

Luke wonders where Ruth is tonight.

Luke felt guiltiest of all that he took pleasure in Barry's performance on Christmas Day. It was a masterclass in sneering disregard. If Barry had made a checklist of all the things that might enrage Norma, he could not have gone through them more effectively; from his crude language and Ballyhaunis accent, a clear challenge to Norma's long-suppressed but still faintly evident Mayo vowels, to the faux-admiring tone of his comments on the Reid wealth, their house, their furnishings, their cut glass, their exotic range of booze, their obscenely expensive Christmas decorations, and, most unkindly, Norma's gorgeously traditional Delia Smith-inspired

Christmas dinner table layout. Throughout the dismal, lack-lustre meal that finally began after his father's late return from Tahilla, Luke cast himself and Barry as a crack complementary team of crimefighters: he the cold intellectual genius of the operation; Barry the hands-on operator, the all-round mechanic, safe-cracker, computer nerd and, as it turned out in reality, electrical guru and arsonist. Together they had carried out their daring and devious plan, then coolly sat down to dine with their hapless victims. Luke had always hoped this project, this mission he had embarked on, would in the end make him feel better. He had not expected it would make him feel high.

'It's freezing. What's keeping Matt? It couldn't take that long to get the old tights and mascara off, could it?'

It is mock exasperation; Frank's twinkle is growing. Luke knows that as long as Dublin 6 parents stop to tell him how marvellous his son's performance had been, shake his hand and sincerely wish him the best for the New Year, then Matthew could take all night with his make-up. The wind could blow as sharp as it liked. Luke even senses that his father might want to use this time to feel his way towards a rapprochement of some kind with him. That has to be prevented.

Two neighbours, a college professor and his psychologist wife, sidle over to praise Matthew's performance. There is something slightly embarrassed in their manner. Luke knows them and their gilt-edged liberal-left credentials. He has no doubt they are making a conscious gesture, probably the result of whispered discussion as they emerged from the hall.

Frank is clearly delighted. He decides to play the pleased but modest parent. 'Ah, I can't really tell. I'm prejudiced of course.'

'It was actually a remarkably mature performance.'

'He wasn't bad, was he? Didn't let the side down, ha?'

'And it is such a complex play.'

'Oh, he rose to the occasion all right. The Reid tradition continues.'

'So, has he caught the acting bug?'

'Oh well now, there's the rub. He'll probably have a bit of a big head for a while after this all right, but he'll cop himself on soon enough. He's wise enough to know he can do better for himself than acting, you know.'

Luke instantly feels the little shadow pass over the professor's eyes. Their olive branch via Matthew was intended to allow his tax-dodging, money-laundering father a chance to recant; not directly, of course, but by implication. Had he shown real deference to the arts, or made some subtle allusion to the ethical power of a play like *A Man for All Seasons*, then rehabilitation could have begun. Frank had missed the point completely. He had blown it and he didn't even realize. The professor and the psychologist smile politely and depart. Luke has no doubt they had simply confirmed for themselves that their neighbour was still the thing he was. His father is oblivious. His smile is now broad and content. He is on a roll. He twinkles again at Luke. In this mood he might say anything. Now. It must be now.

'Any news on Tahilla since?'

Luke's question is calm, simple. The silence after it is short but significant. He feels his father's brain shift gear, slow down, reluctantly turn into a darker, more twisted road. In the hiatus Luke briefly closes his eyes, and sees himself sitting alone in the Tribeca café, the night he returned from Tahilla with his parents. He is handing over his credit card to the waitress. This was the moment he decided it would be the last time he would use it; the moment he decided on this course of action.

He opens his eyes again. His father still has not spoken. Until the unbearable pain of January, Luke's resolution had turned out to be stronger than he ever believed himself capable of. The hardest part by far was saying nothing to Ruth all this while. Only his conviction that he could never ask her to choose between him and her beloved daddy had kept him silent. The rest was easier; the break with Emma much easier than he would have thought. He had asked himself, could he sit her down and tell her what he intended to do? The answer was instant and emphatic. She would be horrified, she would try to dissuade him. She might even warn his parents. The more he had thought about Emma, the colder he grew. He was reminded of a film she had persuaded him to rent on DVD one night because she loved it so. It was *The Dead Poets' Society*. It had a brilliance, an apparent intelligence that was alluring. It was coated in a persuasive layer of thoughtfulness and sensitivity. But its heartbeat was merely a literate, calculating formula, highly polished for commercial success. Yes, it proved easy to say goodbye to Emma.

His father finally breaks the silence. 'Ah sure, what news? It's gone, destroyed. What can you do?'

'Any idea what actually happened?'

His father shrugs. 'Who knows?'

'But what does the insurance company say?'

'How do you mean?'

'Are they sure it was an accident?'

'Sure, what else would it be?'

Luke thinks of Cousin Barry. The instinct to seek his help had turned out to be inspired. The first sight of him after so many years had been a shock. He did not know why Barry had sculpted and honed himself this way; what self-loathing had gripped him. He gauged that somehow he would have to politicize his curiously pumped-up painted cousin to convince him to help. He would have to anger him at what Frank had done; not just the tax dodges, the offshore accounts, but the more particular personal affair of Barry's parents. Luke would have to drive home to Barry how his uncle Frank had bought their little cottage in the depressed market of 1989; 'taken it off their hands', to help them out, when they were in dire financial trouble. Then he simply waited until in 1993 he got planning permission to knock down the old cottage and build two luxury holiday bungalows, which he sold a year later. The boom had begun. As far as Luke could calculate, although he had no real idea what it might have cost Frank to ensure planning permission, he could be fairly certain that his father had made a profit of a hundred thousand or so from helping Barry's mother and father out of their debt. He was sure that this story would rouse Barry, anger him enough to get involved, but in fact his cousin didn't really care about any of that. He did not want to hear anything about the past. He was lonely, depressed and disconnected. Luke soon realized how desperately needy his cousin was; how glad to make the connection again with Luke. He didn't need persuading. He would be up for any plan Luke had in mind, especially if it was destructive. Most importantly, Barry had the technical know-how to make it happen.

'So everything is OK with the insurance company?'

Frank the barrister is suddenly more alert. Luke sees his gaze shift a fraction.

'You mean . . . ?'

'I mean, they'll pay up?'

He knows the directness of this will shock his father, because he never expects Luke to speak about money. As far as his father is concerned Luke cares little about such things. In this respect he is absolutely right.

It had surprised and relieved Luke that he became much happier once he sold his car, threw away his credit card and mobile phone, and moved to the little bedsit in Kilmainham. None of this seemed a trial or a privation to him. He felt no loss. It was costing him 350 euro a month less to live. He had set up a direct debit to pay this sum to Focus Ireland; a charity for the homeless seemed most appropriate in the circumstances. He had given Barry a thousand euro from the sale of his car, as a kitty to finance their Tahilla adventure. Every change he made in his life, with the single exception of not confiding in Ruth, had made him feel more focused, less depressed. It suddenly occurred to him one day that he didn't even miss sex. He hadn't been consciously celibate, but now that he thought about it, the idea tickled him. It seemed to fit. He wondered how long that would last. On Christmas morning, travelling back from Tahilla, Barry had suddenly confided in him.

'You know something . . . I haven't fucked anyone since all this started. Couldn't be bothered. Isn't that weird?'

Luke wanted to laugh out loud at such an unlikely coincidence, but he guessed Barry would think he was making fun of him. Instead he said, 'Same here. It's like we're on a mission. Whether it's Holy or Impossible I'm not so sure.'

Frank shivers a little. Luke is glad that he seems to be feeling the cold at last.

'Of course the insurance will pay out. That was never in question . . .'

He pauses. Luke can tell he wants to ask, why are you asking me about that, but some instinct is stopping him. Luke stays silent. He is sure that his father will not be able to resist for long. He will ask. He can't bear not to. Why, Luke?

'What's keeping them? We'll feckin' freeze waiting here.'

Now there is real exasperation. No twinkle. Silence. They both look towards the open doors of the school hall. There are still some lights on inside. Everyone seems to have left. There will be no more smiles and handshakes tonight. Time slows. Luke is still, controlled, waiting for his father to break:

'Why . . . why are asking me about the insurance money anyway?'

Luke feels a little relief. He suddenly remembers that cliché about barristers; about not asking a question when one doesn't know the answer. Does Frank subconsciously know the answer?

'Because there is something I'd like you to do with it.'

'Really?'

'Yes. Is it a lot of money?'

'It's enough to build another cottage, that's how it works usually.'

'I want you to tell the insurance company to send the money directly to Focus Ireland.'

A little laughing sigh tells Luke that his father is keeping a tight hold on his nervous anger.

'Ah, for God's sake, Luke, will you ever grow up?'

'It seems appropriate. They are a very good charity.'

'Of course they are a very good charity. I've given to them many a time, and plenty of other charities over the years that you know nothing about. Didn't you see what I gave to that tsunami raffle tonight, for God's sake?'

Luke had seen. Two hundred euro-worth of tickets. Two fresh notes handed over to an impressed student. Thank you very much, Mr Reid.

Frank's anger cannot hold.

'I'm sick of this. I've held my peace for a long while now, but you might as well know, I'm sick of your attitude. Fucking moral high ground—'

'I want you to give the insurance money to Focus Ireland.'

'And even if I did decide, off my own bat, to give the money to some charity, hand over the quarter million or whatever it'll be, who are you to tell me who to give it to? I'll decide who to give it to – not that I am going to—'

'If you don't do this, I will inform the insurance company that the fire in Tahilla was started deliberately. By me.'

His father seems to age in front of his eyes. Luke can no longer be moved to tears by his father's pain. That is past. But he understands fully how shattering his words are.

'I did it. I even have a witness, Dad.'

The barrister in Frank still functions. He pieces it together quickly.

'Barry. Did he put you up to this?'

Luke knows that his father doesn't believe that, even as he asks. Luke ignores the question.

'The insurance company will pay nothing. The story may even become public. These things have a way of leaking out.'

He has done it. It is done. It is up to his father now.

'What's all this about? What is it supposed to achieve? Make you feel a bit better about yourself? Make you the great fella? Well, let me tell you, you have it all out of proportion, son. Your father is really sorry he's embarrassed you so much, made your life a bit uncomfortable. Oh yeah, you've had an awful hard time of it, haven't you? Much more than the rest of us. You're so . . . you're so sensitive. It's tragic for you, isn't it? . . . For Christ's sake, Luke, nobody died. Frank Reid didn't do anything that thousands of others weren't doing at the same time. Why do you feel you have to turn it into some huge crusade? What was it? Nothing. In the scheme of things, nothing. Look at the news this week, at random, the collapse of this Medialab thing, Bertie's big idea. Thirty-five million taxpayers' quids pissed away. Look around you. Look at the world. A hundred and fifty thousand people dead in the tsunami, for God's sake, families, whole communities wiped out like that. If you want to go on a mission, get out and do something about that. Save lives for real, why don't you . . . ?'

Luke had known that Frank would end up making a speech, but he never expected him to expose Luke's weak spot so unerringly. Since St Stephen's Day, when he first heard the news about the earthquake on his radio, Luke's resolution had faltered. Suddenly the elation of the previous day seemed petty and ugly in the face of such overwhelming tragedy. As the New Year began, he took to sitting alone in his bedsit drinking coffee and roaming the airwaves, listening to Liveline, Newstalk, the World Service, anywhere he could tune into the stench of death and disaster. He pieced all the events together as one horror: the tsunami, snow storms in California, in Ireland hundreds of hospital patients were in corridors, lying on trolleys, and in mid-January there came another cold, silent shock; a little boy brutally murdered and abandoned on an empty beach. Against this terrible mosaic of pain, his own cause seemed selfish and irrelevant. He had no significance. He recalled that very recently Ruth had asked him fearfully, 'Something is happening, isn't it, Luke?' He had reassured her then. He would not have the strength to do so now. One day, needing her, he phoned Ruth from work. He got her voicemail. He did not leave a message. Luke was still sufficiently in control to recognize what was happening to him. He knew the statistics. In Ireland many young men commit suicide; seven males for every female. Luke knew he was a candidate.

Does Frank sense this frailty now? He is in full rhetorical flow about real death, real tragedy; probing Luke's motives. A barrister's instinct for any weakness? A father's love? Which?

Luke had been at a particularly low point when Barry had caught him at home one afternoon, listening to a catalogue of suffering on Liveline. He arrived out of the blue. Normally he never called to the bedsit without warning. He said it was to find out if there was any more news; had he confronted his father yet? Luke sensed that something else was troubling him. Barry said he was on his way to the gym. He was allowed to bring a guest; would Luke like to come along? Because the request was so unlikely, because there had to be some other significant reason for it, Luke said yes. Despite his own dark state, he still thought of Barry as more or less in his care.

There was a long queue of cars waiting to get into the gym car park. It was the New Year fever. Luke wondered why, if people really wanted exercise, they didn't just walk to the gym. In the crowded dressing area he changed into his gear, feeling more and more diminished as he did so. It was not that his body looked pathetic, but he just felt less visible somehow in the throng of flesh. Barry by contrast seemed to emerge glowing in these surroundings. He marched Luke to the main exercise area, showed him the simplest machines, and left him to attend a 'Body Pump' class.

Luke spent ten minutes jogging slowly on a machine before becoming too bored to continue. He looked through the large glass panels into the studio where Barry's Body Pump class was on. There were about twenty bodies hard at it. Two instructors wearing head-mikes called out instructions in time to music. All the bodies lifted weights, first one way, then another, then another. Luke guessed that each exercise focused on a different bit of body. That's all people ever did now: focus on different bits of themselves.

Barry was clearly top of his class. He seemed to be lifting more weight than everyone less. His body glistened. He looked master of his universe. Luke couldn't bear to look at this class any more, but when he turned away he just saw more bodies: bodies on bikes, bodies stretched on peculiar machines, bodies curled and twisted on mats, pulling weights and pushing pedals; every face sweating and driven, concentrating on my thighs, my biceps, my triceps, my abs, on me me me me me me.

Luke escaped downstairs to the steam room. There at least the flesh was at rest. There was silence and he could see no faces. It was some relief, but the depression would not lift.

When Barry joined him fifteen minutes later he finally got round to telling him that his mother, Luke's Aunt Joan, was in hospital in Castlebar. Nothing life-threatening as far as he knew, but they couldn't find her a bed. He didn't know what state she was in. Barry said he couldn't go down there. His mother had not seen him since the nose job. Now was not the time to confront her with that. He just hoped everything would be all right. He would talk to her on the phone.

Clearly Barry wanted to be persuaded to go. Luke didn't think twice. 'I'll come with you. We'll go early in the morning.'

So for the second time in a few weeks, the cousins set off west together. Once again the journey lifted Luke's spirits. He felt the beauty of winter, the light golden on the bare land. From inside the van it even looked warm outside. He was able to ease the fear and tension in Barry as they got closer to Castlebar. Luke realized he was looking forward to seeing his Aunt Joan again – it would be the first time in several years.

In the hospital reception area, they bought sweets and fruit and got directions. It was Barry saw her first. He stopped, touched Luke's arm and pointed. There was Aunt Joan, on her trolley in a crowded messy corridor just outside St Jude's ward. Luke led the way towards her. She looked directly at him and then a huge smile of recognition opened her face.

'Ah now, Luke, aren't you very good to come down. Are you all the way from Dublin? I heard about the cottage, isn't it awful? Poor Norma was crying her eyes out on the phone telling me about it—'

Luke didn't know what to say because he could tell she had not noticed Barry at all. He nodded slightly in his direction without speaking. He watched his aunt's eyes take in the stranger standing just behind her nephew. He saw her realize that the stranger was her son.

'Holy Jesus. Barry?'

'I know, Ma. Don't annoy me about it now, all right?'

'But I mean, what – are you all right? What happened to you?'

Luke's heart lifted. Only an Irish mother could lie ill on a hospital trolley and worry about the state of her son's nose.

'Tell her to give over, will you, Luke?'

'Aunt Joan. He's grand. It's just a nose job and a sunbed tan. A big improvement if you ask me. How are you?'

'Me? Oh, I'm fine. Gallstones, that's all. I was hoping they'd give me something to, you know –' she flaps her hand, dropping her voice – 'flush them out or something. But no, they're keeping me here until they can fit me in for surgery to take them out.'

She adds, gleefully pointing down her mouth, 'Keyhole surgery. It sounds awful but Dr Aziz says I won't feel a thing.' Her voice drops again. 'He's from the Lebanon. But very good. Those glasses are lovely on you, Luke.'

She turns again to Barry. 'See now, there's Luke, he hasn't changed a bit. I don't know what to make of you. You don't look like yourself at all.'

'Well, so what? What does it matter? I'm here to see you, aren't I?'

And they talked on. It still sounded like an argument but that was just their way. Luke sat back and listened. It occurred to him how, as always, his aunt had to put up with how things were. If a queue was formed poor Joan would always be at the end of it. His mother would never have to lie on a trolley. Luke felt tears rise. He was glad to find that he still had some left inside him. He felt connected to some purpose again, even if it was just the daily grind: hospital trolleys and gallstones and sons who mortify their mothers with dodgy plastic surgery. It was at that moment he remembered Matthew's school play. He had promised him he would go but had forgotten all about it. He hoped he was not too late. He would ring Ruth and arrange to go with her. He really needed to see her again, to talk to her; maybe even to tell her what he had done, and perhaps what he was going to do.

The following day he rang her from work, but again Ruth was not answering her phone. This time Luke left a message, but she didn't reply. He inquired directly from the school about the play. He was not too late. He sat in his old school hall and was moved and surprised as he watched his baby brother's eyes blaze with moral purpose from the stage. A message from a most unlikely source.

Luke suddenly realizes he has not been listening to his father, who is still making his closing arguments. He seems to want Luke to appreciate the wretched nature of Ireland in the eighties.

'You were a child, you were protected from these things. You all were. But what would you have done if you were me? What would you have done with a wife and four children and an uncertain future? The country was facing bankruptcy, for God's sake. It could all have gone west. Savings – investments – kaput! You don't realize the fear that was all around, and the feckin' coalition taxing everything in sight. I wanted to make the future safe and secure for all of you. Do you seriously think I should apologize for loving my family so much? Luke, have you no idea how much I love you all?'

The light of truth is in his father's eyes, even if it is a sentimental truth. Luke knows absolutely how much he loves them all. Frank's hands are reaching out, pleading for understanding. There is no cigar. He must have dropped it in the dirt at some point in the passion of his advocacy.

Luke asks quietly, 'So are you going to do as I ask or not?'

His father's eyes stare back at him in grave reproof. How can his plea be met with such coldness? What sort of son has he raised at all?

'Well?'

Surely Frank has to give him some answer now. He cannot launch into another speech. He must say yes or no. His father glances past Luke. At the same moment he hears voices behind. Luke turns to see his mother approaching, her arm placed tenderly around Matthew's shoulder. Luke steps close to his father, speaking quickly, 'Yes or no? If you don't—'

His mother's voice is brighter and fonder than he has heard it in a long time. 'Sorry we took so long. Matthew was getting a few notes on his performance. Not from me now, from his director. I had no criticisms. I thought he was just out of this world, and I don't mind telling him.'

Matthew shrugs. Just a disengaged teenager again.

'It was pretty OK tonight.'

Frank seizes on the distraction the new arrivals provide.

'Well done. Very impressed, Matt, I have to say. Just how impressed I was, I'll tell you on the way home. Get in out of the cold.' He jumps quickly into the driver seat.

'You'll have to drop him round to Mountain View Road, Frank. There's some kind of cast party – where is it again?'

'Harrisons.'

Only now does Norma turn to look at Luke directly.

'We're not going your way, are we, Luke?'

'No, you're not.'

'Good night so.'

She gets into the car. Luke puts a hand on Matthew's shoulder.

'Well done, Matthew. It was really fine. Inspiring.'

The shrug again. But Matthew is pleased.

'Thanks for coming, Luke. I appreciate it. I'll give you a buzz, yeah?'

'Do. Please.'

Then Matthew frowns, and whispers as he opens the back door, 'Where was Ruth, for fuck's sake?'

Luke shakes his head. Matthew sits in and shuts the back door. Luke bends towards the driver window, trying to catch his father's eye as he starts the car. Frank avoids his gaze. The Mercedes pulls away.

# 7

# *Death and Taxes*

Norma told Joan that she would definitely visit her as soon as she and Frank got back from New York. With any luck Joan would even be out of hospital by then. Norma had intended to be with her in Mayo all this week, only Judy really needed her, and her sister knew that daughter of hers once she got the bit between her teeth. So then Norma thought she might as well go the whole hog, and whisk Frank off for a bit of a mini-break. Joan said she was dead right, sure Frank always loved Manhattan. After the fire and so on, it would be just the thing. Norma said poor Frank was inconsolable about the cottage. They were all very upset. Joan said yes, she could tell that from Luke when he came to see her a couple of weeks back.

Norma did not react. She passed no remark on this entirely new piece of information. She just listened to Joan blather on about lovely Luke; how he really was the most thoughtful boy she had ever met in her whole life, really and truly, always was; how he had never given Norma and Frank an ounce of trouble. Of course the best thing as far as Joan was concerned was, she was thrilled to see himself and Barry had made up after all these years. They were back thick as thieves, like when they were young fellas. As Joan, God help us, burbled away, Norma's brain ticked along trying to analyse what was behind Luke's visit to her sister. Was this some other part of whatever plot he was hatching? And of course Barry in the thick of it again. He was always a sullen, disreputable child. It was the one thing that blackened those summers down in Tahilla for Norma; her Luke having to hang around with that unpleasant boy.

Now Norma really wished she could be in Mayo, where she could have a proper go at Joan; get to the bottom of all this. But the car for the airport was due and truth be told, Norma didn't even have time for this conversation, only she had to, at the very least, give her sister a call to let her know that she was thinking of her. Now she was going to be driven mad all day, wondering what was behind Luke's trip to Mayo. Was it just to visit his auntie Joan? Norma suddenly got an awful fright as it occurred to her, was the house safe while they were away? Matthew would be here, but would that stop Luke if, with whatever madness had taken hold of him, he decided to do damage? She hadn't thought about this at all. Maybe taking off for New York was completely the wrong thing to do. Too late now. The car was on the way, Frank was up to hi-doe about the trip, and it would kill him if Norma suddenly changed her mind and put a stop to it. Anyway, more than anything she needed to sit down face-to-face with Judy, and discuss her plan of action in relation to Luke. Judy was the only one Norma trusted to take a good hardheaded look at the whole situation, which was why Norma had thought up this New York thing in the first place. It was a family crisis and urgent decisive action was needed. The timing mightn't be ideal, but arrangements had been made, so that was it. Norma needed to end this chat with Joan quickly, and have a moment or two to settle her mind before leaving. She interrupted the flow.

'Listen, there's our lift outside, I'd better let you go, Joan love. I'll see you in a week or so. Bye, love, bye, bye, bye, bye.'

Done. Silence.

Norma cocked an ear upstairs, but there was no sound. Hopefully Frank was having a little lie-down. There was no drink anywhere upstairs, was there? No. The luggage was all ready in the hall. Nothing more to do. Norma decided to let him relax until the car came. It wouldn't be long now.

She went to the front room and stood in the bay window, lost in thought. She caught sight of herself in the mirror and turned to check, automatically patting her hips. She was pleased enough; the Richard Lewis complemented the necklace perfectly. She had never dared wear the flawless marquise diamond on a journey before. She wondered if she was getting sentimental.

New York, 1978: Frank had left her resting in the hotel room with little Luke fast asleep in the cot. Norma used to love having a lie-down, totally relaxed, listening to Luke's soft breathing. It seemed hardly any time had passed when she heard Frank slip quietly back into the room. She felt him ease on to the bed beside her. He slid his hand under her elbow round her breasts, then pressed something into her hand and kissed her neck. She looked down. Even in the semi-darkness it was breathtaking. Frank had gone round the corner to 47th Street and bought it, just like that, for her thirtieth birthday. Same age as Luke now.

It suddenly occurred to Norma that Luke would be thirty-one soon. What would she do about a card or a present? It would depend, she supposed. On him mainly. It was all very difficult. The car turned into the driveway, right on time.

Norma had a last look round before calling Frank. She had laid out everything Matthew might need in the kitchen so he could see it all easily: the frying pan, three saucepans, essential cutlery and the cheese grater. She had placed a box of potatoes and assorted vegetables on the table. Not much chance that they would be touched, but they were there for him. She checked in the freezer again even though she knew she had marked each little package clearly. She had prepared all his favourites yesterday: lamb arrabbiata, a beef casserole in red wine, a three-cheese sauce, two portions of pork medallions in mustard and mascarpone, all ready to pop in the microwave. That should keep him going. She was just opening the fridge door when she heard Frank coming downstairs.

'Norma, the car's outside.'

'I know. Coming.'

A quick glance satisfied her that the fridge was well stocked; Low-Low, Matthew's latest fad, milk, eggs, cheese, yoghurt, orange juice, bacon, sausages. Grand: he wouldn't starve. That was it so. She was glad she had decided last night to give him back the keys to the Vespa. Telling him that she would trust him not to use it while they were away was exactly the right thing to do. She could tell Matthew liked feeling responsible, and it was important to keep him on her side right now. Truth be told, Norma was annoyed by how thrilled he had been that Luke had come to the play, and as usual, whatever it was Luke had said to him about his performance had seemed to impress him far more than any praise she or Frank had offered. What was this power Luke had when it came to everyone in the family except herself and Judy? Well, whatever it was, Norma was going to break it once and for all. This lunacy had gone too far—

'What's up?'

Frank was in the doorway looking at her. Norma realized that he would have seen her just standing there, staring at a closed fridge. She wondered what kind of expression he had seen on her face, even as she immediately transformed it into a smile and walked briskly past him towards the front door, pausing only to smooth his lapel. She opened the door and waved out at the driver who was waiting patiently.

'Good, it's Joe. You do the bags. I'll set the alarm.'

She motioned to Joe to come and help with the bags. She went to set the alarm. Did Luke know the code? She couldn't remember. It was too late to change it now anyway. It would take too long and only cause confusion. She had to stop thinking about this. Nothing was going to happen to the house. Time to go. This latest bit of information about Luke visiting Joan was not really what made Norma so jittery. Luke's silence since his outrageous demands last week had been driving her mad. It was killing poor Frank, and it was all Norma could do to stop him giving in to Luke's nonsense. This trip to Judy was make or break as far as Norma was concerned. Yes, time to go. She glanced again to make sure all the bags had been taken out. Yes. She pressed 'system armed'. The beeps began. The voice said 'system armed'. Norma left her home and locked up.

Norma couldn't remember the last time they had used the limousine company, but she was glad it was Joe again. She liked Joe. He was a nice old Dublin gentleman, and he never spoke unless spoken to. She took Frank's hand as they sat silently in the back. The radio was playing quietly. Norma quite liked John Creedon, so she didn't ask Joe to turn it off. Soon her mind drifted back to Luke, as it always seemed to these days. It was the sheer arrogance of him really, when it came down to it. He had Frank's brains but none of Frank's softness, his simple human feeling. No, that wasn't true. Luke used to have it. She used to be afraid he was too soft. For years she never had a minute's trouble with him, he was so eager to please, so gentle and . . . Norma realized she was doing that thing again; remembering her little ten-year-old, seven-year-old, five-year-old Luke. She wanted him back, her precious angel-boy, who seemed to be drifting further and further away, and was nearly gone for ever.

She was so lost in thought that she hadn't noticed the news bulletin starting, so the words 'Former Minister for Justice Ray Burke has received a six-month custodial sentence for tax evasion' seemed to come at her from nowhere. As she looked up she caught Joe's glance in the rear-view mirror. He instantly averted his eyes and said nothing. Norma felt Frank's hand tighten round hers, and she knew he was staring out of the window wishing he was dead. The silence was just awful as the report continued. The first time in the history of the State that a Government minister had gone to prison for such offences. Any normal everyday big-mouth taxi driver would have been off immediately, making cracks about politicians, passing remarks about tax dodgers, as if they were in any position to talk. Joe's silence was so much worse. Norma knew exactly what it meant. He had made a connection between them and Ray Burke, and so was respectfully passing no remark.

Norma wanted to scream. She wanted to reach forward and poke him on the shoulder and say, 'Now you listen here to me, Joe. You've got it all wrong.' She wanted to nail the notion that either she or Frank could ever be compared to the likes of Ray Burke. She wanted Joe to know that she could never stand the man, ever. She had no time for the way he went about his business. He was nothing to do with the Fianna Fáil Party that she grew up in. A gutty, Frank had once called him, and that wasn't today or yesterday either. It was the night of the election count in 1977. Frank was at the count centre. Norma strolled down to see how things were going, with three-year-old Luke in the buggy, peacefully asleep, a huge FF rosette pinned to his chest. It was the best night. Result after result came in, and all over the country Fianna Fáil were sweeping to their largest victory ever. After all the dark days of the arms trial, and the in-fighting, and losing the previous election, it seemed the country was ready to love Fianna Fáil again. Frank was in high good humour, waiting eagerly for the final result in Dublin North-East, where he had been canvassing throughout the election. Fianna Fáil was definitely going to win two seats, but much better than that, the despised, the reviled Conor Cruise O'Brien was dead in the water. It looked like he was going to lose his seat. This would be the icing on the cake as far as Frank was concerned; the cherry on top. He and Norma were hanging over a barrier scrutinizing the latest count, staring hungrily at the little piles mounting for each candidate, when some whoops and cheers distracted them. They looked and saw a jubilant Ray Burke, who had already been elected, and a few of his usual cohorts moving towards them, pressing the flesh of the faithful and accepting congratulations all round. There were fists clenched in the air, and victorious yelps as everyone reached out to touch success.

Frank whispered to Norma, 'Keep me away from that gutty, for God's sake, or I'll puke.'

He just turned his back, using Norma and Luke's buggy as a shield from the Burke gang. Suddenly a big face with glasses was smiling into hers, Ray's huge paw extended. She had no choice but to smile back and shake his hand. Then he bent over the buggy and grinned at the sleeping Luke. 'We'll have you out canvassing next time round, ha?'

His fans all laughed as he took off.

Norma stared at the back of Joe's neck, willing him to understand. That was as much as she and Frank ever had to do with Ray Burke. People should know all the facts. It was totally unfair to link them with the kind of activities that Burke and his type had been guilty of. It was ridiculous. Absolutely ridiculous! Norma voiced none of this. She knew from that tiny spontaneous glance in the rear-view mirror that in Joe's mind they were all lumped in together. It just put the cap on it as far as Norma was concerned, that as the radio report finally mercifully ended, the limousine drove through the crossroads at Collins Avenue and ground to a halt in the mess of traffic worming its way through the unfinished port tunnel works. They were now in Ray Burke's territory, his old North Dublin fiefdom, stuck in a jam. Unnerving though it was, Norma would have sat it out in determined silence, but she couldn't help being relieved when she heard Frank's voice.

'Put on Lyric there, Joe, would you?'

The speed with which Joe changed over to the classical music station told Norma he was relieved too. Placido Domingo. What was it? Something from *Rigoletto*? Whatever it was, it was a merciful relief.

Frank was off and running now. 'Any idea who that is, Joe, is it Pavarotti or Domingo?'

'Oh sure, I can never tell one from another, Mr Reid. They're all brilliant.'

'We need Jack O'Brien here in the car with us now to tell us which one it is, and what year it was recorded. Do you ever listen to Jack's programme of a Sunday?'

'If I'm at home, myself and the wife listen in sometimes.'

'Great programme. He's an education, isn't he?'

'He plays lovely music all right.'

Norma gave Frank's hand a little squeeze. Well done. He gave hers a little squeeze back. No problem. He continued the merry banter with Joe about great tenors as the traffic edged along. The worst was over, surely. Soon they would reach the airport. Soon they would be off and away, far away. It couldn't come quickly enough.

New York held only happy memories for Norma. She forced her mind back again to 1978, that first Manhattan holiday together. Because it was her thirtieth birthday Frank had pulled out all the stops. The first surprise was at the airport itself. He hadn't told her he'd bought first-class tickets until the moment they arrived at check-in. Then he just marched them past the queue at the economy desk with a wink. Oh, the luxury in those days when first-class really was first-class. Mind you, once you got used to something it was always harder to go back. She and Frank had never travelled economy since.

This time, when they finally got to the airport, they stood uncertainly at the self-check-in machines. They had not used them before. They followed the steps a little fearfully, and were surprised and relieved when suddenly it was all over. Two Premiere boarding cards popped out: Norma Reid 2a and Frank Reid 2b. It was handy and quick all right, but Norma missed the personal touch, so when Frank asked an Aer Lingus lady what they should do with their luggage, she was delighted when, having looked at their boarding cards, the lady walked them personally over to the right desk, smiled and wished them a pleasant flight. The young man behind the desk took their luggage, and gave them invitations to the Gold Circle lounge. He pointed out the fast-track security line for Premiere passengers. He also smiled sweetly and wished them a pleasant flight. Norma liked all that. She was beginning to feel more relaxed.

Frank had his first drink of the day in the lounge. He poured himself a Jameson, but had to gulp it back quickly when the flight was called. Norma would have preferred if he had just left it. She had begun to accept that Frank's drinking was now a serious problem and getting worse. She had not worked out a plan of action. Only now was she remembering that of course, there would be any amount of free drink on the flight. Normally that was considered one of the great perks of flying Premiere. Norma started thinking about how she might politely limit Frank's intake. She didn't want to kill the atmosphere, determined that this trip would be a happy one for him. There would be enough trouble to deal with when they returned to face Luke. She didn't want any tension whatsoever between Frank and herself. Neither did she want him drinking himself into an awful state on the plane, with God knows what consequences.

As they got on board, it occurred to Norma that they hadn't been back to the States for four years, not since Judy's wedding. That day twelve of them, family and friends, had all travelled together. It was such terrific fun. They had practically taken over the Premiere section. Norma couldn't help a little bitter thought, that Luke seemed to have no qualms about flying Premiere that day. Today she looked briefly around before sitting down, and realized that she recognized absolutely nobody. This had never happened before. Normally when travelling Premiere on Aer Lingus, there would be someone familiar: an RTÉ personality; one of the Riverdance crowd; Frank might spot another lawyer or Party member, or even just a face that drove you mad because you couldn't work out where you had seen it before. Ireland was small and very few got to fly Premiere. There was a crowd, a gang. Why did it seem different today? Maybe there was just a whole new gang?

She suddenly spotted someone across the aisle staring at

Frank from behind a copy of *Cara* magazine. She was sure she didn't know him. A little fella with black hair and black eyes, with a stare like an evil dwarf's. He didn't seem to Norma like the type who would normally be in Premiere. He suddenly realized that she had seen him and immediately shifted his stare to her, insolent, smirking. They both held their gaze, neither giving in. Norma wasn't going to be cowed by the likes of him.

The flight attendant suddenly came between them, and the spell was thankfully broken. Norma took orange juice and Frank had champagne, followed by another before the plane took off. Norma was a little concerned. On the other hand she noticed that he was brightening up minute by minute, checking through the in-flight entertainment, fiddling with the seat to find the most comfortable arrangement, making little humorous remarks. He seemed very relaxed. Over the last year or so, really since the trouble began, Norma had noticed a certain pattern. There would be a point in any given day when the Frank Reid she loved and treasured appeared. He might stay for five minutes or an hour, then, just like that, he would be gone, and all the other Frank Reids, the strange assortment of morose, frightened, self-loathing creatures that increasingly invaded their lives, would take over. The Frank she loved was sitting beside her now. She did not know how long the happiness would last this time.

The 'fasten seat belt' light went off. Frank reached up to press the attendant bell and ordered a Bushmills. He smiled a long smile at Norma. Out of nowhere he reached over and fingered the marquise.

'The Algonquin, ha? How many years ago now?'

Norma nodded and smiled. Keep this going. This was fine.

'Is that why you asked Judy to book us in there?'

Norma nodded again. Frank almost chuckled.

'Good for you. Remember we saw *Da* that time? I think that might have been the first time you showed it off.'

Yes. How had Norma forgotten that? Frank was right. It had been her first chance to wear the necklace in public. Frank seemed to be filling up. What was he remembering? He bowed his head. She suddenly thought of something from that night long ago. She had glanced over at Frank at a particular point in the play, the moment when the Charlie Now character realizes that his da, now dead, had never spent a penny of the money he had sent him. At that moment Frank had been sitting up, bent forward, his eyes fixed on the stage, tears rolling down his face. He seemed so beautiful to her just then.

It had been one of those unexpected treats. A few days after they arrived in New York the Tony Awards ceremony had taken place in the Schubert theatre. *Da* by Hugh Leonard, which was already enjoying a big success on Broadway, won for Best New Play, and several other categories as well. Frank had arrived back at the hotel with a bundle of papers, absolutely thrilled. He read out bits from the reports, and showed Norma photos of the glitter and glam. What a great night for the Irish! They had to go see this play. How could they not? Of course tickets would be like hen's teeth after news of the awards came out, but Frank would sort it somehow. They weren't leaving New York without seeing *Da*.

When normal channels proved useless, Frank got on to Party headquarters in Dublin. They got on to someone in the embassy in Washington, who got on to someone in the cultural section. Two days later a message was left for Frank at reception. There were tickets awaiting his collection from a Mr O'Connell at the UN building. Norma brought Luke down to Washington Square that afternoon, to let him run around and play safely, while Frank went to collect what turned out to be two prime parterre tickets for that night. She would never forget the sight of him striding towards her under the arch, sweating in the June sunshine, but cock-a-hoop. 'Look!' he called, waving the tickets in the air. 'See what can be done when you put your mind to it?'

They felt such huge Irish pride that night as they stepped inside the theatre. They were tempted to shake people's hands and bid them welcome, saying, we're from Dublin actually, we know Dalkey very well. Frank jigged up and down in his seat, his head spinning this way and that, totally caught up in the buzz.

'Look at this. You see? There's no reason the Irish can't be up there too. Right up there with the best of them.'

Norma stared out of the plane window at a sumptuous setting sun, which had been threatening to drop into night for several hours of the flight, but still somehow hung on. She could remember it all perfectly; the tears of joy and the heartfelt burst of feeling at the end of the performance as she and Frank leaped to their feet. They clapped and cheered for Barnard Hughes when he took his final dignified bow. As they left, Frank could not stop talking. His hands waved uncontrollably in the crush of the crowd. Norma had to take his arm, for fear he would poke someone in the eye, and ease it down several times until they burst out on to a still warm summer night on 49th Street.

'How did he do it? Credit to Leonard all the same. Nail on the head. Nail on the head. That was my old man up there on that stage. That was him, the old fucker. What were we like? What kind of a poxy little country were we at all? He nailed it all right. Did you hear the cheers at the end? Every one of them thinking, that's my da, that's my da; the recognition factor, you see.'

He hardly drew breath as the light and energy of Times Square seemed to wind him up even more and powered them along 44th Street.

'That thing with the money. Da never spent the money. Typical. The rows I used to have with my old man: "But that's what it's for, Dad; making and spending. That's what money is for." Talking to the wall. Another generation. Money wasn't to be spent. Money was for putting away in case you were ever stuck. Sure, God help us, they didn't understand that money makes you money, and more money makes more money, and on and on. They just couldn't think big enough.'

He swept Norma into the Algonquin lift, still talking. He paused only to kiss her, and they held each other laughing. He nearly wrenched her hand off dragging her to the room, kissing her outside the door as he fumbled for the key, and pawing at her clothes, until she reminded him that the baby-sitter was inside. They opened the door as straight-faced as they could. Frank shoved twenty dollars into the girl's hand and bundled her out of the room. She started to tell them what a little sweetheart Luke had been, so peaceful all night. 'Great, yeah, thank you so much. Goodnight, goodnight.' Frank closed the door and turned back, a big dirty grin on his face.

'You're not getting off that lightly, Mrs Reid.'

They kissed again, falling backwards on to the bed, stumbling and fumbling, shoes, a sock, tights pulled down, buttons undone, Frank's face pressed hard against her mouth, his tongue roving; still high from the non-stop talk. Somehow the marquise stayed on, the gold chain scraping hard against Norma's throat, and finally there was the heat of skin on skin as clothes gave way. Judy was conceived that night.

Norma realized that the flight attendant, who was asking her if she was ready to order dinner, must have caught the little grin on her face. She quickly focused on the menu. Truth be told, even in all the anger and frustration of the last week, Norma had enjoyed her private joke, her secret knowledge when she instructed Judy, who had insisted on making all the arrangements, to book them into the Algonquin.

Judy, of course, couldn't just do as she was asked. 'Mum, nobody stays there. I was thinking somewhere really cutting-edge like the W on Union Square or the St Mark maybe if you wanted something more uptown and discreet—'

Norma just insisted on the Algonquin without any more explanation. She even asked Judy to check if Room 205 was free. This made Judy really curious, but Norma had kept herself to herself. If only Judy knew . . .

'I'll have the beef.'

'Same here, and another bottle of the Rioja, would you?'

Norma knew she couldn't stop Frank yet, but maybe she could slow him down, not let it get to the embarrassing stage.

'Frank, do you remember it was my idea to stay at the Algonquin that first time?'

'I do, yeah. God, it was a bit down-at-heel back then when you think about it. But it didn't stop us enjoying ourselves.'

'Do you remember why I suggested it?'

'Ah . . . location, was it? Handy for Times Square?'

'No.'

Pause. Something made her continue.

'You've no idea?'

'Ah . . . don't think so. Should I?'

'Dorothy Parker? That ring a bell?'

'Oh right, yeah, Dorothy Parker and all that Algonquin crowd. Of course, yeah. What about it?'

'You've no idea?'

'Ah Jaysus, Norma, what's the interrogation for?'

It was only a little snap, but Norma knew it was time to shut up. Let it be.

'Nothing special, love. I was just a fan of hers, that's all.'

'Sure I knew that.'

Dinner arrived. Norma could have kicked herself for pushing so hard just then. What was she trying to do? She already knew Frank had never spotted why she suggested the Algonquin all those years ago. Why not just let it be?

It happened about a week before the 1967 *Irish Times* debating final. They were alone in one of the small old lecture theatres in Earlsfort Terrace rehearsing their speeches. Teamed for the competition, inevitably they had been spending a lot of time together. Norma listened to Frank's speech, in awe as usual of his scurrilously witty turn of phrase, his ice-cool delivery. She started apologizing yet again for how plodding her speech seemed. He just grinned and said, 'I keep saying it's good we have complementary styles. It makes us better as a team. Why do you think we've got so far?'

'It's because of you we've got so far.'

Frank took a book out of his bag.

'I knew you'd be beating yourself over the head about this, so I got you something. The funniest woman I've ever read. She might inspire you.'

It was a Dorothy Parker collection entitled *Death and Taxes*. Inside he had written, 'From one brilliant lady to another,' followed by his name in full, 'Francis Reid', and '*Irish Times* final, February 1967'. It had felt so romantic to Norma that, just for a moment, she had allowed herself to wonder if Frank was falling in love with her, as she already knew she was with him.

Dorothy Parker never inspired Norma to be a wittier

debater. That didn't matter in the end. She was content for Frank to be witty enough for the both of them. She also grew to love the writings of that oh-so-clever lonely woman.

Oh, for God's sake! Plastic cutlery? She understood about September 11th and dangerous weapons and all that, but still . . . plastic knives and forks in Premiere? One more change. One more step backwards.

Frank was gulping down the wine and chomping his beef happily; Norma could see a little dribble of gravy run very slowly down his chin. Frank wasn't aware of it. She reached over with her napkin.

'Here, love.'

She wiped. He pulled away, and said just a little too loudly, 'What are you doing? I can wipe my own fucking chin.'

He took his napkin and rubbed his face roughly. He emptied and refilled his glass. Norma knew for sure now that happy time had passed. At least Judy and Alan would be waiting at JFK. However bad Frank might be, she would have them for support. Would she get to talk to Judy about Luke tonight? Probably not. By the time they got to Midtown, checked into the hotel and were all settled, it would be too late for a proper conversation. Norma would get Judy on her own first thing tomorrow, get her onside before revealing her plan to Frank. Having come to the conclusion that Luke needed psychiatric help and that if he refused to seek it voluntarily, then he would have to be forced to do so, Norma needed support from inside the family. Judy was the best option. She was least under the influence of Luke and the least sentimental. If Norma had Judy on her side then Frank could not resist. Judy was also the only one who might make Ruth understand that this course of action was genuinely in Luke's best interest. Faced with all of them, Luke might even agree that he should have himself looked at, though somehow Norma doubted he would. She sensed it was much more likely to be a fight to the death.

Norma felt so tired. She used never to notice her age but recently she had started to do so. Now it seemed to her she aged two days for every one, and each day went by twice as fast. After dinner she dozed and woke several times. It did not seem like time was passing at all. Outside her window the plane still chased the setting sun. When would the inevitable darkness come? Each time she glanced at Frank, he seemed to be constantly chuckling at *Shark Tale* and ordering more Bushmills. Finally she woke to hear the flight attendant saying, 'No, I can't, sir, we're beginning our descent and the captain has asked us to suspend service.'

'A last little one, pet, come on.'

Norma turned and her eyes met the flight attendant's. They were slightly pleading. Norma said to her, 'That's fine. We understand. Thanks very much.'

Her eyes said walk away now, and the flight attendant was happy to take the hint. Norma grabbed Frank by the arm and pressed very hard. She hissed, 'Stop it now, Frank.'

Frank turned to say something, but she pressed his arm even harder and even his bleary eyes understood her look. He said nothing. Norma spotted the Black-eyed Dwarf smirking from across the aisle, but she just turned her face away. She sat rigid with tension for the remaining twenty-five minutes of the journey.

Premiere passengers were allowed off the plane first. Frank could still walk, albeit a little unsteadily. In these situations Norma knew he would follow her like a well-trained dog. It was another twenty tedious minutes before they recaptured their luggage and emerged at the arrivals hall. They looked around. There was no sign of Judy or Alan. This was not what Norma needed or wanted. They stood for several minutes, tired, uncertain. Then Frank pointed and said, 'That's me, isn't it?'

An Arab-looking man was standing, like many other drivers, holding up a sign. It was a sheet of paper on which he had handwritten 'Mr Frank Reid'. They approached and Norma spoke.

'This is Frank Reid. We're supposed to meet my daughter. Where is she?'

The man shrugged. He consulted a piece of paper.

'Frank Reid. Algonquin Hotel. West 44th Street.'

'Yes, but is my daughter here with you?'

He shook his head. 'No daughter. Just me. It is OK. It is paid already.'

The man brought them to a shining black Lincoln town car. They set off in silence for Midtown. Norma was now close to boiling point. Where was Judy? How could she have done this? Maybe there would turn out to be a reasonable explanation but Norma didn't think so. No, Judy had simply let her down again. Judy had suited herself as she always did. There would be nothing much Norma could even say about it, because she needed Judy now. There was no one else. Norma's frustration began to overwhelm her. For the second time today she wanted to scream at a driver. This time there would be no words, just a long exhausted impotent howl.

How had she finally got to this awful failed place? It would be possible to blame many things but truth be told, she knew she was the one who could have stopped it somewhere along the way. That power had always been in her hands. Norma could have said no to Frank at any time. If she had said it and really meant it, then he would have stopped. She wished she could fool herself that there were factors, forces, events that had all conspired to overwhelm her and her family, but in the end, Norma was not someone who would fool herself. She knew what she knew.

She could even pinpoint the exact moment when she should have said no; when Paschal Finnan walked into Morrissey's in Abbeyleix back in August 1984 and did his big pretendy 'Well, will you look who's here' to Frank, as if their meeting there was pure accident. Norma knew, even at that moment, it was nothing of the kind. She knew what Paschal Finnan was; everyone in Fianna Fáil was in awe of his financial wizardry. If Frank had arranged to bump into Paschal Finnan in a country pub, and not told Norma, then he was ashamed of something. She should have made Frank leave as quickly as possible. She could have stopped all the schemes, the fake foreign addresses, the money transfers, the whole tiresome shenanigans, before they even started. Instead Norma took the children for ice cream, and left the men in Morrissey's to do their talking.

Frank was asleep now, slumped against her shoulder, pressing Norma against the passenger door. It was all she could do not to burst and blub. Would Luke find it amusingly ironic if he knew she had let things alone that day for his sake? He loved his irony after all. As they had left Tahilla she had flown into a rage with Frank, because he suddenly announced that he was going to drive home by Abbeyleix instead of taking their usual route; no explanation was offered. Well, Norma was not letting that go. She was determined to best him; even more so when Frank dared to argue back. Then Luke had put his little face between their seats, his eyes pleading with them not to fight – he hated it when they fought. Sometimes at home if their shouting reached a certain pitch, even if it was just loud friendly debate as it often was, Luke would run upstairs and wait at the top. He'd say a prayer to make them stop. When Norma saw that little face between them, so full of hurt and fear, she let it go for his sake. Ten-year-old Luke was right. Whichever road they took home wasn't worth fighting about.

If only. If only.

They arrived at the Algonquin. Norma took Frank's wallet from his inside pocket. The smallest note he had was five dollars. She gave five to the driver and could see his shock when she asked for two dollars' change. She was well past caring what he thought. She sat Frank down in a fine old armchair in the oak-panelled lobby, thankful that there were not so many people about. She explained to the large friendly black man behind the desk that her husband wasn't feeling too well. He waved a sympathetic arm, pursed his lips in a very homo sort of way, and asked if she required a physician because he'd be more than happy to arrange it. Norma said no, some rest would be fine. The large black man suddenly flapped and said, 'Oh there's a message!' He handed Norma a sheet of paper, while he got through the formalities very quickly. He was sure they must be totally exhausted. The message was from Judy:

'Delay. Usual Washington nonsense. Flying up first thing tomorrow in time for brunch. Will ring later. Love.'

The large black man apologized that they could not accommodate the request for Room 205 because it was a non-smoking room, and they had requested smoking. He hoped Room 405 would be satisfactory? Yes, yes, yes, fine. She got Frank to the room without too much embarrassment, and gave the luggage man two dollars. He seemed happy with that.

Frank slumped in an armchair and took out a Partagas. He

picked up the remote control and started flicking through TV channels as he lit up. Norma turned on the ceiling fan to keep the smoke moving about and undressed to have a shower. The strong hot spray was some relief, and she stayed under it as long as she could. As she was drying herself, she heard Dan Rather's voice announce the death of Arthur Miller.

'My God, Frank, you hear that?'

Frank did not reply. Asleep? Norma listened as she put on a robe.

'. . . most remembered for three plays that defined an American generation. *All My Sons* caught the mood of post-war depression as the nation mourned its lost children, *The Crucible* confronted the tyranny of McCarthyism . . .'

Norma stepped out of the bathroom towelling her hair.

'That's very sad, isn't it? Still I suppose he—'

She saw Frank's head bowed, the Partagas still lodged smouldering between his fingers.

'Ah, for God's sake, Frank. You'll burn the place down.'

'In *Death of a Salesman* he presented the tragedy of a man who craved the American dream so much that he became its victim, struggling desperately against the onrushing knowledge that he had slaved in service to a false ideal of worldly success . . .'

Norma stepped quickly over to Frank. Only when she took his limp hand and removed the cigar from between his fingers did she realize what had actually just occurred.

# 8

## *Lent*

Emma finally knew on the first Sunday in March that she was totally, totally over Luke. Spring had arrived. She sat at her Mac facing the window, enjoying the uncommon warmth from the early afternoon sun. She presumed it was still chilly enough out in the open air, but from where she sat it felt glorious. Although the deadline for her occasional column was later that evening, she felt no stress. If anything she was feeling an old, nearly forgotten, tingle of pleasure and anticipation. She had just written the following:

First Arthur Miller then Hunter S. Thompson; who's next, I ask? Why are radical voices on the left of the equation suddenly departing this vale of tears? Now there are some dullards who will point out that Mr Miller lived a long fruitful life and his time had come anyway, while old Hunter had been killing himself softly for several decades, and it was inevitable that he would go with a bang; but there are others, more hardened to the sinister machinations of Big Politics, who will see the lethal claw of the Bush administration in all this. (Apparently the spiralling price of the pint is also part of the Bush imperial agenda, or is that linked to Sinn Féin money-laundering? It's so hard to keep it all in one's head, isn't it?)

Anyway, the idea that assorted darlings of left-lit are being 'taken out' might be a tantalizing plotline for Hollywood, but rather difficult to prove in the real world, as with all the best conspiracy theories. Should Gore, Noam or whoever, suddenly pop their clogs in the very near future though, it really will be time to think, 'Maybe . . . just maybe . . .'

Emma liked it. It had a lightness of tone, a flirtatiousness, a teasing quality that she recognized as her signature, the essence of Emma McCann; a quality that, frankly, she had lost over the last four months. She had wandered in the wilderness, basically going out of her mind, frustrating all her friends, pretending everything was fine when it was not, and simply NOT LETTING GO!!! Now, as she got up to make coffee and have a think about the next two hundred words, Emma knew that was all behind her. She had sensed it ever since the funeral really, but it was only now, a couple of weeks later, holed up in the apartment with a deadline happily beckoning, alive and in the moment, that she felt the absolute proof of her recovery.

Emma recalled once enduring a searing, blinding headache when she was out Connemara way, writing a travel piece on eccentric Hidden Ireland houses. She had to finish the article that night. It was ten miles to the nearest chemist's shop, which was closed anyway, and she had no car. She so regretted not having done something about it earlier. She had felt a bit heavy-headed that morning and skipped breakfast, assuming that a power walk through the woods of the old estate would put her back on track. The fresh air seemed to help all right, but as she worked on into the afternoon, the headache returned, and whereas at first it just affected her concentration, it had finally reached the point where she could barely form a sentence.

When she was reduced to kneeling by her bed, her head drooping low, Emma knew she had to do something. She lurched downstairs in search of the lord of the manor. He was terribly sympathetic in his slightly too loud staccato manner. Emma guessed he was taking for granted that she, being of the Fourth Estate, as he would have said while whinnying nervously, had a mother and father of a hangover but she didn't care at this stage as long as he helped in some way. He went off to rummage in the kitchen, and came back with a fizzing glass. Emma had never taken Solpadeine before. She rarely suffered from headaches and wasn't keen on pills as a rule. She gulped the drink back in one hungry go, and staggered back upstairs to lie down, possibly even to pray, if things didn't get any better.

No more than ten minutes later she began to feel a curious shiver run from the base of her neck to her temple. Some gentle but super-strong type was ooooozing up the block of stone that was her pain, and easing it out, causing this strange, but emphatically not unpleasant, vibration inside her head. Then, just like that, the migraine was gone. Emma felt a blessed elation, along with the slightly more nervous feeling that any pill that could do that should frankly be avoided except in an absolute crisis.

It was that giddiness, that same elation Emma felt now on this sun-filled March Sunday. She did a couple of silly dance steps to herself as she stood over the coffee machine. The fever had truly passed and would not be back. She was rather pleased with the metaphor that now presented itself to her: Frank Reid's funeral was the Solpadeine that eased her emotional pain. To think she had no awareness, even the day before the funeral, that the end of her ordeal was so near! Emma had actually thought she might be closer to another beginning, that events were bringing Luke and her together again.

Even the way she first discovered that poor old Frank had

suddenly died was significant. She overheard something on the DART, literally as she was thinking about Luke. She was lost, staring out of the window, as the train approached Pearse Street, thinking as she often did about what she would say to Luke if she happened to see him standing on the platform as the train pulled into the station. These thoughts always came to her whenever she used the DART or LUAS instead of taxis – she still couldn't bring herself to travel by bus. One of the things she definitely knew about Luke since he had removed himself from her life was that he had developed an obsession with public transport. So as her train or tram approached a stop, she would imagine Luke standing there, always alone of course, perhaps a little forlorn. He would see her through the window and look shocked. Emma would meet his gaze steadily and step out on to the platform. She would look closely at the expression on Luke's face as she drew nearer, and what she would say to him, how she would treat him, would depend on that expression; how contrite he seemed, how much she gauged he needed her at that moment, how delighted he was at the serendipity of the occasion.

'See Frank Reid died suddenly.'

'Frank Reid?'

Emma looked to see who had said the name. Two men in suits opposite her were talking. One was pointing to something in his *Irish Times*.

'Remember him now?'

'What page is that? Oh yeah, I see what you mean, yeah . . . one of those faces you can never put a name to.'

'Always lurking behind someone important.'

'Does it say how much they took off him in the end?'

'The Revenue? Over four million apparently. That includes penalties and so on.'

Emma knew it must be the same Frank Reid. It had to be. The next comment confirmed it.

'Hear this: "Often tipped for Attorney-General, it's not certain if it was his tax problems, or the fact that he never get on with Bertie, ended that hope . . ."'

Old Frank was dead. Died suddenly. When? Where? How? Emma suddenly panicked, thinking she might have missed the funeral. She had to find out. She hoped it wasn't too late. She would be furious if she missed the funeral. It might seem like a deliberate snub. She desperately wanted a quick look at the paper. If it were at all possible, she would go. Emma stared at the man through his paper, willing him to put it down, so she could casually ask him for a look. She didn't want him to know what item interested her. It would certainly be the proper thing to contact Luke now. Absolutely. After all, if this had happened a few months ago Emma would have been one of the chief mourners, sitting in the family pew holding Luke's hand. He might be really glad to get a call from her at this time.

She got off at Tara Street and went straight to the nearest newsagent. She had briefly stopped buying the *Irish Times* in protest during the controversy over Kevin Myers calling children born outside of marriage 'bastards' in his column. Then she realized that her mornings were no emptier without it, so even though she wasn't actually boycotting the paper any longer, she hadn't bothered to buy it since then. This morning Emma snatched at a copy, and shuffled through the pages searching for the item on Frank Reid's death. It was a small piece in the Home News section. She was in luck; the lying-in was that evening in the church of Mary Immaculate, Refuge of Sinners, Rathmines, at five-fifteen; the funeral, tomorrow at eleven. Emma was relieved and a little excited.

She could probably get to both. Tomorrow would definitely be fine. Today was more awkward. Working back from five-fifteen, she would need to leave home by quarter to five at the latest, to be at the church on time. That meant she would have to get back to the apartment by four, to shower and find something suitable to wear. That was tight. It was now twenty past eleven. If she kept going and just grabbed a sandwich on the run for lunch, then she might manage it. Should she send flowers? Get a card? Flowers. Flowers were easier. She could organize that over the phone while on the move. A card would involve finding a shop and spending ten or fifteen minutes sifting for something appropriate. She wasn't sure what one did these days anyway; was it just solemn-looking cards with a suitable personal message, or was it still the thing to get a mass-card and find some priest to sign it for a tenner or whatever? Emma vaguely recalled that it was possible to buy them pre-signed now, from the Veritas shop or somewhere like that. Anyway, where Norma Reid was involved there was no way Emma was going to chance getting it wrong. Flowers were definitely by far the safer option; lilies for preference.

A savagely cold wind blew along Burgh Quay. There were still ice patches about from the night before. Would this winter never end? Emma, now on the tightest of schedules, silently cursed the weather, as she racked her brain trying to remember the name of the florist nearest the apartment. Joy's. That was it. Excellent. Walking quickly towards the Clarence Hotel, she dialled 11811 to get the number.

Emma was going to see Luke again at last; the first time since that awful end-of-October evening. It felt a little peculiar suddenly to know this piece of the future, especially as time and time again over the last four months, Emma had speculated about how they might meet, and what the outcome would be. None of her efforts to force an encounter had worked. Christmas seemed to offer an opportunity, but attempting to make Ruth the mediator had come to nothing. Phoning Norma herself to explain why she would be absent from the Reid Christmas dinner had failed to ignite a chain of events that would lead to Luke contacting her. Norma had simply said thanks for letting her know. Ruth had heard no more. Now she knew the location, time, circumstances, even the likely atmosphere of this sudden rendezvous with Luke. She would be able to look at him during the brief lying-in service. It was unlikely that he would see her until the end, the part where everyone lined up to shake hands with the family and mutter something suitable. Face after face would pass in front of him. Suddenly Emma would be there. In the church of Mary Immaculate, Refuge of Sinners, she would take Luke's hand again and gaze into his eyes. Would he instinctively reach out and hug her? Would he maintain a posture of dignified mourning, even though his eyes flamed again with a renewed intensity, composed equally of shock and delight? Would he be cold? Would she be just another face in a sad parade? Of course Emma knew that so much of this would depend on how Luke was dealing with his father's death. Had there been any kind of reconciliation? If not, then might Luke, being Luke, be in deep distress, racked with guilt and self-recrimination? Frankly, the more Emma thought about the drama that lay ahead, the more its delicious possibilities excited her; that delicate combination of what she could foresee, and what remained a teasing mystery, made it all irresistible.

Emma was particularly aware that the typical Irish funeral had a crucial two-act structure. It was vital to work that to her advantage. It would, for example, be foolish to overplay her hand tonight at the shorter lying-in bit. She should build slowly to the more extended and climactic funeral mass and burial the following day. With that in mind she had already decided not to try to force, or even hint at, an invitation back to the Reid home tonight, unless of course Luke himself really pressed her to go. No, she would merely signal her presence on the edge of things, quietly offer her availability as a potential shoulder to cry on, wait thoughtfully and respectfully in the background, not press her claims in any way. Be there for him. Emma whispered the phrase softly to herself. Anything more proactive than that should be left to the graveyard scene the following day.

Trying to make this exciting new scenario gel with her working day was always going to be frustrating. The freezing nagging wind worked actively against her, slowing everything down as she moved about the city, making her long for a break, even fifteen minutes in the warmth of a coffee shop. She knew that was not on, if she was to get to the church on time. She had to be disciplined.

Emma was relatively satisfied to get back to the apartment at seven minutes after four. She was only slightly behind schedule. In the bedroom she laid out every item of black clothing she had. While there could be some crossover of minor items between today and tomorrow, essentially she needed two separate and distinct outfits. A key problem, she discovered, once she slipped on an old favourite, was that a lot of her black clothes were really of the party dress variety. They just didn't strike the correct sombre tone. She could get up early tomorrow, go to Zara, get a suitable outfit, and literally wear her purchase to the funeral. That would allow her much more attractive mix-and-match possibilities for this evening. Frankly, her present wardrobe couldn't cope with two funeral scenarios.

It was nearly four-thirty. She would have to do her thinking in the shower, rather than in front of the mirror. By the time she was towelling herself, she had decided on the early shopping trip tomorrow. This meant her outfit for this evening now fell into place more or less automatically. She dressed and left the apartment at four fifty-five. It was getting very tight. She still had to collect the flowers from Joy's. She decided to walk along Sandford Road and keep an eye out for a taxi.

Joy's didn't let her down. Everything was ready, and the bouquet was exactly what she had in mind; sombre beauty but with a hint of individuality. She knew Luke would appreciate it. It would remind him of just one of the things that had made her special to him. As she came out of Joy's, someone was exiting a cab across the road. It was free. Emma felt luck was with her, but the traffic all the way into Ranelagh village was horrendous. By the time they got to the Swan Centre it was already five-twenty, and the driver's monologue about how the politicians had made a complete bollocks of the whole transport situation was like a deadly drumbeat in her head. Stuck at the lights opposite the Stella Cinema for what seemed like hours, Emma began that process of judging whether it was better to stay where she was, or get out and walk. If she walked now she would certainly get there before the end, if she didn't mind being out of breath and perspiring when she arrived. The driver was of the opinion that if the fucker in the fuckin' BMW X5 trying to pull out would only get back in again, then they all might be able to move.

What was most tantalizing and frustrating was that she could actually see the church. On a clear road she could be there in thirty seconds. The BMW thing, far from pulling back, had now forced itself out further to the exact point where it could not move another inch, while preventing everyone else behind it from going anywhere. Emma was now actually jigging in the back seat, suppressing the desire to scream at the driver to shut up and drive. Frankly, there was nowhere for him to go.

She couldn't take it any longer. It was twenty-five past. They had progressed no more than twenty yards. She looked at the meter, took out a tenner and shoved it at him, saying, 'Sorry, listen, I'll walk. That's fine.'

Emma slammed the door and was gone at speed. It was as she passed the BMW or whatever it was, and turned to glare meaningfully at the driver, that she realized she had left the funeral bouquet in the cab.

She ran back and saw the cab turn on to the relatively calm Leinster Road. By the time she reached the corner it was well out of reach. Emma was beginning to perspire despite the infuriating cold. Forget the flowers, just get to the church. She was not going to run. She would walk quickly, but as calmly, as possible. There was no point in getting hysterical. She would arrive at the church shortly. Things were now entirely in her hands, and nothing more could go wrong. It was with thoughts like these that she passed the time as she power-walked along Rathmines Road. Keeping her eye fixed on the dome of Mary Immaculate, Refuge of Sinners also seemed to help.

People were already leaving as Emma arrived. She pushed through the porch area inside. She was very much struggling against a departing tide. Only absolute determination to see it through kept her going. Distracted by the odd familiar face moving in the opposite direction, nodding or gesturing at her, she tried to see what was happening with the family at the top of the church. To her relief she could see that there was still a line of mourners shuffling forward. Emma bowed her head a little and drove towards them as directly as possible. She attached herself to the end of the line. She had a few moments to compose herself. She felt hot, flustered and enraged, but at least she knew that the family would know nothing of her late arrival. Emma could have been doing several decades of the rosary on her knees before presenting herself in front of them, for all they were aware.

She could see the line of Reids now. Norma, then Luke and Matthew, the men of the family first of course, then Judy and Ruth. Someone had his arm around Ruth. Viewed from behind, she seemed more crumpled and distressed than the others. Emma was utterly shocked when she realized the comforting arm belonged to that awful Cousin Barry. What in God's name was he doing up at the top pew, and all over Ruth like a rash?

Having begun to compose herself, Emma now started to feel the tightness again. She counted the line ahead to gauge how long it would be before she came face to face with Luke. Thirty seconds each, she figured, and there were two, four, six, eight, ten – oh! Who was the black guy? Emma saw a young black man look around as he waited in line. He was in his mid-twenties, elegant, with such a beautiful face. Emma wondered who he knew. She watched, fascinated, as he reached the family. She could tell as he moved along that he seemed to be introducing himself briefly. When he arrived in front of Ruth, however, it was different. Her head hung low, and he angled his face a little closer to hers. He took her hand in a familiar way. Some friend of Ruth's, clearly, but what made this more interesting was that, while Ruth acknowledged whatever he said with nods, she never met his eyes. The poor guy seemed not to know what else to say or do. His eyes were sad and frankly, rather enticing. He nodded at Barry and moved on.

Emma saw no more of him because at that moment, she arrived in front of Norma. She had already decided what to say so that it would be clean and simple. Nothing inspired. Just 'I'm very sorry for your loss', and take it from there.

Emma looked into Norma's eyes. They did not look tired or red from weeping; nor broken or haunted. They were strong, clear, in control. Frankly, Emma would always have bet on Norma being a magnificent widow. So it seemed. She was very glad that she hadn't decided to attempt anything more inventive or personal than 'I'm very sorry for your loss'. It was clear as she took Norma's hand and said the words that was all the Reid Widow either needed or required. She responded with a magnificently sad measured nod of the head, and the tiniest pressure on Emma's hand. Then her eyes moved decisively to the next mourner.

Emma felt her whole body tighten and focus as she turned to Luke. It was the live radio moment; the red light went on, and suddenly there was the electrifying consciousness that every word would be heard by tens of thousands of people. Emma was about to look into Luke's eyes again. She would feel his skin again. It was a moment of intense emotional turbulence.

Luke smiled at her and took her hand. It was as if she was an old school pal he hadn't seen in a few years, and was pleasantly surprised she had bothered to turn up for the funeral. It was sincere and passionless. There was no special message, there was no surge of feeling behind his eyes. Frankly his eyes were . . . what were they? Not dead, they were . . . disengaged. Emma didn't know what she said, she didn't know what he said. As she turned to Matthew, she felt as if she had come to the wrong funeral by mistake, and had ended up sympathizing with complete strangers, who tactfully covered up the embarrassment. That feeling was dispelled by Judy. Once she'd politely shaken hands with a stern-looking all-grown-up Matthew and moved on, Emma was suddenly enveloped in a remarkable girlie hug of solidarity. Judy whispered urgently, 'Thanks so much for coming. It means so much to me. We're all on your side, you know.'

This was followed by an extraordinarily penetrating 'if only you knew' stare, and a mouthed 'really'.

Emma couldn't wait to turn away, even though it meant confronting the dread sight of a blotched, shattered Ruth. Like some Brontë sisters creation, Ruth seemed scarcely able to stand. Emma kept her eyes fixed on her. She couldn't help but be creepily aware of the presence of Cousin Barry's arm, clearly offering real support as well as comfort. What else might this physical closeness suggest? Emma didn't want to go there. At that moment she just yearned to be back home, showered and curled up tightly in bed. Ruth managed a grimace and a single whispered, 'Poor Daddy'.

Emma nodded with what she hoped was a look of sad understanding. Then she timed a quick acknowledging nod at Barry, the merest eye contact, and moved on. She couldn't get home fast enough.

Emma showered again but didn't go to bed immediately. Wrapped in an enormous dressing gown, she lay on the sofa, Luke's expression nagging at her. What did it mean? If there had even been anger or coldness or contempt, that would have been acceptable. Instead it had been merely friendly. Who did he think she was, some young one who had done work experience with him in the museum during the summer?

They had lived together for three years. What in Christ's name *did it mean?*

Emma decided to avoid another taxi disaster. The solution was to borrow her brother's car. She wanted to control events tomorrow. She was confident that if she could get to Zara on time, she could find everything she needed, fit it, buy it, wear it, and still have a full hour to get to the church by eleven. She phoned her brother Cillian and forced him to bring his car around to her later that night. She even checked the Zara website for opening times and catalogue details.

Emma was in bed before midnight, but still couldn't sleep. Whenever she dozed off, she was taunted with hysterical trapped dreams. She couldn't open some door . . . *even though she desperately needed to get inside. Cousin Barry grasped her hand and the more she pulled away, the harder and more painful his grip became. Norma kept saying to her, I'm very sorry for your loss. She could see Luke standing behind, with his back to her, but Emma couldn't reach him. She couldn't get past Norma, who just kept saying, I'm very sorry for your loss. I'm very sorry for your loss.*

At six-thirty Emma sat up, sweating and hyperventilating. She decided to kick-start the day with yet another shower and coffee. At least there was no danger of being late for the funeral mass. She left the apartment at seven, and was in Henry Street by half past. She idled time away until Zara opened. She knew her instinct had been right the moment she crossed the threshold. Almost at a glance she could see half a dozen options and combinations in black. There were skirts, dresses, a surprisingly attractive trouser suit, a perfect linen/cotton overcoat. Far from being a frantic runaround, it was oddly relaxing. By the time the shoes were chosen and fitted, it was still only quarter to ten. Emma looked at herself and smiled. For less than 250 euro she looked rather gorgeous.

With over an hour to spare, she was able to sit back in the car and listen to Ray D'Arcy, whom she really admired. She began to wonder if there was some kind of slot she might do on his show. Being from the country like Ray, she felt they might find a common language or attitude to 'click' on-air.

Emma found parking, and arrived in good time to pick her spot in the church. She chose a centre-aisle position about four rows back on the other side from the family. She figured this would give her a good back-profile view. Frank's coffin was now snowed under with floral tributes. Emma realized she had entirely forgotten to get another bouquet. Oh well, frankly she didn't think it would ever be noticed.

She viewed the gathering crowd. It was going to be a big one all right. Suits were now arriving in numbers. A party of older schoolboys in uniform trooped in, presumably Matthew's pals, looking determinedly sombre. Surely they were delighted to have the morning off? By the time the family appeared and mass began, the church was bulging with mourners.

Part of Emma's strategy in choosing her seat was to be directly in Luke's eyeline whenever he glanced left. The theory was, when he looked at his mother, he would see her too. The problem, as soon became clear to Emma, was that they were not looking at each other. At all. Norma and Luke stood or sat shoulder to shoulder, wife and elder son, chief mourners at the funeral of Frank Reid, but they were not in communication with each other on any level. Frankly, the only real physical and emotional togetherness anywhere in that front pew seemed to be between Barry and Ruth. Having more or less avoided looking at him the evening before, Emma now began to think that actually Barry seemed different to her memory of him. What was it? Had he eased off on the fake tan? His face certainly seemed less orange. The hair was longer, which made for a softer effect. Yes, looking at him now, Emma didn't find him so repulsive.

She couldn't resist checking out the mourners again. It became clear to her very quickly that there was a certain absence of familiar political faces. If Fianna Fáil was paying tribute to one of its devoted old soldiers, then it had sent its more anonymous emissaries to do the honours. Despite the layers upon layers of distinguished grey and navy and black, Emma could not recognize a single front-line Government representative. Nobody who might be easy prey for a tabloid photographer or columnist had shown his face. The Bar was clearly made of sterner stuff when it came to respecting their own, even those in disgrace with fortune and men's eyes. Well-fed faces and greyheads were out in force. Every pew seemed to be stuffed with Frank's honourable friends. It suddenly occurred to Emma, where was his old hero? Had Haughey himself shown a face? After all, he had pulled out all the stops back in 1970 to get to Frank and Norma's wedding. It would surely round it off nicely for him to turn up today. But she could see no sign of him.

Despite her growing mood of relaxed cynical detachment, Emma had no conscious realization that the demons might be departing her body, until the moment she had to stop herself laughing out loud. It happened when the priest came to the lectern, bowed solemnly, and announced, 'A reading from the Holy Gospel according to Luke.'

Emma glanced around. Did nobody else see the joke? Did Luke himself not find this amusing? She searched the faces – most were bland, some bored, some genuinely sad – but no one, including Luke, seemed to get the joke. What was the matter with these people?

Pilate then called together the chief priests and the rulers and the people, and said to them, 'You brought me this man as one who was perverting the people; and after examining him before you, behold, I did not find this man guilty of any of your charges against him; neither did Herod, for he sent him back to us. Behold, nothing deserving death has been done by him; I will therefore chastise him and release him.' But they shouted out, 'Crucify, crucify him!' He said to them, 'Why, what evil has he done? I have found in him no crime deserving death; I will therefore chastise him and release him.' But they were urgent, demanding with loud cries that he should be crucified. And their voices prevailed.

This is the gospel of the Lord.


From this moment on, Emma began to enjoy the whole event. She felt like a country girl again, observing, at a remove, this ludicrous charade of South Dublin respectability. She found herself wondering how she had ever got involved with this family. There was another moment of comic bliss when the priest was slipped a note by an obsequious church clerk. Without even a trace of an ironic smile, he requested the owner of a black Lexus, number plate blah-de-blah, to move as it was causing an obstruction.

The sense of bathos deepened. Judy stepped forward with 'Daddy's favourite poem', O'Rahilly's dirge, 'Is Fada Liom Oíche Fhírfhluich', read in Dublin 6 Gaelic by way of Washington. After 'Ag Críost an Síol', hordes of men in suits queued for communion. It took more than fifteen minutes to satisfy their Christian hunger. Throughout it all, the Reid family performed with awesome professional discipline. Finally, Luke and Matthew, side by side but managing not to touch each other, shouldered the front end of the coffin and helped carry their distinguished father solemnly down the aisle. Someone sang 'Going Home'.

There was no way Emma was going to miss the final scene in Deansgrange cemetery. She didn't waste time chatting outside the church, and got to her car quickly. She noticed her reflection in the door window and thought she looked fantastic. She suddenly saw the handsome black guy from the evening before. He was standing on the path alone, looking a little uncertain. Emma couldn't resist the urge. She was feeling quite giddy. She called to him, 'Hello. Did you want a lift to the graveyard?'

The young man seemed very surprised.

'Oh sorry. I, ah – well, I wasn't sure if . . . well, what was appropriate.'

'Are you a friend of someone in the family?'

'Well . . . I am a college friend of Ruth.'

'Then of course you should come. If you have the time.'

'Yes . . . well, yes, I have.'

'Come on, I'm going now.'

'Thank you.'

The young man got in. Emma smiled and offered her hand.

'I'm Emma. I'm actually Luke's ex. All finished with now. No tension thankfully. But you know at times like these . . .'

The young man seemed a little relieved at this news.

'Yes, yes, absolutely. I'm Benjamin.'

'Nice to meet you, Benjamin. Are you Ruth's ex?'

Benjamin was taken aback, as Emma had intended him to be.

'Sorry, no, no, well . . . ah, no. I mean we were never . . . a couple, you know.'

'But? I hear a "but" there somewhere?'

'No . . . well, no.'

Benjamin laughed nervously.

'I'm sorry. I wasn't expecting such a conversation.'

'I know, I'm being very cheeky. It's just, having been through it with the Reid family myself, I was delighted I might have found a fellow-traveller. Luke was – is, ah, a very . . . complex person.'

'Yes, so is Ruth. Actually I think that she – well, she did like me, I think.'

'Aha!'

'But . . . well, it was very complicated. You know, perhaps she is going through some difficult times.'

Emma eased into fourth gear. She was going to enjoy this little chat. By the time they arrived at Deansgrange, she had extracted a pretty full picture of the extent of the humiliation Ruth had exposed herself to, in her efforts to bed the very attractive Benjamin. Poor Ruth. It seemed like Benjamin had sent out as many polite signals as possible, but she just wasn't listening. Yesterday evening's performance suggested she was not over him yet.

Emma and Benjamin drifted apart as they joined the small gathering around the grave. A decade of the rosary had begun. No sign of Cousin Barry. The women of the family were clinging together for support. Luke and Matthew stood on either side of them. Luke now just seemed to Emma one of those thin, intense, serious-minded young men, good-looking in a milk-fed sort of way. Nothing more.

The coffin was lowered as the priest gave the final blessing. At the last moment Norma stepped forward and threw something on to the coffin. It struck the wood with a muffled metallic thud. People began to shuffle off, leaving the family alone to have their last moment. Some went straight for their cars. Emma merely eased back to a more protected vantage point. Ruth broke down completely. Judy held her. Led by the Reid Widow, they all began to move back towards the limousine.

Then suddenly, quietly, the whole facade crumbled. Just for a moment, the reality of this family revealed itself. Emma, to her huge delight, saw it happen. As the women got into the car, Matthew, just behind them, turned to Luke. He jabbed an accusing finger at him and spoke quietly, quickly and, it seemed to Emma, with real anger. Luke didn't respond verbally, but he nodded and turned away. Matthew, looking just a little too pleased with himself, followed the women into the car. As Emma turned back to look at Luke, she was distracted by Benjamin, standing a little way off, but very much looking in her direction. He smiled and gestured to her car with a question on his face. Emma smiled back and nodded. Yes. Inside, she felt, Yes, Ben! Absolutely!

Coffee in hand, Emma sat again at her desk. Sunshine still poured in through her window, and she realized that she was smiling at the memory of that moment. What time was it? Nearly four o'clock. Benjamin had said he would get to the apartment at around six. There would be no more writing done once he arrived. She had better get on with it. She had an idea for a paragraph on Sinn Féin, Fianna Fáil and criminality. She hadn't formulated it properly yet, but it would be something about stark choices for the voter in Modern Ireland. On the one hand the vulgarity of armed robbery, and on the other the finesse of rezoning scams and shady property deals. If there was the crude savagery of punishment beatings, then there was also Fianna Fáil's much more civilized portfolio of secret offshore accounts and dodgy tax schemes. Frankly, who needed to money-launder, when there were always nods, winks and amnesties at one's disposal should anything go awry? And of course any Exchequer shortfall could be made up by taking pension books from the elderly in care. In the end Fianna Fáil, having presented a compelling argument as to why voters should reject the politics of Sinn Féin, could only offer the politics of Mé Féin as their alternative.

It took her longer than expected to get the shape of the piece exactly to her liking. In the end she was a little surprised by the underlying tone. It was that of the disdainful outsider. Emma rather liked that. She had just sent the finished column, when Benjamin came walking across the front lawn below towards the apartment building. He seemed to be holding something gift-wrapped under his arm. She was pleased. It might be an early Easter egg. How things work out!

Her mind drifted back to the moment they drove out of the cemetery together. When she turned on to the busy road she saw Luke standing alone at a bus stop. Benjamin didn't seem to notice him, and she felt no need to point him out. Luke did not see them pass by. Emma realized she just felt glad he did not look forlorn or lonely. Frankly, he seemed quite at peace, standing waiting, as if the only agitation in his heart at that moment concerned the very mundane Dublin mystery of when the next bus would arrive.

# 9

# Cousins II

Barry found out in the weirdest way that the Pope had finally died. He woke up suddenly at nearly four in the morning. His mouth was sticky dry. He needed water. He slid from under Molly's arm and left the bedroom. While he stood naked in the living room, sipping the cold water, stretching and arching his back and shoulders, he flicked on the telly just to see what was what. He was never normally awake at that hour, but he and Molly must have conked out around eight o'clock. Barry tried to figure out the time. They had got back from the Summit before seven. They started fucking in the kitchen while they were getting ready for dinner. That continued into the bedroom, where they fucked again, until the last thing Barry could remember was lying on the flat of his back soaked in sweat, with Molly's little rubbery body curled on top of him, her arms clutched around his neck. Then total blackout, until he woke up parched. Why wasn't he starving? They had ended up having no dinner. They hadn't even looked at telly, so it was a bit of a shock for Barry to flick it on now and find Pope stuff on practically every channel. Of course it had been on the cards for days. When exactly had he died?

Barry immediately thought of Luke. He couldn't ring him at this hour, could he? Yet Luke mightn't mind in the circumstances. He'd probably still be up, glued to the radio. Barry, hopping from channel to channel as he thought about this, was distracted by shots he recognized of the Pope's visit to Ireland. He waited, hoping to see the Galway mass. He had been there. He was only six at the time, and as he looked now at the fuzzy old film, Barry tried to remember stuff about that famous day. The truth was it was more or less a complete blank to him, except maybe for two things. The first was they had left the house that morning at some mad hour, six o'clock or something, to get there on time. This was kind of unbeliev-able, because Barry could never remember his ma and da being on time for anything. The second memory he definitely had was of his ma having a row with his da at the mass itself, because da insisted on leaving during the communion to get a headstart.

'Look at the crowds, we'll be all day getting out if we wait till the end.'

Ma got into an awful snot over that. She thought it was an insult to the Holy Father. It put a bit of a damper on the journey home.

Watching the film from Galway now didn't help jog Barry's memory. He knew the Pope said, 'Young people of Ireland, I love you', but that was only because he had seen it on telly hundreds of times since. No way did he remember it from being there. Bishop Casey turned up on screen waving his pudgy hands, winding up the crowd. Barry had no memory of him that day either. He wouldn't even have known now who he was, if it hadn't been for the scandal years later. Barry wondered what age Casey's secret child was at the time of the Pope's visit. He had never thought about it before. Was he at the Galway mass? What was the story there? Would John Paul have known about him? Then there was a shot of that other guy, what was his name? The priest with the beard who, it turned out, was riding his housekeeper. It was funny really looking at it now; Beardy and Casey up on the platform singing away. Jesus, you had to hand it to them for nerve. The pictures looked so washed out and long ago now. Barry flicked over to hard bright live Sky News.

He was beginning to feel a bit chilly. He rubbed his dick softly, wondering if he should go back to bed, or put on a dressing gown and watch some more. Could he chance ringing Luke, just to see if he was up? Get his read on the whole thing. Barry decided. He tiptoed into the bedroom and felt for his dressing gown, He noticed Molly was now curled into the tiniest ball on the far side of the bed, and he grinned. He knew he'd get the horn if he stayed looking at her, so he wrapped the dressing gown warm around him and went back out. He closed the door really silently. He sat himself into an armchair with the phone. Turning down the telly sound, he dialled Luke's number.

He had decided to give it no more than four rings. Just in case. Luke picked up after just one ring. Barry thought his 'hello' sounded a bit surprised, which wasn't surprising.

'Hi, Luke.'

'Oh, Barry? It's you.'

'I hope I didn't wake you.'

'No, no, I was up. Funny, I thought it might be Ruth.'

'Oh, are you expecting a call from Ruth?'

'No, no. Absolutely not. It's just . . . well . . . it's sort of what she used to do in this kind of situation.'

'You mean the Pope dying?'

'Kind of thing.'

'That's why I was ringing. I just saw it on the telly.'

'Oh, you only found out now?'

'A couple of minutes ago.'

'He's been dead since half eight. Were you out?'

That was around the time he and Molly fell asleep. Weird. Luke kept talking.

'Of course, that's what they announced. I think he's been dead since Friday, but there was no way they could allow him to die on April 1st, so they kept it going for another day.'

'You really think, yeah?'

'Well, it's a good conspiracy theory. In the end, does it matter anyway whether he died on April Fool's Day or April 2nd? He's dead now. I think we can definitely believe that much. It's nice to be certain about something, isn't it?'

Barry didn't really know what to say to that. Was Luke drunk? He was kind of rambling. Barry wasn't so sure now exactly what kind of chat this was going to be. There was a little awkward silence. Then Luke spoke again.

'Actually, I'm glad you called. I was going to get in touch to ask you a favour. Do you think you could talk to Ruth for me? Persuade her to meet with me?'

'Yeah, sure.'

The answer was automatic. It was not the answer Barry wanted to give. For fuck's sake, he didn't want to meet Ruth again anytime soon. How was he supposed to explain this to Luke, who didn't even realize that Barry had avoided going to the graveside on the day of Uncle Frank's funeral, because of Ruth? The simple fact was her clinging had become way too much. It had been OK at first the evening before; flattering even. Barry really liked his little cousin. He thought it was cute the way she was so deadly serious, and a bit awkward around people, and her hair was gorgeous, and her big eyes were actually sexy, though she didn't even seem to know it herself. When he arrived at the church that evening for the lying-in bit, he had no problem going straight over to Ruth as soon as he spotted her. He gave her his big cousin's hug. The poor little thing was in a desperate state. She looked like she'd been crying non-stop for days. Barry meant just to give her a bit of a squeeze and a peck on the cheek, but she clung on to him like he was going to save her from something. Suddenly the priest came out, and the thing had started, and he was stuck there, his arm locked around her, afraid to take it away. Aunt Norma, at the far end of the line, wouldn't even glance in his direction. That made Barry think, fuck her, and he started to enjoy being up at the top seat with the Reid family. The fact that he was really helping Ruth by being there felt good too. He was glad.

Thinking back on it, Barry figured that the weirdness really started near the end of that evening, when the black guy came up to sympathize with Ruth. Barry felt her whole body go rigid, like someone lifting a weight that's beyond them, and they know they're going to have to drop it. Barry didn't know who this guy was, but he could tell that Ruth knew him, and he was the last person she wanted to see; at least, right then. The black guy looked a bit shitless too, to be fair, like he was worried she'd suddenly start screaming or something. Barry didn't know what the story was, but he recognized the vibe. It reminded him of that thing, when you suddenly turn a corner, and bump into someone you've fucked and not bothered to call since. It never bothered Barry too much when it happened, but sometimes he could tell that the girls were really squirming, like they were going to be sick or something. Barry had no patience for this stuff. It was bollocks, and anyway it was a lie, because mostly they knew it was only a fuck in the first place, the same as he did, so what was the big act for? Say hello, how're you, good luck and move on. But he felt really sorry for Ruth at that moment, hooked on to his arm. Actually he felt a bit sorry for your man too, poor fucking eejit. What possessed him to turn up? Did Aunt Norma know about him? Barry thought there was no chance of that. She'd have a fit if she thought her precious baby was riding a black.

It was when Ruth came speeding over to him outside the church the following day, and pulled at his hand as they walked inside, that Barry thought, whoa now! He felt a bit panicky. He started wanting her to back off. All through the mass Ruth became more and more like dead weight on his arm. The big shock, though, came in the middle of one of those Irish hymns. He happened to look down and caught Ruth's big eyes, all cried out, looking up at him. She wanted him to reach down and kiss her. On the mouth. He was sure of it. He nearly did too. Jesus Christ, what was he thinking of? He had to get away. By the end of the mass he had worked out a straightforward enough story about having to get back to work on the double. He had only barely been given the morning off, and if he went all the way out to Deansgrange he'd never get back in time. He escaped. Luke obviously didn't have a clue about any of this.

'You have a way with Ruth. She'll do it for you, I'm sure of it. If we could just get talking again, you know . . . ?'

Suddenly Luke said, anyway thanks, goodnight, and he put down the phone. Barry felt a bit empty. Usually Luke would talk to him for hours about stuff: even when Barry didn't really know what he was on about, he could feel how fired up Luke was. That was what Barry liked. Tonight Luke just sounded odd. There was no energy. Barry remembered that at the funeral, he had thought Luke looked a bit too thin. Maybe he wasn't eating properly.

There was nothing for it now but to go back to bed, but he knew he wouldn't sleep. He slid off his dressing gown and pressed himself against Molly's back. It warmed him but it didn't distract him. He kept thinking about Luke. He could imagine him sitting alone in his crappy flat, listening to all the Pope news on the radio. Why hadn't he wanted to talk about stuff? Barry was dying to know what had happened since with the family. What about Uncle Frank's will? What was Luke's next move? Would he want Barry to help? They could have talked about all of these things. The Pope would just have been the kick-start. It never happened. Instead, Barry had made this stupid promise to go and see Ruth. That made him very uneasy. He didn't like being a go-between in the first place. He was a bit fucked off actually, the more he thought about it. Another two hours passed before he managed to sleep again.

More and more, Barry regretted his promise to Luke. He spent all Monday at work, letting his resentment build up. When Dougal came snaking round, Barry snapped at him, 'Are you checking up on me?'

Dougal was genuinely surprised. What was eating him? Barry was his top man, surely he knew that. He was the fastest and neatest spark on the team. Far from checking up on him, Dougal had dropped by to tell Barry there would be a bit extra in an envelope for him at the weekend – not a word to the East Europeans or the Turks. He held up his hand and rubbed his finger and thumb together, with a little wink. Go fuck yourself, Barry felt like telling him, but didn't.

Later in the day he ignored two text messages from Molly. It was the first time he'd done something like that since their big scene started three weeks ago. That made him even more annoyed with himself. By the time he finished work, he had changed his mind again about going to see Ruth. He'd do it tomorrow. Instead, he phoned Molly and apologized for taking so long to get back to her. Did she want to call over tonight? Molly did. Of course she did.

Later that night, as he lay in bed with Molly snuggled into him, sleeping like a baby, Barry began to figure out what it was exactly that was wrecking his head. Lately he had started to feel like a better person. He didn't want anything to mess things up. He had started to count his blessings. There was Molly for a start; the fact that he wanted her to be around so much, and he was even willing to change his ways to make that happen. Another thing was, he visited his mother all the time. That was good. When she finally got out of hospital last week, he went down to Mayo especially, with a welcome home present for her. He had even nearly brought Molly to meet her.

Barry linked all this change to Luke. He was sure of it. The thing that really convinced him, funnily enough, was when he realized that, little by little, he was spending less money, even though he was still earning fuck-loads. He hadn't really noticed how much cash had been building up in his account until the last time he went to the bank. The manager had called him aside. It was the first time he had ever spoken to him. Barry didn't know what to say when he was told he had far too much money doing nothing in his current account, and really he should think about how to make it work for him. The manager said the bank had a number of interesting products, and he suggested an appointment to discuss Barry's affairs.

Somehow, creeping up on him unnoticed, there were many things to feel better about. His looks even. The night, a few weeks ago, when Molly called out of the blue to see him, she had told him he looked even more gorgeous and sexy than when she had last seen him months before. Barry had stopped taking sunbeds before Christmas, his hair had grown, even the nose job seemed less weird. When he had looked into Molly's eyes that night, the face reflected back at him seemed softer, kinder.

Lying with Molly, thinking and thinking, Barry wondered why he traced all these things back to Luke. For starters, he could never decide if he just didn't understand Luke at all or had completely the wrong impression about what he was at. Barry had felt this for the first time the night they burned down the cottage. He had never analysed in any detail why Luke wanted to do this. It seemed obvious. He was angry at his father. He had copped on that old Frank was just another liar, as greedy and weak as all the rest, and he wanted to punish him; his mother as well probably. Barry had no trouble buying into that. He had spent so much time in his own life thinking out elaborate revenges on people, especially his own family. When Luke asked him to help with his scheme, he jumped at the idea. Working out how to burn down the cottage, and then actually doing it successfully, was such a buzz. The heat of the blaze had toasted his back as he ran back to the van. He turned round expecting to do a high five with his cousin like something in a movie, only to find Luke had not followed him from the burning cottage. That was the moment Barry first felt there was something else going on with his cousin; something he didn't understand at all. Looking through the window of the open van door, he saw Luke's silhouette like a black cut-out against the flames. He seemed to be in deep meditation, maybe even praying. From the angle Barry was at, his cousin looked like he was so close to the fire that all he had to do was fall forward where he stood and he would be engulfed, as if in some kind of ritual death. Barry's shout to Luke at that moment was really a spontaneous cry of panic.

Afterwards, travelling back to Dublin, Barry found himself confessing things he never thought he would reveal to another person. That night and since, he always felt completely safe talking to Luke. He believed in him.

So what now? Luke had asked him what seemed like this simple little favour, but something in Barry was fighting against it. Some instinct. He felt very guilty, and very stupid. What was he nervous about, going to see Ruth with a simple message from her brother? He really misses you. You are his favourite. He really wants to talk to you again. She would either say yes or no, and he would bring the message back. What was the big deal? Barry wasn't fooling himself. He remembered that look from Ruth in the church. It was a hungry look, the black holes of her eyes were trying to suck him into some horror. He didn't want to see that look again. Especially not now he had Molly to think about.

Tuesday passed on the penthouse floor above the canal dock, with rain rapping constantly against the all-glass front. Barry worked on automatic, his brain focused on building himself up to visit Ruth that evening. He told himself, get it over with, do it tonight. He hoped that being decisive would stop him thinking about it too much. Instead, the mind-fuck just went on and on, this version and that, none of it happy, none of it with an ending he liked. When Dougal stuck his head in again, he was a welcome distraction. This time he had a real reason for interrupting Barry. He was in one of his vile moods. Some of the Poles had started looking for a day off on Friday for the Pope's funeral. Dougal told them go fuck themselves, but now a few of the Irish lads were jumping on the bandwagon.

'Some of that shower if you asked them last week who Karol Wo-teela was, would have said she was a Bosnian lap-dancer. Now they're saying they need a day of reflection. Jesus, those fuckin' phone-ins on the radio have a lot to answer for. What about you? I need someone on my side here.'

Barry knew what that meant. Another few bob would be slipped his way if he said he was happy to work on Friday. Barry thought about it. Working on Friday was no problem, but he hated doing Dougal any favours. To his shock he suddenly found himself thinking, 'What would Luke do?' The answer came.

'Of course I'll be working Friday. And I don't want anything extra for it.'

Dougal's eyes narrowed. The little rat was waiting for the sting in the tail. Instead Barry just said, 'That OK?'

Dougal recovered his tongue just in time. That's grand. Great stuff. That's the spirit. Fair dues. He wished there were more like Barry. A fair deal all round for everyone, that was all Dougal asked for. Too many gougers and cowboys around these days. Barry stopped listening. He was trying to convince himself that straight after work was the best time to call on Ruth.

He didn't call straight after work, or at any time that evening. He couldn't do it. He went to bed alone; Molly wasn't around. Barry didn't sleep. He got up at six and checked his emails. As he feared, there was one from Luke:

5/4/05. 23.50

Did you talk to Ruth yet? Any news? Don't worry about telling me if it's bad. I can take it.

Luke

There was no way out of it. At the gym Barry pushed himself harder than he had for ages, and afterwards soaked in the jacuzzi for twenty minutes. He was spotless, drained, but a bit less wound up when he arrived at Ruth's front door just after eight-thirty. She opened the door only slightly. The eyes peeping through the gap were suspicious, then amazed.

'Barry. Hello. Come in.' She opened the door fully. She was still in pyjamas.

'Sorry about this.'

'No, you're grand.'

'You know students. Never out of bed before midday.'

The remark calmed Barry. It was so ordinary. He hoped this meeting was going to be ordinary. Simple cousin to cousin.

'Tea or coffee?'

'Tea.'

Ruth went out to her little kitchen. Barry settled into an armchair, feeling more relaxed. Then the silence began to seem a little too long, and he started to get nervous again. More than three minutes passed without a word between them. Barry could hear little kitchen sounds: the clatter of a cup, the bubble and click as the kettle came to the boil and turned itself off. It was all still ordinary enough. Ruth returned with two cups of tea. She had done something to her hair.

'No sugar, isn't it?'

Barry nodded.

'I suppose you noticed I've been crying . . .'

Barry hadn't. Now that he looked closely, he could see the signs.

'It's terrible, isn't it? I always seem to be in tears whenever I see you these days. You must think I'm a complete hopeless case, but it was just . . . it's just more terrible news. More death. It seems to be everywhere.'

Barry wasn't too surprised that the Pope's death had made

Ruth cry, except it was four days ago now. She really was in a bad way. Barry thought the best thing was just to let her talk.

'I couldn't help feeling that . . . you know . . . that the world is emptier somehow without people like Saul Bellow. Does that sound really crappy? Is that just a real student thing to say?'

Barry didn't know who the fuck Saul Bellow was. Was he supposed to? Ruth talked on anyway.

'First thing I heard when I turned on the radio this morning. First thing. You know you wake up hoping maybe this day at last will be a good day. I didn't know who they were talking about, because it was in the middle of the report, but I knew someone was dead. Then they mentioned the Nobel prize in 1976 and it hit me. Saul Bellow was dead. I just started crying. I mean, he was ninety, you know, it was time, it wasn't like it was a tragic thing, but, but, but . . . I can't seem to start a day any more. Without feeling some loss.'

To Barry's horror Ruth started crying again. There were no crying sounds. He wasn't even sure she knew she was crying. Tears just appeared and trickled down her face, as she talked about Saul Bellow who was dead. The poor girl was utterly lost. There was nothing Barry could do. This wasn't the same as Molly, even though she had cried too. When Molly arrived at his apartment out of the blue three weeks ago, she was looking for a way back to something. She was throwing the dice. When Molly suddenly burst into tears in mid-sentence, Barry hadn't felt afraid; he felt desire. He started to get a hard-on. Molly had blubbed on about this horrible boyfriend she had never told Barry about; how she had finally succeeded in dumping him because she missed Barry so much, and finally realized that he wasn't just an occasional fuck for her, and she knew Barry probably didn't feel the same way, it had been so long since he had seen her anyway, but she had to tell him at least, just to get it off her chest. Sobbing uncontrollably, she had held out her arms like a little girl. Barry felt in himself no hesitation, no resistance, no doubt at all. He wanted nothing more than to draw Molly's trembling body into him. He had kissed the top of her head softly, and suddenly understood why he hadn't fucked in five months. It was suddenly obvious that all he wanted, all he ever wanted really, was Molly.

Because of her, Barry had some sense of the difference between the pain of hope and the pain of despair. He knew he had to resist making any move to comfort Ruth now. She wasn't looking him in the eye. She hadn't even asked why he had called at half eight in the morning. These were danger signals as far as he was concerned. She was still rambling on quietly about Saul Bellow, who Barry had now figured out was a famous writer. Jesus Christ! Crying over someone she'd never even met. How was Barry going to drag the subject round to Luke, deliver his message and get out of there? Suddenly, chillingly, Ruth looked directly at him. Black and empty eyes.

'But then, just when I think there is nothing, you always seem to turn up. You're amazing, Barry.'

Barry watched Ruth stand up and walk towards him. She wanted a hug, an embrace . . . something. He knew he would have to give her something. It was that or run away.

'Lately there's been nobody. Even my own friends in college keep dropping hints about therapy. I know they care about me, sure, but at the same time they're thinking, she's a million-aire now, she should get on with it. Deal with stuff. They think there's reasons for it all, that can be worked out. They don't know it's just all empty . . . and endless.'

Ruth put her arms on Barry's shoulders. He was forced to take her waist and she fell into his chest. He could feel her wet mouth and her hot breath through his shirt. At least she had stopped talking. Barry still hoped that in a few moments he could sit her down and explain why he called.

Ruth's mouth left his chest and reached up to him, open and hungry. At the same moment her hands tugged his neck down. Their lips met and he felt her tongue shoot into his mouth. Barry came as close as he had ever come to fainting. The kiss didn't stop, and when her hands started to tear at his shirt, reaching for the skin inside, Barry finally put a violent stop to it. Almost as if he was throwing up, he thrust her back, luckily on to the sofa.

'Jesus Christ, Ruth. We're cousins. Jesus.'

It came out as a babble. It was all he could say. He ran for the door as fast as he could.

Once Barry got to work, he turned off his mobile for fear Ruth would try to contact him. He worked even harder and faster than usual. By eleven o'clock he had signed off on an apartment he wasn't due to finish until the following day. He had decided to move on to the next immediately, when his stomach suddenly heaved. Barry knew what was coming. He ran through the glass doors on to the balcony. He reached the edge just in time and vomited over the side. Luckily there was no one below as the liquid puke landed splat!, harmlessly on the pathway beside the canal basin. Barry hung there, his body shaking. He spat to rid himself of the vile taste in his mouth. When he was sure it was over he went back into the apartment. He leaned into the sink, drinking directly from the tap, gargling and spitting until he felt clean again. Then he went to start work on the next apartment.

\*

Gigs were not Barry's thing but he was very relieved that Molly had persuaded him to go to Eamonn Doran's that night. There was a battle of the bands on, and Molly wanted to support Guests of the Nation. In the noise and the buzz Barry was glad there could be no serious conversation. Afterwards, in the taxi, they were both too drunk to say anything meaningful. They got back to the apartment at around two-thirty. Barry genuinely felt so exhausted that his 'I'm off' as soon as they arrived sounded completely sincere. By the time Molly came to the bedroom, he could pretend to be asleep.

In the gym the following morning the TV screens were still full of the non-stop Pope coverage. Millions of people had poured into Rome and were queuing up to see John Paul's corpse. The commentator kept going on about the huge number of young people in the crowd. It was a sign of some deep spiritual void craving to be filled, some theology professor in the studio suggested. The queue had become too large. There would not be enough time before the funeral for everyone to see the body. A line had to be drawn. There were shots of young people on the right side of the line, delirious with joy to be among the chosen ones. On the other side, a young woman who just missed the cut sobbed like a baby on camera. She would never get to look at the dead Pope. Barry wondered how far the young girl had travelled to end up with nothing.

What was he to do? At least Ruth hadn't tried to phone him. Hopefully that meant she wasn't going to. Luke hadn't contacted him again, but he would soon. Barry was only sure of one thing. There was no way he could tell Luke what had actually happened. This was something he would never tell anyone.

Perhaps the biggest surprise of Barry's life was that he broke that vow within a few hours. Later the same evening, as they sat together watching *Footballers' Wives*, he found it really hard not to say something to Molly. In the end he couldn't stop himself. Barry had never in his life shared a problem with a woman. Tonight, once he made the first remark, he discovered that the rest was surprisingly easy. Molly was in stitches at the latest plot-line in *Footballers' Wives*. One of the footballers was supposed to have got two women pregnant at the same time. Or had he? The two babies were born within minutes of each other, and one of the mothers, who Molly explained was fantastic because she was such an über-bitch, switched the babies to avoid a DNA test, because she knew that her child was not fathered by the footballer guy after all. It was some other character who, Molly explained, had died in the last series, murdered by über-bitch in fact. Barry was only learning to enjoy this stuff through Molly. He still didn't really see why she found it so funny, but he loved watching her laugh. He found himself wanting to know what she'd think about Ruth and Luke and him and the whole Reid setup. As an ad break started, he suddenly found the courage to say, 'What would you think about cousins having sex – for real, I mean, not on telly?'

Molly's reaction to the question told Barry he would have to explain everything. There was no way she would let him leave that one hanging. Maybe he knew all along that was what would happen. Coffee was brewed and *Footballers' Wives* was forgotten, as Molly questioned the whole story out of him. She was totally into it. Barry realized very quickly that he did not need to worry about Molly being jealous or suspicious. She thought the Reids were unreal, and felt very sorry for the poor girl Ruth. She was dying to know what Barry was going to do now. Did he want advice? Yes, he did. Absolutely.

Molly was very straightforward: 'You don't want to be stuck in the middle of some weird brother–sister thing, do you?'

'No. Exactly.'

'Then lie. Just tell Luke that Ruth wouldn't give you an answer. Tell him she refused to say anything to you about Luke and her. You tried and it didn't work out.'

'You think?'

'Barry, your cousins are going to have to sort themselves out. Don't go there.'

It sounded right to Barry. They continued talking the whole thing back and forth for hours all the way to bed. Now that he had started, Barry couldn't stop talking about it. Molly was more than happy to listen and join in. He even laughed when, as soon as they got into bed, Molly slithered her hand towards his crotch, whispering, 'Cousin Barry, please be nice to me.'

He slept a deep, peaceful sleep.

A compromise had been reached about the Pope's funeral. Dougal had sort of given in. Work would begin at twelve noon, so everyone had the morning free to watch the Requiem Mass. As soon as Barry woke he decided to use the time to follow through on Molly's advice. Go see Luke, get it all over with. She wished him luck with a grin. She was looking forward to a full blow-by-blow later on. Her attitude made Barry feel a bit more relaxed about the whole thing.

Luke was listening to the Requiem Mass on the radio when Barry arrived.

'You just missed Aidan Matthews.'

Barry didn't know who Aidan Matthews was. He wasn't going to ask.

'He wrote a special meditation for the occasion. It was very beautiful. Another Jesuit boy like me, funnily enough. They got to us all, one way or the other.'

Luke seemed in no hurry to find out Barry's news. He made coffee, talking all the while over the voice of Cardinal Ratzinger on the radio, droning in Italian or was it Latin?

'Wouldn't Joe Ratzinger be a great name for a hitman in a spy thriller? *"Coolly, with precision, Ratzinger fitted the silencer to his custom-made magnum 45 point 4, the only gun of its kind in the world. He took careful aim. Ratzinger was paid never to miss, and he never did!"'*

Luke thought this was very funny. Barry was feeling uptight already. If he could just tell his lie and get away. He didn't want to be stuck in Luke's bedsit any longer than he had to. He hated the crap flowery wallpaper and the cheap furniture. It felt so poor and out of its time. Nobody lived like this any more. Why had his cousin chosen it? Hadn't Ruth said something about being a millionaire? She must have been left loads of money in her father's will. So what about Luke? Was he a millionaire now as well? It sure didn't look like it in this kip. Why was he telling Barry nothing about all that stuff? Barry began to feel resentment returning. What did Luke see him as? His cousin, his friend? Or just some little assistant? A go-between?

Luke handed him his mug of tea. As he sat down Barry moved an upturned book out of the way. He looked at the cover. *Mr Sammler's Planet*. Barry read the author's name: Saul Bellow. Luke too? That was it as far as Barry was concerned. Whatever was happening between this brother and sister, it was nothing to do with him. He had to get out from between them. He decided he wasn't going to wait for Luke to get bored listening to the Pope's funeral before finally asking about his sister. Barry tried to recall what Molly had suggested he should say. He did his best.

'I saw Ruth. She, ah . . . she didn't want to talk to me about you. So I have nothing to tell you really. Sorry.'

There was a few moments' silence, filled by a rich radio voice describing the Pope's simple cypress coffin. Then Luke asked, 'So she didn't say that she would not talk to me, is that right? She just said she wouldn't discuss it with you? Were those her exact words?'

Barry was terrified of an interrogation from Luke. He felt sure he would be caught out and end up revealing everything. He couldn't even look directly at him. He nodded and gestured in agreement, hoping that would be enough for Luke. There was another long silence, filled this time by crowds chanting *'Santo subito!'* When Luke finally spoke again, Barry could hear the real sadness in his voice.

'Well . . . thanks for trying anyway.'

Off the hook. Now was the moment for Barry to escape. The usual excuse would do it. He had to be at work. The Requiem Mass was nearly over. He managed to stand up casually enough, looking at his watch. Luke probably wouldn't make any kind of fuss. He seemed distracted, lost now in some other train of thought. All Barry had to do was excuse himself and get out. Goodbye. Good luck.

'Right, I'd better be off. Work at twelve.'

Luke nodded, rose, and put an arm around Barry. He led him to the front door.

Perhaps it was an instinct that this might be the last time he would ever see Luke that made him ask one more question, even though Molly's voice in his head told him it was one question too many.

'So what will you do now?'
Luke spoke very simply.
'Well . . . if I could, I'd kill myself.'
He closed the door.

# 10

# A Letter

Luke notices the look when his colleagues see him arrive back at work. The stare that becomes a glaze. He passes several workmates as he crosses the barracks square to the museum itself. They all say Morning Luke of course, as normally as they can. He smiles back. He knows they are too kind and sensitive to say anything more. He completely understands their surprise at seeing him. It is after all only two days since the funeral. Do they think he is being very brave or very coldhearted? Or perhaps just a little bit mad?

Luke goes to the first floor and wanders through the history of Irish coinage and currency until he reaches the little room devoted to money in the period since independence. Looking at the exhibits, his eyes are drawn, as always, to the famous 'Lady Lavery' banknotes, the first ever complete set designed for the Irish Free State. Luke has always thought these notes seem so much more than mere objects of transaction. They are beautiful, dignified. In its time it was a bold statement of independent spirit from a tiny new nation. Luke wasn't even born when this design was abandoned in the seventies. His appreciation is purely aesthetic, historiographical. He cannot know what it felt like to count and spend this money; to earn and bank it. He is very aware of a curious need in himself to sentimentalize. He had to remind himself of harsher realities.

When these banknotes first appeared in the 1920s very few newly independent Irish citizens could ever hope to hold in their hands anything larger than the jovial orange ten-shilling note or perhaps the more sombre green pound. Who in those days could readily have unfolded the enormous, deep-hued £100 note from a back pocket? Graceful and proud as they looked, was there any reason to suppose that unlike the flimsier, cruder successors of the seventies and nineties, these banknotes had escaped the taint of corrupt practice?

Luke wants to reorganize this exhibit in a way that would ask such questions. What image of the nation is projected through its currency design? What aspirations? What truth? His plan is to display the four versions since independence and, alongside their artifice and self-importance, create exhibits that would reveal something of the actual relationship of people to money. He has observed over the thirty years of his lifetime how a dark suspicion has grown in people's minds that they have been hoodwinked, the victims of an elaborate counter-feit. This feeling has coincided with three changes in currency design since the seventies, each one looking more and more like joke money. The original Lady Lavery notes had lasted for fifty years. The trust in and affection for them had never diminished. Was the more distant past really different, or was that faith misplaced? Luke gazes into Lady Lavery's saintly eyes and wonders if in fact this elegant serious money was the most sophisticated con-trick of all. The fraud that had never been found out.

Luke realizes it would not be easy to encompass so many complex ideas in a museum display. He isn't even very confident that his proposal would find favour and funding. It would certainly be a long hard slog to get it approved. This was simply the way of things when one worked for a National

Institution. Would he have the stomach for it? He wonders if he has the stomach for anything any more.

Luke returns to his desk to find a clutter of post and memos which are the result of his three-day absence. He starts to sort them. There is only one handwritten letter, so it stands out. Luke recognizes immediately that it is from Ruth. He picks it up and stares. In the top left-hand corner she had written 'Private and Confidential'. Ruth's handwriting always showed the mark of successful primacy school training. It was neat and pretty. As she grew older she had clearly never felt the need to force some flourish of individuality on to it. It retained its simplicity and honesty. Anyone receiving a letter addressed in this hand might well feel anticipatory pleasure before opening it. Today, Luke is shocked and afraid. He continues to gaze at the envelope.

Luke Reid
c/o The National Museum of Ireland
Collins Barracks
Dublin 7

The postmark is four days ago. Was the word 'Dublin' the last she ever wrote? The envelope feels quite thick. What does it contain? After some minutes of silent staring he gets up and goes to lock his door. He stands at the window. There is an odd silence. Even a school group trooping across the barracks square to the public entrance seems subdued. It is as if the whole world has gone sshhh! Luke opens the envelope and takes out Ruth's long letter. A slip of paper falls to the floor. Luke picks it up. It is a cheque. He places it on his desk and sits down to read.

Dear Luke,

First of all, let me say sorry. Many times in the last week I have wanted to pick up the phone and talk to you. I nearly did it so many times, please believe me. I might still do it yet, who knows? Maybe when I've got all this off my chest I'll just tear up the letter and call you. No, I shouldn't say that. I can't call you. I'm fairly sure of that now. That's why I have to write to you at least. You're the only one I'm writing to by the way. I don't know if that makes any difference but I want you to know.

Anyway. Please think of this letter as a first draft. I want it like that. That's why I'm writing it by hand so that I won't be tempted to correct or redraft it. I just want it to come out whatever way it comes out. I know you'll say that's not like me, Little Miss Particular, and I'll say, well, you don't know everything, Mr Clever Luke Reid, so there!

You know I'm on your side, don't you? That's the first thing. I have to make sure you know that so I'm saying it straight away. If by the time you read this you are having any guilty thoughts about anything that's happened, stop it now. Have you stopped? It might be hard but I want you to. Because if you're too busy feeling guilty you won't be paying attention to what I'm trying to say to you. I hope I'll make enough sense so you will definitely have stopped by the time you finish reading this.

It's been a few minutes since I wrote the last bit. Thinking. See, I still can't help trying to put things in order. I was angry with you for going off with Barry and burning down the cottage. I was right to be angry about that. You probably think you know why but you don't. I'm sure that Barry told you I came looking for you on Christmas Eve just before you took off for Kerry. What you don't know is, I was still there when you left. I was standing outside Venetian Hall in the cold dark, watching the two of you. I was so sad and lonely that night, Luke. It was because you hadn't confided in me. I always thought you would tell me everything that was important to you, and vice versa of course. So on Christmas Day I really hated – no, I was really angry with you. I ate myself up with it for weeks afterwards, but I had to stop because, you see, in truth, I knew all the time in my heart that I had done the same to you. So in a way it had been vice versa after all. We had both avoided telling each other important things. It took me a while to see it that way, but eventually I did. You know when you know something but you can't even admit to yourself that you know? Of course eventually you have to. I hadn't told you about Benjamin. I still haven't, but I will now. I'm going to tell you about everything if I can. I mean, I know you know there is a person I know called Benjamin, but I hadn't told you about me and Benjamin, if you see what I mean, and that was the important bit. Neither had I told you the even more important bit about myself only. That was definitely the big thing I knew, that I could not tell even myself I knew, until finally now in these last few weeks.

Let me try to be clear. I can't say exactly when I realized that I had no right to be so angry with you. It was a few weeks after Christmas, definitely before Daddy died. The problem for me then was I didn't know what that meant for the future. Was something broken for ever? Had the cord between us been cut and we were floating free now? I didn't want that to happen, but maybe this was the way it had to be. Another truth was beginning to haunt me, that having you for a brother had helped keep me going much longer than I might have managed otherwise. I tried to imagine what if there had been no Luke? If I had grown up with just Matthew for a brother and Judy for a sister? It didn't bear thinking about. I couldn't have gone on. What I'm trying to say Luke is, I realize I'm kind of leaving you in the lurch, because there will be people who will think it's all about Daddy and you. Judy and Matthew and Mother will definitely be even more convinced that you are to blame for everything, and I know you won't even show them this letter and say, 'Look, I told you so' because you know this letter is only for you, but I want you to know from my heart that the exact opposite is the truth. You were part of keeping me alive, Luke, it's as simple as that. For years really. I love how much you want the world to be decent. I wish I could have been by your side for everything. I don't think you have betrayed the family. I don't think you need therapy, not remotely. I don't think you are responsible for Daddy dying although you have to admit you were very hard on him. Poor Daddy, he just didn't know any better. He wanted to take care of us and he thought money was the way to do that. If he lived another hundred years he wouldn't learn to think any other way, certainly not the way we do. But you know something, Luke? You and I don't really think alike either. Here's a question. Do you think things can be made better in this world? You do, don't you? You really have faith that something might be said or done that will bring us all on to some new plain of happi— no, not that word, some new sense of rightness, of beauty and dignity and honesty. I'm not poking fun, I swear. You have made my life as joyful as it could be for years with your hope, but over the last while I have realized how, in a really fundamental way, I am different. Mother always went on about how alike we were – remember? Usually implying something freakish about it. As usual she completely missed the point – I'm sorry, I find her insufferable, even now when it hardly matters any more I can't get past that. Anyway. You know she'll pursue you for as long as it takes, Luke, don't you? You've exposed something, probably something she's ashamed of, I don't know, but whatever it is, she will not, or maybe just cannot, forgive you. I met her the day after the reading of Daddy's will, that I couldn't face going to at the last minute, although God knows what reason Mother gave for me not being there. I bet it was a lie. She called me up first thing the next day and insisted on seeing me to tell me all about it. She said it was terribly serious, and she wanted my advice immediately because action was needed. Can you believe she said that she wanted advice from me?

We met in Donnybrook Fare and it was unsettling because there were loads of girls from Muckross having their lunch and boys from Gonzaga too. I just kept thinking, my God, how old am I? How completely out of it am I? Since when did school students go for cappuccinos and panini in Donnybrook Fare? I presumed Mother must have been very sure that Matthew wasn't suddenly going to stroll in with some tanned little Muckross babe on his arm, otherwise she would never have suggested meeting there. Anyway. She fixed me with her eye and began recruiting me to her side. She was clearly paranoid that you might have poisoned me already with your version of things. According to her your insanity – no, she didn't say that to be fair, she used a very funny old-fashioned phrase, your parlous mental state. Apparently at the reading of the will, it had been obvious for everyone to see. She was so embarrassed in front of the executor. She wondered what it was exactly, she wouldn't be entirely surprised if you turned out to be some kind of sociopath, which was a cross the whole family would have to bear if that was so. I suppose to someone like Mother the idea of donating an inheritance of over a million to charity was obviously madness, de facto madness. I have to tell you that while she was talking away, the look on her face made me want to laugh and clap my hands for the only time in months, so you can thank yourself, Luke, for inspiring that little bit of joy in me. She was trying to create an aura around herself that was somewhere between Mother Theresa and CJ from the *West Wing*, but she couldn't do anything about her eyes, which glittered with a sort of carnivorous frustration as she described your behaviour. I was able to imagine you so easily sitting at the big dining-room table. I bet you never raised your voice. I bet you had the famous explanatory expression on your face, that patient look you have when you decide to help someone understand a proposition which you appreciate seems very complex to others, even though you know it is relatively straightforward. It really can be annoying, you know that, don't you, Luke? I'd say Mother was at boiling point. Anyway, she clearly thought she could rally me to her cause by telling me that this was all for your benefit. Strong medicine to make you better. You would be thankful in the long run when the therapy worked and you could grieve for Daddy properly and accept the good fortune life had bestowed on you.

Apart from the oddity of Mother needing my support for anything, there was something strange even in the way she spoke to me, something in the rhythm of her sentences, the vocabulary. It just wasn't Mother. This is really what I was puzzling over as she talked on. It filled the time nicely. It wasn't until she used the word 'closure' that it hit me. She said something about you needing to find 'closure'. I swear. I bet you're laughing now, aren't you? You've guessed, haven't you? It had Judy written all over it. Imagine, the two of them, maybe Matthew as well, no, I doubt it, sitting down and working it all out like a plan of campaign. The whole thing was freakish because I always thought that my family really needing me would make me feel good. When she finally finished talking I said maybe it wasn't Luke who needed therapy. She reared up at that and asked me what I was talking about. Naturally she thought I meant her. I suppose I knew she'd react like that, but I wanted to say, look at me, look at your baby daughter, can't you see something's not right? But I didn't. Instead I said, sorry, Mother, I was just being a clever boots. She said Daddy had worked himself into an early grave to make sure we were all secure. It was up to all of us in the family to honour that memory.

Which reminds me, I presume I don't need to explain the cheque I'm putting in with the letter. You can tell by the amount what it is. I'm giving it to you to make sure that even if they manage to stop you getting your share, you will have mine. I must be getting a bit paranoid myself because I waited until just before closing time this evening to withdraw it, in case someone in the bank felt the need to break confidentiality and contact Mother. Do what you want with the money. The charity idea is fine by me, but I have a special request. Use some of it to buy something for yourself. Anything, all for yourself. To remember me by.

I stopped again. Longer this time. I had to think. It's harder than I thought, Luke. I'm just not used to spontaneous writing. I made coffee and lay down for a while. What a lovely sunny day it's been. I watched the last light fading outside my window. Remember the story I showed you when I was eight, the one that you said was so brilliant it proved I was going to be a writer when I grew up? You knew, I suppose, that I really wanted to be the little girl in the story, living in a house that slowly turned 360 degrees every day. She didn't ever have to get out of bed because she got to see everything she needed to see out the window as the house turned.

Anyway, it's after nine, nearly dark now. I'd better get on with it.

I fell in love with Benjamin soon after term began in October. It's more complicated than that but I have to tell you that first, like a sort of headline. He seemed perfect to me. I had no trouble in recognizing and accepting that part of the attraction was, he was so like you (you know all the things I think you are, Luke, so I don't need to describe any of that), but there was one extra element, the thing that made me believe for a while that a wondrous thing had happened. I felt such desire for him. That was obvious straight away, a genuine *coup de foudre*, from the first long conversation sitting in an alcove on the history department corridor. It started so simply, talking about the seminar we had just been to on the role of women in the 1913 strike and lock-out, then I had a rant about the recent citizenship referendum, then to the Kerry babies which he had never heard about, and it seemed like he really wanted me to tell him that whole story, so I did, and somehow we drifted on and on, on to all sorts of topics, like what had he discovered about Dublin that most amused or intrigued him, what were his favourite places? It seemed so right when both of us ended up agreeing how brilliant it would be to go for coffee and cake in the National Gallery and then see the Yeats collection together. It was the perfect easy endless meandering conversation of romance fiction. Afterwards I was sky high with pleasure. It was like several fantastic things happening together; as good as being in your company, Luke, plus the frisson of sexual attraction; then an aftermath of radiant longing, the thrill of looking ahead to the next encounter. I thought maybe that was it, that was the trick. Maybe staying alive was as simple as that. Maybe, until now, I had just misinterpreted the signs, because I had not met Benjamin and did not know what life really had in store for me.

Sure enough, every time we met after that, all kinds of casual encounters, you know the way it is around college, the feeling just got better and better. The trip to the art gallery became like a comedy riff between us, a flirtatious thing, a melodious duet. Benjamin's smile whenever he saw me coming towards him, the pleasure in his eyes as we chatted were unmistakable signs, I was sure. Finally, in early November, we had what in my head was our first date. I was also determined it was going to be our first kiss. When it happened it all seemed to me amazing and perfect. We were looking at Jack B's *On the Tram*, and that started us on about the LUAS, how someone should be commissioned to do a matching *On the LUAS* painting. Benjamin told me how he liked living in Rialto near the Red Line, but one of his housemates was leaving Ireland soon, so there would be the hassle of finding someone else to take the room. Somehow, yet inevitably, the idea that I might like to move in came up. I said yes, absolutely. This seemed to be just the right moment to kiss on the deal. Quite genuinely I swear I did not notice any lack of passion in Benjamin's kiss. It all seemed so perfect. In a way I'm glad I was able to delude myself completely at that moment. It's terrible to know everything all the time.

There is always a particular moment when you know that you know something. After that you cannot not know it any more. Do you agree with that proposition, Luke? I think most of us spend a lot of our lives wanting not to know, wishing we could stop knowing certain things. But it's not possible, is it? Do you remember in Tahilla the thing Auntie Joan used to say if she wanted us to admit we were telling fibs? 'In your heart of hearts'. Well, sometime near the end of last summer my heart of hearts had started a faint but persistent beat. I began to put a name on a feeling. I suppose, in truth, this feeling had been a tiny seed propagating silently inside me for years. Finally last summer I found myself able to think the word. I still couldn't say it. Can I write it even now?

Suicide.

There you go. Anyway. It made me more depressed and scared of course. I didn't want to be one of those people. Then, out of the blue, the miracle of Benjamin. I told myself it was OK, false alarm, I must have been mistaken about myself. My heart of hearts was just plain wrong.

I was able to keep the whole fantasy going more or less until Christmas. Of course I can see now it was only by denying some of my faculties – simple observation, intuition, reasoning. We had never made love, and since the day of the kiss, the glow in Benjamin's eyes had ever so slightly dimmed. His touches had, incrementally, grown fewer. There was something in his manner towards me that I couldn't quite put my finger on. I can now. He was behaving more like a pal. His housemate didn't leave after all so that plan died. By the New Year I had stopped telling myself that it was just because he was too shy, or gentle or cerebral. When term started again

Benjamin never seemed to be in the places where he used to be. It was becoming harder to close my mind to the possibility that he did not feel the same way about me as I did about him. Do you remember how cold and full of death January was? All that month, deep in the hole of my heart of hearts, I knew my love story was a lie.

Right. I have to just tell you this and get it over with. I begged Benjamin to have sex with me. I knocked on his door late on the night of 19 January. As soon as he opened it, I saw a little wave of anxiety ripple across his eyes, but I smiled determinedly and he smiled too. He asked me in, what else could he do? We stood in the kitchen talking away while he made me coffee. He had his back to me so I could look at his body all I liked, while we talked about whatever. The tsunami, I think. Apart from the kiss in front of the Jack B. Yeats, all my physical contact with Benjamin had hovered on that excruciating borderline, stretched longingly between friendly affection and desire. I had shyly encouraged but never openly invited a passionate response. Nothing had happened. So here we were in his little kitchen, chatting. Benjamin reached up to take coffee from a shelf. His body, stretched and beautiful in that moment, was irresistible Luke.

I stepped closer and put my hands on his hips. I slid them round his waist, pressing each hand flat against his tummy, waiting, praying for him to melt into me, to turn and take my face in his hands, to kiss me deeply. Instead his head sagged slightly, I heard a little agitated exhalation of breath, and I was forlorn. It was all over. My heart of hearts whispered to me it's over, but I fought back. I can't remember what I murmured to Benjamin as I slid my hands down to his crotch, but I know that right then, I would have done anything to arouse him. He turned to me, forcing my hands away. He started to say something. It would have been some kind of no, some form of words, some explanation that, in the end, meant no.

I didn't want to hear no. I dropped to my knees wrestling my hands free. I started to open his fly, pressing him against the cooker. Some part of me must have thought there was a chance that for whatever reason (and by then I didn't care what reason) he might yet just go with it.

Benjamin ran away. He pulled himself free and ran upstairs. I heard a door slam and lock. I lay on the floor and my heart of hearts said I told you so. It was then the crying started. Crying that would go on for weeks and weeks and weeks. Eventually, after half an hour or so, I pulled myself off the kitchen floor and left the house. As I was walking away I heard a window open. Benjamin called my name. I turned around and saw him at his bedroom window. He said he was sorry. He did not mean to hurt me. I looked up at him and said it's all right. It was like some sad inversion of the balcony scene in *Romeo and Juliet*. Of course then he felt he had to start explaining himself, so I told him again it was all right. I tried to stop the flow but not before I heard him say this: 'It is not that I am not attracted to you. But you are too dark, Ruth. Too deep.'

Benjamin had turned out to be my banshee, a male version of La Belle Dame Sans Merci, seeming to be my salvation but only drawing me more quickly to the end. Oh God, Luke, believe it or not, it gets even more embarrassing now, but I have to get on with it, it's getting late.

When I was little, Daddy used to tease me when I came to him crying over something. 'It'll get worse before it gets better, my little angel.' Poor Daddy, he never knew just how terrifying that sounded to me. He meant it as a joke. He didn't mean any harm. He could never really have understood what it's like, when all your life it gets worse before it gets better. I'd say even at the moment he died Daddy still thought things were on the up and up.

In the cemetery at the very end of that awful day, I saw Benjamin get into a car with Emma McCann. I couldn't believe it. I saw it out the back window as we drove away. Emma McCann and Benjamin? What did that mean? It was suddenly all I could think about. I didn't even ask Matthew what had just happened with you and him, why you weren't with us in the car. Then when we got back to the house, I escaped as soon as I could and took a taxi to where you and Emma used to live. I had to find out what was happening. I was able to work out which window was your old apartment. The light was on and every so often I saw a shadow, but never two shadows. Once I saw Emma herself as she passed near the window. I waited until the lights went off at the end of the night. I couldn't say for certain that Benjamin wasn't there, but I didn't think he was.

I had to find out more. Who would be easier to follow around? Both of them knew me, so the chances of being spotted were equally high. Emma would be less likely to notice anything because she's much more stupid and self-involved, but Benjamin used public transport more, or walked, so that would make tailing him easier. This really was the way my mind was going, Luke. It was now jumping up and down in my head that there was something going on with the two of them and I had to find out what. I even told myself I'd kill myself if I discovered she was sleeping with him, but to be honest, in that context, that was just a figure of speech.

Anyway, I decided to follow Benjamin. This turned out to be my first real step away from this world – no, actually. Not talking to you since Christmas was the first step away, but I didn't realize at the time how significant that was. You see, Luke, you have to understand that if I hadn't stayed away from you, you'd have made me feel it was worthwhile hanging on. Even today, I was on the LUAS and when it stopped outside the museum I wanted so much to get off and find a place where I could hide and watch you, just to see you one more time. But I was afraid you'd find me out. You'd sense I was there and you'd turn suddenly and catch my eye. You would know what was in my mind and you would smile at me, tempting me to stay a little while longer. I couldn't let that happen. Let me tell you why. Once I started following Benjamin around I discovered something extraordinary. I felt like a ghost and I liked it. My invisibility allowed me to see Benjamin's aliveness happening. I could see it minute by minute in so many ordinary moments, the way he just walked along, or the expression on his face when he stood looking in a shop window. I realized I was looking at the face of someone who expected to stay alive, who was comfortable with that, just like billions of others in the world. But seeing it play out, observing it just happen in so many simple obvious ways, it helped me recognize how different I was. More recently as I walk the streets just looking around, I now notice other people like me. I followed one for a while the other day to confirm my feeling. He was a young man doing nothing more than going into Tower Records to buy himself an album, but watching his face as he flicked through the rows of CDs, I saw the black, empty hole of his eyes, stretching back and back. Someone who knew him said hello. As he looked up his eyes flicked back on 'smile', but I had seen his death-wish hover about him. He left the shop without buying anything.

Even though from early on in my brief career as private eye it became obvious that I was right about Benjamin and Emma, that there was some kind of relationship happening, it already seemed less important, though it still hurt. I couldn't deny how happy and alive they both seemed. I have to say, Luke, and I don't mean to sound bitchy, Emma seemed more genuinely happy with Benjamin than I ever thought she was with you. Do you know what I mean?

On 5 April I saw them making love. It was the day Saul Bellow died although I didn't know that then. The strange thing was, I had more or less stopped following Benjamin around at that stage. I had already stepped so far away I was scarcely relating to the living world any more. It was actually the first time I had been to college in several days. Just as I was leaving the Centre for the Humanities building at lunchtime, I saw Benjamin crossing the car park towards me. Emma was with him. They were holding hands. I had never seen her in Belfield before. There was no way of avoiding them except to step back inside the building. I ran to the top of the stairs and listened. When they came in, Benjamin said something to Emma, and she did that annoying laugh she does. Then he walked away somewhere, and she started up the stairs. I panicked and retreated up to the second floor, which was now completely deserted because it was lunchtime. But Emma came up those stairs too. The door of a seminar room was open so I backed in, closing it until there was just a crack for me to see through. Emma appeared at the top of the stairs and came towards the room I was hiding in. I pulled back out of sight. Seconds later the door began to open. There was nothing for it at that stage but to duck down behind the teaching desk. Can you imagine it, Luke? I'm curled up, terrified to make a sound, too scared to try and see what's happening. I know you're not a fan of farce, but I bet you are on the edge of your seat now.

Emma put her head in, had a little look round, and then went back out again, leaving the door hanging open. I tried to hear if she was walking away. Instead I heard another pair of footsteps coming up the stairs. Benjamin said something as he came closer and Emma did her laugh again. They both came into the seminar room. He smiled as he held up the key he had borrowed, and he quietly locked the door.

So there you go. There I was. The thing I had been trailing after, hunting to find, had arrived plop! on my doorstep, like a cat proudly delivering a dead rat to her mistress. I crouched on the floor behind the desk. Through the little forest of tables and chairs I watched and listened. The surprise was, Luke, who they were didn't matter any more. They were just two people talking intimately. They laughed and kissed and touched and, it seemed like with real ease, found that state of grace, that place of ecstasy everyone who loves being alive can expect to find at least once, maybe often. But not me. It was like my heart of hearts had tired of being gentle with me, and was going for Tough Love. Look, my heart of hearts was saying, why do you not understand? This is what it's like for so many. Stop fooling yourself. This will never be for you.

I am exhausted from this writing, Luke. Please forgive me if I finish quickly now. I haven't written much more than my name with a pen in such a long time. You and I were always so proud of the fact that we were the only left-handed ones in the family. It was another sign of our special connection. Now my left hand is so tired, I've had to stop a couple of times and do little exercises to get the stiffness out. And of course I'm scared, of course I am, I won't tell you I'm not. Remember I used to cling on to you in the sea down in Tahilla? And you'd go down and down and down and I'd let you take me all the way underwater, because it was fantastic to be scared when I was certain you would lift me up again safe and sound.

Anyway. From that moment under the table until tonight it's really a fairly simple story. And everything's been much easier, to be honest. I saw no point in lingering there. I stood up and walked quietly to the door. I could probably have slipped away without being noticed except that I had to turn the key. It might as well have been a gunshot or an alarm clock, the effect was so melodramatic. They both swung round, two terrified naked people. But they were not my concern now. I just opened the door and left. I haven't seen them since. I haven't been to college since. My nearly finished thesis will stay nearly finished. I think everyone I've met since then has smelled danger from me. Poor Barry certainly did. I never even found out why he called round to my flat in the first place, he ran away so quickly. Tell the poor guy I'm sorry, Luke, the next time you're talking to him. Tell him he just called at a bad time. Matthew got a scare too. On the afternoon of 11 April I waited for him outside school and pestered him to give me a lesson on his Vespa. I tried to make him let me ride it on my own, but I think he suddenly realized what I might do. He knew it in his heart of hearts. He's no fool, Matthew. He'll do fine though. He'll be able to tell himself he never saw it coming. His conscience won't trouble him.

The last few weeks have been a kind of adventure, Luke, once I accepted how it would be. I stopped lying in bed all day and got out and about. It's amazing how different Dublin looks when you're intending to die in it instead of live in it. It's not as obvious as Venice maybe, as a city of death, but it's getting there. Last week I saw a young woman trap her bike wheel on the LUAS line at the corner of Capel Street. A tram was approaching and people rushed to help her dislodge it. The obvious thing would have been to abandon the bike, but she was hysterical of course and not helping herself at all. I watched wondering what it was going to be like, the impact, the horror, if the tram could not stop on time and she could not break free. It stopped several yards from her. The driver had too much warning. Suddenly there was cause for celebration amongst the group of people that had spontaneously become involved in this little reality drama. A life had been saved. I was pleased for them and I moved on.

At the beginning of May I was walking along Nassau Street when I saw a protest march. I recognized Joe Higgins at the head of it. The protest was in support of the underpaid Turkish construction workers. For old times' sake I joined in and walked with them up to Leinster House. I floated along smiling encouragingly at the Turkish guys waving their placards. I was dazzled by the life-force pulsing from them, their lifelines suddenly visible beams to me, stretching out and on and on, unstoppable. I couldn't be envious of them, it was so beautiful to see.

Everyone's been complaining about how it's the middle of May and summer is still refusing to begin. There is hardly a day without rain and even when it's bright and sunny as it was all day today, there always seems to be a cold breeze chilling the atmosphere. I feel as if it's partly my fault, I should get on with it, let summer begin. Fair enough. Today seemed as good a time as any, and you know, Luke, Dublin will get along fine without me.

I don't know if I'll have the time or energy to read back over this to see if it makes any sense at all. In fact I won't. I have the envelope, I have the stamp. I'll just seal it up and post it.

Anyway. I love you so much, Luke, that's really the main thing. I'm sorry to leave you but I'm tired, Luke, so tired. I know you'll understand. I won't linger.

Your baby sister

Ruth


It is several hours later. Luke still sits at his desk. He has been thinking of so many things, reading and re-reading passages from his sister's letter. He still hasn't cried. He hasn't cried at all since he heard the news of Ruth's death three days ago. He doesn't know why. Right now only one thing is clear to him. He takes out a sheet of headed notepaper and begins to write his letter of resignation.

## II

# *The Lady Dances*

Norma was in shock. She did not like to admit it but it was so. Part of her could hardly believe it had happened. The key, the cheque and the letter were on the table, so that was some kind of proof. Anyway, she was not a woman given to imaginings. According to the clock, barely five minutes had passed since she had last noticed the time. That was before Luke had arrived, and he was already gone.

Five minutes ago Norma had been upstairs sitting on the bed examining the photograph when the doorbell rang. She was not expecting a call. She had no idea who it might be. Norma had never been one of those people who got annoyed and thought, 'Who the hell is that?' when the doorbell rang unexpectedly. It was one of several little country ways she had held on to throughout her years in Dublin 6. For Norma, someone dropping by was generally an unexpected pleasure. In thirty-two years in this house, she had never had a moment's distress about a surprise knock on her door. Admittedly, right at that moment she had been enjoying the little mystery of the photograph, and had no particular desire to be interrupted. On the other hand, the doorbell had not rung at all for several weeks. No one called casually any more. So she was very curious to see who it was. Norma put down the photograph and went downstairs to the front door.

Luke stood outside. Norma noticed immediately that he

was even thinner than when she had seen him at Ruth's inquest. Why did he ring the doorbell when he still had a key? Had he forgotten it? No, Norma guessed that he had decided not to use it. He was making a point. Luke smiled. His shy smile. Norma remembered the rest of what happened like a scene from some family drama.

'Hello, Mum.'

'Luke. Did you forget your key?'

(Luke holds up key.)

'Can I come in?'

'Of course.'

(He walks past her into the dining room. He puts the key down on the table.)

'Beeswax. You've been polishing?'

'Yes.'

'Mmm. Smells lovely. I have something for you.'

(A plain white envelope.)

'What is it?'

'Open it.'

(She does. A bank draft for one million three hundred thousand euro, made out to Luke.)

'Oh.'

'Ruth sent it to me. So there it is.'

(Silence.)

'We wondered what she had done. Of course it would have been stopped, you know, in the circumstances, if you had tried to do anything with it. So it wouldn't have been any use to you.'

'I didn't think of that. Anyway, there it is. And this is from me.'

(Another white envelope.)

'It's just so you have it in writing, officially. I'm giving up my claim on any part of the inheritance. So it will come to you, I suppose. I hope that might allow us to – well, you know, sometime in the future . . . anyway, it just clears away the clutter. It's been very depressing, Mum, to be honest. Nothing has happened really the way I'd have liked it to. No reason why it should I suppose. It's hard to see clearly, know what to think about anything. So . . . I'm going away.'

Then, as Norma remembered it, before she could begin a proper answer, before she could tell Luke how she really felt, because it did now seem like the time to do it, maybe he was ready for it now; before she could open her mouth, he had stepped forward and embraced her. She wanted to resist. If he had said, give me a hug, or asked, can I hug you? then it would never have happened. Luke didn't say anything. He took a few steps and reached out. His hug was quite natural, as relaxed and pure as when he was little Luke, running in the door from school. His body felt so thin and brittle against her. Norma's whole being exhaled. She gave in to the moment completely. She could not help but reach for his hair. It was still the same, wispy blond and soft to touch. Her lovely boy's hair was still the same. Then she heard him whisper in her ear, 'I will pray for you, Mum.'

She was sure she had not imagined it: 'I will pray for you, Mum.'

Luke let go. He smiled at her and walked to the front door. He left his key behind. It was there now on the table along with the cheque and the letter, proof that all this had really happened. Norma followed him, but she heard the door close before she got to the hall. That was it. Luke was gone. When she reached the front door, she just stood looking at it. She wondered if she opened it now would he have just disappeared into the air, or would she see him walking away down the road? Norma could not bring herself to find out. She was afraid that if she opened the door, and he was still in sight, she would completely lose control. She would run on to the road after him screaming, 'How dare you say you will pray for me! I don't need your prayers. I command respect. I am respected in the community!'

She shuddered. God, imagine! Norma turned away from the closed door. That was when she noticed the clock again, and realized that no more than five minutes had passed. Alone now in the empty hall, she could not avoid admitting that what had really upset her was how strange it was, how really very peculiar, that Luke should call just then. How had that happened, just after she had found the photograph? It was as if . . . Norma once again asserted her normal brisk self, refusing even to finish that thought. Nonsense, she said out loud. It was just one of those . . . just a simple coincidence. Yes, her decision to do a clearout of Luke's room had been a sort of act of vengeance, Norma had no trouble admitting that to herself. Could anyone blame her for being angry and frustrated? It was perfectly normal anger. She hadn't unleashed some strange spirit that brought Luke to the door at that moment. It was much simpler than that. She was simply not satisfied with the solicitor's letter on the desk in her bedroom which assured her that any attempt by Luke to 'misuse or recommend misuse of' his inheritance, would automatically allow Norma to intervene and contest. It wasn't enough for her to have every legal right to insist on a psychiatric report, to establish if Luke was in a fit state of mind to handle his good fortune properly. Norma had been waiting for weeks now for any action on Luke's part to trigger this legal assault, but already she realized that this alone would never appease the hurt she felt. Truth be told, she needed something else, some more immediate revenge.

Joan's visit gave Norma the perfect excuse. She was able to tell herself that there was no way she was going to allow her sister to be a servant around the house, constantly cleaning and cooking and doing things for her. That might suit Joan just fine, but Norma was not going to put up with it. She would make sure the house was spotless by the time Joan arrived. She could also tell herself that the best idea was to put her sister into Luke's old room, even though there was a regular guest room, because of the lovely garden view it had. She could tell herself that after all, Luke had been away from home for five years now. Anything he wanted he had surely removed by now. It was more than time for a clearout. These excellent reasons had been enough this morning, finally, to allow her act of vandalism. Everything that was left of Luke was stripped out of the room and piled up in the hall. When Matthew returned she would instruct him to dump it all in the shed.

Until Norma saw the photograph, there had been no surprises: his old tennis racket, some dusty tapes with names of pop groups (she didn't bother to read who), a Live Aid poster, the only one on the wall, a very old cheap clock radio that he had bought in a street market on some school trip abroad, in the wardrobe his school uniform, his schoolbooks in a chest of drawers, packed away very neatly, his Junior Cert in one, his Leaving Cert in another, and some college texts and notebooks in another. Norma resisted the urge to open anything as she tossed it all into the hall. By two o'clock the room was nearly ready to be vacuumed. Looking at it, Norma thought it could also do with being stripped and repapered. That could wait. There was an awful garish eighties feel to the wallpaper. She had allowed Luke to pick it as a reward for something. He loved it, and she gave in to him. At least he had never gone in for those heavy metal posters. It was as she closed the drawer that had contained the Leaving Cert books that she noticed the photograph. It was face down.

Norma turned it over. It took her a moment to realize it was a photograph of her; well, her in the middle of a gang. A snap grabbed somewhere. There was nothing immediately familiar about it. In fact Norma was sure she had never seen it before, which in itself was strange. It was definitely years old. She looked more closely at the image of herself, her clothes and hairdo. It could be twenty years ago, maybe not as much as that. What was the wild laugh about? She was dancing. In fact the picture was a bit blurry, so she must have been dancing very fast. Or maybe whoever took it was so drunk. The whole photograph had a mad drunken feel about it. She was clinging on to her dancing partner, and he seemed to be laughing his head off too. He was swinging her around. There were another half-dozen people in the background, but they were even more blurred.

Suddenly Norma recognized where it was. She sat down on the bed with the shock of it. It was in the cottage. When? Who took it? Definitely not Luke, he never had a camera. Where had he got this? Why had he kept it? Well now. Norma knew she wouldn't be satisfied until she pieced this together in her head. She seemed to be having a fantastic time of it, that was for sure. Whoever she was dancing with, it wasn't Frank. Was he there in the photo at all? She squinted to see. That was the moment the doorbell rang.

Still standing in the hallway, not really knowing what to do next, Norma couldn't shake off this unease about the timing of Luke's arrival. She knew what Joan would say if she told her the story: 'It was as if he knew what you were doing.'

Their mother, God rest her, would have said exactly the same thing. Norma was not remotely like her mother and sister in these matters, but still, this disturbance persisted in her mind. She wished Matthew would come home, so she would not be alone. He could clear away Luke's things from the upstairs landing. Matthew was trying really hard to be a proper grown-up these days. In a funny way the terrible events had been the making of him. He had stood up to the challenges.

Norma knew that she really wanted to look at that photograph again. She gave in to the urge and went back upstairs. She couldn't bear to stay in Luke's room, however. She simply picked up the photograph and came back downstairs. She made a cup of tea, put some biscuits on a plate and sat at the dining table, enjoying the scent of beeswax, pleased again as it occurred to her that Joan would be very hard put to find a single cleaning chore when she arrived. Norma would encourage her to put her feet up, take her ease. Hopefully she would get the message that Norma might be perfectly pleased to see her, but she didn't need her sister by any means.

The photograph captured some kind of reckless joy. The drink must have been flowing that night; a hooley in the cottage. She had begun to think maybe it was Paudie took the photo. It was coming back to her now. Some Yank relative of his had left behind a Kodak Instamatic, and for a while, Paudie drove them all up the wall with this fad for taking photographs; to mark the occasion, he would always say. Frank loved to have Paudie fawning over him. He'd laugh about it as though it was all just a bit of gas, being part of the local scene. Really it was so important to him to be thought worthy of respect, a significant player in national politics. That was the great time.

Norma and Frank were in their prime, at the top of their game. That was when, after they had got back into power in 1987, Frank heard on the grapevine that he was next up for Attorney-General, should a vacancy arise; the sessions they had in the cottage. Norma could tell by how happy and alive she looked that the photograph was definitely from around that time. Where was Frank? There was a pair in the background on the left-hand corner, heads together. It was too dark and blurry to be certain but did the taller one have the shape of Frank about him? It could be. She wished she could be sure. She wished she could place it precisely. She decided to treat it like a crossword puzzle. She would start with the obvious clues, then use the information to work out the more uncertain elements.

First and foremost, who the hell was she dancing with? He was either a local, or one of the Fianna Fáil gang down for the summer like themselves. He was really swinging her off her feet: even in profile his face had a bit of madness in it; the head thrown back, and his hair falling over . . . oh.

It was Paschal Finnan.

Suddenly she knew it with an awful certainty. She could even hear the reel, and feel his grip as he hoisted her through the air. When he was drunk enough, usually only on the Saturday night of an Ard Fheis, Paschal always lost the run of himself completely. He would stomp around and grab girls roughly by the waist. He'd do a 'Yeow!' with all his might, but his 'Yeow!' was never convincing. It was the 'Yeow!' of a man who didn't know how to enjoy himself sober. If it was Paschal Finnan, and it was, then already Norma knew so much more about this photograph. She had even begun to understand why Luke had kept it.

Norma thought it through carefully. If it was Paschal

Finnan, and it was, she was sure of it, then it could only be one night. If it was Paschal Finnan, and there was no doubt about that now, then it was the night that Frank dragged CJ and the gang back for a late night session. Paschal never came to Kerry at all except when summoned by CJ. Was he even there that night? Norma put it this way, she couldn't think of any other night when he would have been in the cottage. How she had ended up dancing and laughing with him she had no idea. Norma tried to summon up a clearer memory, but could not. The more she thought about that night, only one face emerged; that perfect little face. She squinted closely once again at the two blurred figures in the left-hand corner. Was it Frank, the taller one, in intimate consultation with An Taoiseach, the shorter one? It could be. It might be.

She remembered moments; the moment Frank, standing at the bottom of the stairs, had caught her eye. No matter how much drink Norma had taken, she never lost her sense of when something was awry. Frank's nod told her there was some trouble. Even with the noise and whoops and music, she remembered him practically whispering for fear of being overheard, 'We've a bit of a situation here but I think it's sorted, so I don't want you blowing a fuse. There's a young one in Luke's room, you know what I'm saying? I sent him to our room and locked the door. She's above now putting her clothes back on.'

Norma didn't blow a fuse. She listened quietly. She remembered thinking how unbelievable it was that Luke should have caused trouble of any kind. There must be an explanation. Frank was still talking, out of the side of his mouth: 'The Boss has had a word with his driver, fair dues to him. He'll take her wherever she needs to go in his car. Be better if you went up to her, talk to her you know, find out where she's from and slip her out. It'll be all right I'd say. They're all too pissed to notice.'

Norma remembered opening the door of Luke's bedroom and seeing the light from the landing fall on her beautiful young skin, such a perfect little face. Even more she remembered her posture. She sat proud on the edge of the bed, neck and shoulders arched back, her eyes glistening a little but not giving way to tears. Adult and child were fighting it out inside her. Norma knew before she heard the delicate accent that she was not Irish.

'Where is Luke?'

'Luke's gone to bed.'

'You cannot treat him like this.'

'What would your parents do?'

No answer. This girl knew the rules all right.

'You are on holiday?'

'Of course.'

'French?'

'Yes.'

'Quelle t'appelle, s'il vous plaît?'

What was her name? Had the girl told her or had she merely sneered at Norma's little effort in French? There was no great trouble though. Once she realized that there was no possibility of seeing Luke again before leaving, she told Norma where she was staying. As they went down the stairs Norma put her arm around her, partly to shield her from view as they went from the bottom of the stairs to the cottage door, but partly also in genuine reassurance. The girl let her head fall into Norma's breast. She was very tired. Norma told the driver to take her to Parknasilla. He gave the little serious nod that was the assurance of discretion. The girl got into the back of the car. She stopped the door as Norma was closing it.

'You know, do not think I am a girl who . . .'

'I don't. Honestly.'

'Luke, I think, is a very special boy.'

Norma nodded. The Garda driver took her away. Norma knew there would be trouble with Frank tomorrow, and she would have to go along with it. It was fair enough, Luke wasn't even sixteen yet. These things were bound to happen sooner or later. Truth be told, it was a relief to find out that Luke was flesh and blood after all. She could hear the throb of drink and music inside. Through the little steamed-up windows she could see flailing, stomping bodies. It was a while before she could bring herself to go back into the madness. She was happier standing out in the night air thinking about her son. She felt a bit embarrassed at how proud she was of Luke at this moment. She certainly wouldn't be saying so to Frank. What a sophisticated, intelligent girl he had picked out. He would always set his sights high, she was sure of it. Maybe that would be the difference with the next generation. Maybe they would lift everything on to a whole new level. When Norma did go back inside, she caught Frank's anxious eye and nodded. It was all sorted out. As soon as she got a chance, she slipped upstairs and quietly unlocked the bedroom door.

The photograph reminded Norma of how happy she used to be; not particularly that night, but on so many nights and days back then. The fun, the laughter, the pleasure, the devilment. Why were her children not happy? Poor Ruth. What had gone so wrong and why had she never come to her? Luke had so much going for him, but he had made himself so arrogant and unhappy. Even Judy was not happy, though she worked herself into a frenzy trying to be, over there in Happyland. Maybe Matthew. Maybe he would be all right. He didn't seem so . . .

burdened as the rest of them. What was it at all? What was wrong with them? Norma heard the front door open, and a cheery voice call, 'Hellooo. Is the Aged One home?'

'She is. Are you hungry?'

'Starving. Everything OK with you?'

'Yes, everything's fine, pet. Will you come up for a minute? I have one little job for you.'

'Oh, all right, work work work, that's all I am to you, a packhorse, an indentured serf, work work work.'

Listening to Matthew's jokey extra-loud thumps on the stairs, Norma smiled.

# *Journey Home II*

Luke is not looking forward to the rest of the journey. He feels a little tenser as the LUAS veers away from the canal, heading towards Bluebell. The heat in the tram seems to be increasing all the time. It is still so crowded that a battered-looking junkie couple at the previous stop could not face getting on. The woman, shading her eyes from the sun, had peered into the carriage. When she saw the crush of bodies, she jerked back.

'I'm not getting on that. No way.'

'Well what'll we do so? The next one'll be the same.'

'I don't care, I'm not getting on that.'

The door closed on their discussion, and the packed tram moved on. Luke had taken the LUAS outwards from Rialto only once before. Unlike his pleasant route to the museum every day, he had found the journey in this direction profoundly depressing, and avoided it since. That this chunk of South-West Dublin had been entirely developed in his lifetime made it worse. He felt implicated in some illogical way. Maybe the LUAS offered some hope? At least people could travel more quickly and directly back to the canal, and the beginnings of some connection with urban grace. Perhaps the outer zones of the Red Line could be used for school outings; a live action horror train where children would chug up and down, gazing in queasy fascination at the devastation outside, while teacher speaks in a scary voice: 'And remember, children, if we're not careful the whole city could become like this.'

Luke finds it eerily appropriate that departing from Kyle-more, he suddenly sees the Face again on a huge billboard on the left. The tram brings it closer and larger. The huge lettering is designed to be readable at almost any distance:

## HAUGHEY

Not having a TV any more, Luke hadn't been watching the documentary series the billboard poster is advertising. He suspects he would have enjoyed seeing the old yarn played out again: the arms trial, the land deals, the backhanders, the backstabbing, the mistress; our very own cut-price version of the fall of the Roman Empire. He might even have seen his father play a bit part in the background of a shot somewhere; a loyal centurion, delirious with excitement at some rallying moment or other, shaking a fist or slapping a back. It would have been stirring entertainment, no doubt about that. Had his mother been watching it, reliving her heyday? Luke half regrets not asking her earlier. He had been so anxious to get in and out of there without pain. Thinking about it now, he can't imagine Norma putting herself through it. She had appeared so mummified when he called. Luke had the feeling that she partook of nothing any more, not even nostalgia. The competing smells of various cleaning waxes and fluids were noxious. They had created a powerful image of Norma moving slowly but sternly, relentlessly through the house, scouring room after room; beginning again as soon as she had been round the kitchen, two reception rooms, the study, the six bedrooms, two bathrooms and the downstairs toilet. Luke pities her of course. How could he not? Even as he was saying what he had to say, an old part of him still wanted to make things better. He is glad now that he did not give in to that weakness. He is beyond that. Still, when he left, he couldn't resist turning at the gate, to take a last look back, even though he was half afraid Norma would have followed him out with some plea for renewal, some last stand for family solidarity. The front door remained closed and Luke had been satisfied to discover that, standing on the path just outside the gates, he didn't feel like he was looking back at his home at all, but an attractive front-page photo in the *Irish Times* property supplement. The angle was perfect and it presented an enticing prospect for any investor.

The Face looms larger and larger. The famous eyes stare and Luke stares back coldly. The lettering grows huge against the landscape.

# HAUGHEY

# HAUGHEY

# HAUGHEY

Then the tram goes by, and the brooding image is gone. Luke has only the ugly here-and-now to stare at. We used to be poor but respectable, he is thinking. That was our story, our narrative. Ireland was poor but respectable. The world loved us for that. It was such a comfortable place to be. It was a lie of course. Now? Luke turns from the dreary landscape. The woman standing next to him is reading the *Evening Herald*. There is a photo on the front page; a smiling Bertie Ahern, throwing dice on a Monopoly board.

Bertie launches Boomtime Monopoly.

The leader of the country has spent part of his day launching the new Irish edition of the famous board game about money and property. Here and now. The heat is making the tram smell. Luke feels the sweat gather on his forehead, under his arms, in his crotch. He can smell himself now. Standing with his arm up to hold on to the yellow rail, he feels intensely the unwanted proximity of others. How do those kids wear tracksuits in this weather? The tram stops at Red Cow. Luke is relieved when a large crowd spills out into the sunshine. At least it won't be long now.

He finds two empty seats on the left side. Perfect. Sure enough, soon after the tram leaves Red Cow, it speeds up and he can feel its potential force as it moves towards Kingswood. He watches now with absolute focus. He presumes the birch trees will be easy to spot. Sure enough, there are two high walls running on either side of the tracks, just as he had read in the reports. So far all the young birch trees are on the far side of the left-hand wall. Rounding a curve, he sees them; a little grove on the trackside, no more than ten feet back. He sees the cross and bunches of dying flowers that mark the spot. Apparently discussions are still 'ongoing' about cutting the trees down, following the tragedy. Luke can hardly wait now for the tram to reach Kingswood. He knows it will be better to wait for passengers to walk away, and for the tram to leave, before he walks back. He does not want to draw any attention to himself. As his train departs, one for the city centre approaches. Luke waits patiently. He checks the time-table display. The next tram for Tallaght is due in eight minutes. The next for the city will be in ten. He looks down the tracks to the trees. There should be enough time. The city tram leaves. Luke is now completely alone on the platform.

He walks back quickly along the forbidden area beside the track. The trees must have seemed so much further away in darkness. Ruth would have known of course that she had about fifteen minutes before the last tram to Tallaght would pass. It would have been about one in the morning. It is only a small uneven scattering of birch, but at night they would have provided ample cover to stand out of sight. Luke reaches the spot. He steps into the trees and rests against the wall, looking out at the track. The heat is heavy and moist. There would be a tram in the next couple of minutes. Luke wonders how long Ruth had to wait. Did she falter in her resolve at all? He can hear a tram now, some distance away. He takes a peek. There it is. He measures the distance to the track with his eye. It would take hardly four seconds to rush forward; the driver would have only about two seconds to register and react. Was this the only reason she had chosen this spot? The tram is close now and Luke can feel its power. He waits and waits. He makes a guess as to when Ruth would have run to the track. He starts counting down from four. At zero he feels the horror of what happened to her, as the tram reaches where she would have been, and powers by. Only now does he fully appreciate the brutality of how his sister chose to die.

Luke slumps down against the wall. Not in a million years could he do what she had done. He knows for sure now what he always suspected, that he could never give away his life, and certainly would not have the courage to face such violent self-destruction. Having stood there and felt the fierce rage of her end, Luke is certain now that was precisely the point of it for Ruth. His little sister desperately wanted her body to be smashed and broken somewhere far, far from the city of beauty and dignity she knew of as home. To end it all she had deliberately travelled to where Dublin had become as despairing as herself; to the malnourished wasteland beyond the Mad Cow roundabout.

Since he first decided to come out here, Luke had secretly been hoping that this pilgrimage would finally bring him tears. He was sure that he would feel his little sister's presence once more, and simple sentiment would prevail. Ruth had outwitted him again, however. Standing where she died, he mostly feels awe and respect at the depth of her understanding; how carefully she had picked out this place. He turns now slowly clockwise, all the way round, searching as far as his eye can see, for anything built by those who created this corner of Dublin, that might speak of love or respect or joy or civic pride. There is nothing anywhere.

It is cooling off nicely. The late evening sun softens the flat Midlands landscape. The train is quiet and comfortable. Luke is almost relaxed, trying to remember the last time he hitch-hiked. He cannot. He is a little ashamed of that. He wonders if anyone even does it any more. More to the point, does anyone give lifts any more? He will find out when he gets to Killarney. So close to midsummer there should still be about two hours of daylight to allow him to try his luck. If not, he will just have to settle for some Killarney hostel, and go to Kenmare in the morning. Luke smiles to himself, recognizing his lifelong, inbred resistance to staying in Killarney. It's only a night's sleep, for God's sake. Snob.

Luke puts his bag on the table and opens it. He feels a trickle of contentment that he has succeeded in fitting everything he wanted to keep into just one bag. He has nothing else now apart from the two cheques in his jacket pocket: his savings, and the lump sum for his ten years' service at the museum. He rummages for the page he had printed off the Internet property site. Cottage in Cloneen, Cahirciveen. In need of considerable repair. Luke doesn't think it looks so bad in the photograph, but he is not so foolish as to underestimate what those dreaded estate agent words usually mean. It might, just might be possible to live in it; at least the way Luke intends to live. Anyway, what are the choices in South Kerry? He would go see it tomorrow. Then what? What is he doing exactly? Starting from scratch. Is this just another futile, blundering gesture? Luke no longer has answers. He only has instincts, and a limited number of things he knows to be true. He doesn't know why he needs to go on living, but he does. He doesn't know why he is going back to Kerry, but he is. He doesn't know why he can't cry any more, but he can't.

Earlier, when he had walked from his mother's house down to Ranelagh for the II bus, he had noticed some fuchsia pot plants on display across the road, outside Joy's florists. He had suddenly decided to buy one for Ruth. He would bring it out there. Such a sentimental gesture might help his heart to fill and burst at last. He had stepped on to the road, and was checking right and left, when he saw the Vespa approach. There was no danger of a collision, but he and Matthew could not avoid seeing each other. Luke stepped back on to the path and watched Matthew, who glanced at Luke as he passed. Just as Luke was sure he had decided to ride on, the Vespa stopped. For a moment nothing more happened. Matthew still faced away from his brother, who didn't quite know what to do. Then Matthew turned around. Even though he still hadn't taken off his crash helmet, it was enough of a cue for Luke to walk towards him.

Matthew spoke from inside the helmet. 'What are you doing around here? Were you at the house?'

'Yes.'

'I thought I told you stay away. If you were hassling Mum I'll fucking kill you.'

The effect of his voice inside the helmet was peculiar. It certainly wasn't convincingly dangerous. Luke wanted to smile, but that would just have enraged his baby brother more. There was no point in doing that.

'You'll be glad I called, I promise. Mother will tell you everything. Believe me, it's all over now.'

'What do you mean? Did you make it up with Mum?'

Luke noticed Matthew could not conceal his dislike of that idea.

'No, I . . . let Mother tell you everything, but it's fine. I'm going away so there'll be no more trouble. Come on, Matthew, take it off. Let me see your face.'

A pause, then Matthew took off the crash helmet. Luke smiled gently.

'You look great. Very cool.'

'Yeah. Well, you look shit. What are you doing to yourself?'

'I know, I know. I have to sort myself out.'

Luke noticed the iPod dangling. He used it to change the subject.

'So what are you downloading these days? X and Y?'

The big sigh. Luke felt eighty years old.

'That's so lame that you'd think that. Haven't you heard it? No, what am I saying, of course you haven't. But if you had heard it and sort of knew anything, then you'd know I wouldn't be listening to it. It's so shit. I didn't get past like the fourth track. And what was really annoying was, I knew already I'd hate it, so I hadn't even downloaded it, but Eanna kept saying to me, you have to hear it, especially you, you know. And I knew what he meant when he was like going, especially you, you know. I knew he was talking about Ruth and all that stuff.

And he kept saying it with these totally meaningful looks, like he knew I'd have some kind of big fuck-off catharsis if only I listened to Coldplay. So just to shut him up I did. And it was so crap. It was so like . . . nothing. Ruth would have laughed her head off if she'd heard it. She'd have said, what are these wankers talking about? Is this supposed to be – you know what's it supposed to be – deep?'

He stopped. He was trying desperately not to give in to tears.

'So what, like, where are you going? Away?'

'Oh . . . not sure yet.'

Luke shifted the conversation again.

'I hope you're going to get away during the summer. For a break.'

'Yeah, well . . .'

Matthew seemed to be trying to decide if he should say something. He couldn't stop himself.

'Judy said that maybe, you know maybe, it'd be good to head over to her on Long Island, you know, Alan's place. They go there for most of the summer.'

'That's fantastic. You'll love New York.'

'You think?'

'Of course. You'll be able to hop in and out to Manhattan any time you want.'

Matthew nodded. His thoughts exactly, it seemed.

'Yeah, that'd be so cool. But you know . . . I have to see what's happening with Mum.'

Suddenly he remembered all of Luke's transgressions again. His eyes became sullen.

'Being the only one around now.'

His lip quivered very slightly. He fought back again.

'I mean, I'm sure she'll say it's fine, you know, staying with

Judy and so on. I mean, she needs her own time too. I'm sure I'm a real pain around the place sometimes.'

He hesitated, wary again.

'Judy rang Aunt Joan and talked to her, got her to, you know, offer to come and stay for a while.'

Clever Judy. She and Matthew made a great team.

'Which is the best thing for Mum. Much better than me getting in her way all the time.'

A terrible thought seemed to strike Matthew at that moment. 'Jesus, if you've done anything to upset her again—'

'I didn't, I promise. The opposite. Believe me.'

'You've been a real prick, you know. Like what are you trying to prove?'

The tears were getting the upper hand after all. Luke tried to soothe him.

'I'm sure you'll get to go. Judy will persuade her. She always—'

'I'm going anyway. I'm going no matter what.'

Poor little rich kid. Luke saw Matthew couldn't hold back any longer, and reached his arms out just in time, holding him close as he blubbed. Even Matthew could cry. It might only be from spoilt self-pity, but Luke was sure the pain still felt real to his baby brother.

Luke jerks back as the train stops. He had begun to slump forward and doze. Why not? It seems like a very pleasant idea. He checks the station: Limerick Junction, a long way yet. He moves the bag to the seat beside him and lays his head on it, still thinking about Matthew. Even as he had comforted him, Luke knew that Ruth had got it right yet again. Matthew would be just fine. He'd wipe his eyes, put his crash helmet back on, and go, telling himself he'd had a difficult, but quite deep in a kind of fucked-up way, encounter with his brother.

He'd get his way and go to New York. He'd hang out, playing the damaged, hurt, very attractive young man to perfection, and score regularly throughout the hot Long Island summer.

In the awkward moment after Matthew had relinquished hold of Luke, some kind of techno birdcall had provided distraction. Matthew fished out his mobile to read a new text message. Luke saw the 11 bus approach. Matthew grinned at whatever he was reading, and automatically began to text back. Luke gestured towards the bus and offered a little wave goodbye. Matthew nodded, distracted by his texting. The brothers left it at that. Luke caught the bus all right, but as it pulled away, he realized he had forgotten to buy the fuchsia.

Warm, easy sleep is creeping up on him. Luke asks the man across the carriage, 'If I'm asleep when we get to Killarney, would you mind waking me?'

'No problem.'

Luke relaxes, lets go.

The morning sun is already warm by the time the bus arrives at Kenmare. Luke goes straight to the estate agent's. The plan to hitchhike from Killarney the night before had been a predictable failure. He had stood near the roundabout across from Lidl's for at least an hour before accepting that there was not the remotest possibility of anyone acknowledging his outstretched thumb; not that he felt any resentment or even agitation. The truth was he had found it rather soothing to watch the cars speed by as a huge red sun disappeared. When he returned to Killarney town, he found the Railway Hostel easily enough. He got a bed in a dorm with three Italians and slept like a baby.

Inside the estate agent's office in Kenmare, a young man,

more or less his own age, is on the phone. He smiles a warm welcome and indicates that he won't be long. Luke twirls the carousels of gorgeous properties as he waits. He is surprised to recognize views from the old cottage in Tahilla. He stops the carousel to examine the leaflet more closely.

'Magnificent new architect-designed five-bedroom home on site of burnt-out cottage. Total privacy, extensive sea frontage, glorious views of the Beara peninsula. Complete plans available for viewing. House ready from September 2005. POA.'

So Norma had made proper use of the insurance money.

'Are you interested?'

Luke guesses from the slightly jokey tone that the young man now at his shoulder had looked at him and already made an expert assessment of that possibility.

'Price on application? I doubt if I'm in that league.'

'Well, have you the guts of a million to spare? It's a fantastic spot.'

Luke smiles. 'Actually . . . no.'

He opens the bag and takes out the Internet printout. He holds it up. 'This is more what I'm after.'

'Oh, right. Cloneen. Been on the market a while now. You know it's in an awful way.'

The warning expression on his face is even more revealing than his tone.

Luke nods: 'I suppose I expected that.'

'An awful lot of work. Very remote.'

'That's OK.'

'No view to speak of.'

'Will I just go away?'

'Ah, no, no. I don't mean to put you off. It's just I don't want you going off down the peninsula on a wild goose chase either. You might as well know the worst, yeah?'

'Sure. So . . . can I go see it?'

'No problem. I won't be able to go down with you . . .'

Naturally. Not for pin money like a hundred thousand euro.

'But I can give you the key. Drop it back later on or to-morrow, there's no big rush. I'll be honest with you now, there isn't exactly a queue of people looking for that particular property.'

'Suits me.'

'Oh yeah, it might do. Sure anything's possible.'

He finds the key for Luke. He prints out detailed directions to the property. Luke doesn't tell him that he doesn't have a car. He must buy some food before he leaves Kenmare.

By three o'clock that afternoon Luke had found the cottage, unlocked the door, and stepped into the cold, smelly dark. By four o'clock he was sweating in the heart of a brilliant sun as he dragged everything that was moveable out into the air. There was an ancient Kosangas cooker, a huge rotting ward-robe, lumps of other scarcely identifiable furniture, a tin bath, rubble everywhere. By five o'clock he was able to stand, aching and filthy, in the stripped-down musty interior and feel the shape of the little building. The floor was still caked in cow manure, window panes smashed and frames rotten, there were large cracks in the wall, and a hole or two in the ceiling. Now it is six o'clock. He is lying on the grass looking at the cottage, eating what, for Luke, is a very large meal. He is ferociously hungry. He can hear a bell toll miles away. He is thinking that the corrugated tin roof doesn't look like much, and the chimney is more or less a goner, but the building is very nicely positioned.

So what about this idea then, Luke asks himself, this starting from scratch? This was scratch all right. How does it feel right now? He thinks about it. He decides it is slightly better than the black hole he had fallen into over the last year, but only slightly. Yes, but how does it compare to before all that? Luke thinks again for quite a long time. He is shocked to find he cannot remember anything at all about his life then. That can't be, surely? He thinks about it again. There was one day, more than a year ago now, when his father came to him and said, 'Luke there's some things I need to talk to you about.'

Frank urgently needed to explain himself to his eldest son, because if he didn't, Luke would read all about it in the papers the following day. So OK, that was that day, and nothing was the same afterwards. What was Luke doing with his life before that day? Surely he had seen signs, picked up hints, had doubts, suspicions? Luke stretches back in the warmth of the scrub, and tries as hard as he can to remember. It is a blank. What used to occupy his mind then? He was with . . . what was her name? Emma. He knows that because he left her a few months ago, but what did they do together for however long they were a couple? What did they talk about?

Luke is distracted from these thoughts by the sound of a car approaching. He listens intently. He feels a little more tense as the sounds come closer. Then it starts to go away again, and he relaxes. The car hadn't come very close at all. Of course it wouldn't. The nearest proper road is nearly half a mile away. Nobody would bother turning up the dirt track that led eventually to the cottage unless they really needed to. Luke finishes his bread, ham and tomatoes. What had he been thinking about before the car? Oh yes, things he couldn't remember. It would all come back to him eventually.

Full now, he fancies a walk around the nearby land to get the feel of it. He would return just before dark, and bed down here for the night. He is sure that by the morning he will have made up his mind if this is a good idea or not.

Luke walks up the little incline to see what is on the other side. It is scrub and rock mostly; a few sheep in the distance. Before exploring further he turns to look back at the cottage from above. Could he live here? Really? Might there come a time when all the home comforts would be in place, whatever those were? Would friends call and stay the night? Would he meet someone who loved him and he could love, sometime in the future, in this place? Hard work; so much hard work even to stay clean and dry. Luke thinks aloud, 'You might live to regret it,' and immediately wonders what that can possibly mean now.

When he was a child, part of what made Kerry enticing was that it was so far from Dublin. Even though there is no sea view from this property, not for a mere hundred thousand, Luke knows the sea is not far away, just three or four miles west: Valentia Island and the Atlantic. He is near the edge, starting from scratch. He looks down at where the late evening sun shines directly on the back wall of the cottage. It feels so warm. It would be easy enough to buy a cheap comfy chair and a table. He could sit out enjoying the sun. That would certainly be possible at least. It seems to Luke quite a pleasant prospect to spend time there on a sunny day; to read perhaps, and drink something cool. Who knows, if the summer continues this way, and the sun shines more often than not, it might even begin to warm his cold heart.

# *Acknowledgements*

Thanks to
Donal Beecher, Anne Richardson, Peter Crawley, Evelyn
Grant, Sean Moran and all at *The Dubliner* magazine.

# He just wanted a decent book to read ...

Not too much to ask, is it? It was in 1935 when Allen Lane, Managing Director of Bodley Head Publishers, stood on a platform at Exeter railway station looking for something good to read on his journey back to London. His choice was limited to popular magazines and poor-quality paperbacks – the same choice faced every day by the vast majority of readers, few of whom could afford hardbacks. Lane's disappointment and subsequent anger at the range of books generally available led him to found a company – and change the world.

*'We believed in the existence in this country of a vast reading public for intelligent books at a low price, and staked everything on it'*
**Sir Allen Lane, 1902–1970, founder of Penguin Books**

The quality paperback had arrived – and not just in bookshops. Lane was adamant that his Penguins should appear in chain stores and tobacconists, and should cost no more than a packet of cigarettes.

Reading habits (and cigarette prices) have changed since 1935, but Penguin still believes in publishing the best books for everybody to enjoy. We still believe that good design costs no more than bad design, and we still believe that quality books published passionately and responsibly make the world a better place.

So wherever you see the little bird – whether it's on a piece of prize-winning literary fiction or a celebrity autobiography, political tour de force or historical masterpiece, a serial-killer thriller, reference book, world classic or a piece of pure escapism – you can bet that it represents the very best that the genre has to offer.

**Whatever you like to read – trust Penguin.**

read more
www.penguin.co.uk